and now a Triangle

Although the names of some of the shows are factual, the events and characters are purely fictitious Any resemblance of these characters to any person, living or dead, is co-incidental

To Eileen

and now a Triangle

Margaret Duckett

two down now, one to go.

Margaret Duckett

PENQUITE PRESS
SHINGAY

and now a Triangle

ISBN 0 9540367 0 0

First Published 2001 by
Penquite Press
Shingay Herts

Printed in Great Britain for Penquite Press

I should like to dedicate this book to all true dog lovers throughout the World, who exhibit their dogs.

List of Abbreviations

KC	Kennel Club
CC	Challenge Certificate
Ch	Champion (3 Ccs)
BIS	Best in Show
RBIS	Reserve Best in Show
BP	Best Puppy
BOB	Best of Breed
RBOB	Reserve Best of Breed
BOS	Best Opposite Sex

CHAPTER ONE

Simon Philips opened his eyes, sat up in the bed and groaned, "Curse that bloody woman," he muttered between clenched teeth. Without turning on the light, he got out of bed and went to the bathroom. Half an hour later, sitting having a cup of tea in the kitchen, he sighed heavily, it was several months now since he had left Fiona over that bloody Alan Burgess business. He knew that his pride had got the better of him and had landed him in the mess he was in now. He also knew that he still wanted her like hell and was having far too many of these nights where he woke up just as he was making passionate love to her in his dreams. Something had to change. He finished his tea, told the dogs to settle down and made his way upstairs to bed.

He lay there thinking about the very first time that he had met her; he had gone to her house to look at a litter of pups she was selling. It had turned out to be her first litter and she was very unsure of herself. He had been immediately attracted to her physically as soon as she had opened the door to him but had thought her too middle-class and blue-stocking for his taste. As they had talked over a cup of tea it had been obvious that she was naive about most things to do with dog showing and, it appeared, about the ways of the world in general as far as he was concerned.

Their subsequent affaire had surprised him a little and had overwhelmed them both destroying both their marriages; not that his needed destroying! After she had left Duncan, she bought a cottage and he had gone to live with her. Those were the days, he thought, they'd both worked so bloody hard in all weathers to get that kennel up and running. They'd begun to make a name for themselves and for the Simfell kennel. They'd given parties, presents, dinners to all the right people and were just getting into winning ways when she.... He turned over in the bed and wrestled with the pillow until it fitted his tired head. Surely to God, he'd taught her something in the years that they had known each other, she surely couldn't have still been that green when she had that bloody afternoon with Alan Burgess! My God, if Alan hadn't bungled it and wanted to keep it quiet, he would not only have been cuckolded but they would have both been the butt of ridicule throughout the breed, ruining everything they'd done. The unyielding pillow got another adjustment.

Then there was the baby! They might just have managed to survive the Burgess business but for the baby, that, for a time, put a different complexion on the whole affair, you really couldn't blame him for thinking that it wasn't his! He turned over to his other side and again hammered the pillow into shape. How could she have been so stupid! She'd been so good to live with, she'd been marvellous in and out of the bed , he smiled at the memory of some of the places that they had made love, once, of course, he'd shown her what to do. They had had such a damned good life together and he'd really appreciated it after his frigid bitch of a wife, Mary. Sighing, he gave up on the pillow, turned onto his back and stared at the cracks in the ceiling. Yes, he must sort this out with her, but how?

The contours of the furniture were just becoming visible in the dark grey light of morning. Fiona opened her eyes and looked at the display on the clock on her bedside table. She could hear the dawn chorus outside the window and guessed that it must, once again, be about four-twenty in the morning. The figures which glared at her in the dim light told her that it was actually four-thirtyone. She groaned and pulled the sheet over her head covering her eyes and drawing her knees up into the foetal position. I must get more sleep, she thought. Every morning I wake up so early, almost at the same damn time. It doesn't seem to matter what I do. She turned and lay on her back stretching her legs out until her toes found the cold sheet at the bottom of the bed. She was so tired and the day's tasks lay ahead of her like a mountain to climb. Ten minutes later and wide awake, she decided to get up. Sally, her Cumbrian terrier, came up to the bed wagging her tail. As she splashed her face with water she look for signs of grey in her fair hair but, with relief found none. Cheered by this she called to Sally, "OK Sal let's go and make a cup of tea."

Sitting by the Aga and sipping the hot tea her thoughts were on what she could do to sort her life out. She was lonely, very lonely and miserable, she had to admit it. She had discovered that she did not like living alone. When she was growing up and living with her parents, when she was at university, when she became a librarian and married Duncan, even when she left Duncan and came to live here with Simon, she had never had to live entirely on her own. If only she'd had children.

"Sally, this is no time to dwell on that, I've got to let the dogs out."

As the morning progressed her spirits rose. It was one of those rare Spring days when the sky was blue, the sun was shining and everything was coming back to life. All the dogs were well and seemed to be benefitting from the warm sun.

"Hello Fiona, are you in one of the kennels? Its me, Beryl."

Fiona put her head around the door of the main kennel, "Hello Beryl, Am I glad to see you. Put the kettle on, I won't be a minute."

Finishing the cleaning, she hurried down the path and into the cottage, "Oh, Beryl, it's lovely to see you. I can't thank you enough for coming over. How are you and Peter?"

"We're fine and before you ask, no, we haven't seen Simon. He did deign to phone his brother the other week but only to let him know that he's alright."

"Oh, he didn't say anything else then?"

"If you mean did he ask after you, I'm afraid the answer is no. Enough of that. How are you? You look tired. Are you sleeping well? I don't think that I would want to be here alone at night."

"To be honest, I'm not sleeping too well at the moment but it's not because I'm frightened. I don't know what is stopping me from sleeping really."

She knew that this was a lie but she didn't want to burden Beryl and Peter with any more of her problems. They had been so helpful and supportive when she and Simon had split up. Peter had been really annoyed at the time with his brother and had told him that he deplored the way he was behaving towards Fiona. He didn't know the full story though. True to her word, Beryl had not told Peter about the Alan Burgess fiasco.

"How is the new job in the book shop?"

"Fine, just working those three afternoons helps out the finances and doesn't interfere with the routine here and I think that it helps Ruth as well having the extra money for coming in those afternoons. I have really enjoyed talking about books again."

Beryl was not fooled by this bright and breezy attitude. Fiona looked pale and tired.

"Well something must be troubling you or else you would sleep like a log with all this fresh air and exercise."

"Come and look at the dogs. They are all looking wonderfully well and the dog that I ran on from the last litter is turning out to be a very handsome boy." As she was speaking, Fiona had been walking towards the kitchen door. Beryl, realising that she was not going to say anymore, finished her tea and got up and followed her.

"Are you going to show him?"

"Oh, I don't think so. Well I'm not sure really. It's a pity because I think that he is rather good."

"So why not show him?"

Fiona just smiled and opened the door to the run so that Beryl could leave.

When, later, they were having a spot of lunch, Beryl once again tried to get Fiona to tell her what was troubling her.

"I phoned you a fortnight ago, a man answered the phone. It wasn't Simon's voice. Oh, Fiona, is everything all right?"

"I didn't know that you'd phoned. What day was that?"

"I don't know. Wednesday I think. I was going to ask you if I could come over to see you."

"Wednesday, Oh yes, that must have been Paul Aston. Do you remember him? He shows Cumbrian Terriers and is an old friend of Simon's. He had a puppy from the last litter. What did he say?"

"Only that you were in the kennels and that he would tell you that I'd phoned."

"Oh, that explains it. He must have forgotten. Now, let's have another cup of tea and you must tell me all your news. Did you have that day in London that you told me about? Did you go on the bus tours?"

"Yes, and it was wonderful. We both learned so much about the history of the buildings and the tour guide had quite a sense of humour. We are definitely going again and doing another route. You must come with us, you'd love it."

"Yes, I'm sure that I would. I just wish that I had the time."

Just at that moment the phone rang and Fiona hurried into the hall. Beryl, sipping her tea, could hear Fiona's side of the conversation, "Yes, this is Fiona Philips. No, I'm afraid Simon is not here. Can I help? Ah! a judging appointment, well, I'm sorry but I can't help you with that at the moment. I don't quite know where he is. Try the secretary of the Cumbrian Terrier Club, she may have an address for him. Right, goodbye."

She came back into the kitchen with a rather tight smile on her face, "That was a championship show secretary wanting to book Simon to judge for them. Apparently the judge they had previously asked had not been available. I told her that I didn't know where he was."

"Oh dear, couldn't you have done it?"

"Yes, I could have I suppose. She didn't ask me and I certainly didn't tell her. I'm blacked I think and before you ask, I don't think that I ever want to judge a championship show ever again anyway. It caused so much trouble between Simon and me the only time I did judge one."

"Why was that then and what do you mean by blacked?"

"Oh Beryl, you don't really want to know. It's all too involved and besides that, it's still too painful for me to talk about it. I'm sorry Beryl."

"Oh my dear, I do understand, but it does seem such a pity not to use all the knowledge you must have about the dogs. With the expertise you have between you, you and Simon should be judging all the time. Both Peter and I are still so terribly upset that you and Simon have parted and..." Beryl stopped talking, she could see the gleam of tears in Fiona's eyes, "now before I go, I must get your measurements for that waistcoat that I promised to knit for you. You've lost such a lot of weight since your miscarr.... recently, I don't know what size to knit."

That night, as she checked the lock on the driveway gates, a precaution she had taken since being on her own so that no-one could get their car up to the cottage and kennels, she looked up at the clear, starry sky. It looked as if there might be a frost. She would fill a water-bottle and put it in her bed. Putting her hand to her aching forehead she slowly walked back to the cottage.

That phone call from the show secretary, had disturbed her far more than she let on to Beryl. All the angry, bitter words that had passed between her and Simon over her first championship show judging appointment when she had tried to be fair and put up the best dogs and not the people. That was what had finally finished their relationship. God, how she missed him. She stopped in the process of taking off her jumper. Missed him! My God, she must be more tired than she thought. Miss someone who had treated you like dirt! Miss someone who wouldn't be seen with you! Miss someone who couldn't care less how you were managing! It was better to be lonely! Tomorrow, she must get to the chemist's and get something to make her sleep!

"Goodnight Sally, see you in the morning." She turned out the light and the dog settled more comfortably into its' small duvet.

Viv Butcher had woken up that morning feeling terrible. The tablets that she now had to take from time to time to get to sleep were absolutely marvellous but they made her feel so heavy and slow in the mornings as if her brains were scrambled. She looked at the clock and crawled out of bed. She had to feed and walk the dogs before she went to the local doctor's surgery where she worked as a receptionist At least the walk would clear her head.

CHAPTER TWO

As Fiona got out of her car a woman's voice said, “Why, Mrs Philips, what a coincidence. I was going to phone you this week How are you now?” She turned and looked at the woman's face without recognition for a moment, “I'm sorry but.... Oh, I remember now it's Mrs. Bennett isn't it. Of course, how are you?”

“I'm very well thank you. I've often thought of phoning you but didn't like to after.... well you know.”

“After my miscarriage. Yes, well that's all in the past now. I don't think I ever thanked you for all your help did I. Did you mate your bitch after all?”

“Oh yes, didn't your husband tell you. I got a lovely litter and, in fact, I kept two of the puppies. That's what I wanted to talk to you about. Have you got time for a coffee now?”

“No, I'm sorry but I only popped into town to go to the chemist's. Why don't you come round tomorrow though for a cup of tea. About 3 o’clock?”

"Yes, I'd love to. Thank you very much."

The following afternoon as she put two cups and saucers on a tray with a plate of shortbread fingers, Fiona thought of that awful day when she had miscarried Simon's baby. How ironic it had all been, married to Duncan for all those years, all those failed IVF treatments and then, to lose the only baby she had ever conceived. She sighed heavily, it still hurt so much. Hearing a car draw up, she filled the kettle, put it on the Aga and opened the kitchen door.

“Hello again Mrs Philips, I’ve brought the dogs, they’re in the car, it is so kind of you to see me like this, do you want me to get them out now or....” She paused for breath and walked into the kitchen, “What a cosy kitchen, you’ve got an Aga, I have often thought that I should like one and...” she paused, “Here I am chattering away, I do hope that I'm not holding you up. It must be quite hard work with all the dogs, though I suppose that your husband helps a lot.”

“My husband is not here at the moment and not likely to be.”

“Oh, oh, I'm so sorry Mrs Philips.”

“Please don't be and please call me Fiona.”

“I'm Natalie.”

“Now, you said that you wanted to talk about your puppies.”

“Well yes, as I told you, I kept two of them from my litter to your dog and I was thinking of showing them. Just for fun of course.”

Fiona looked at the woman across the table from her, she must be about her age. Around fifty anyway. A little plump but smartly dressed, which disguised it, brown, wavy hair which had been very well cut, make-up which had been well applied to accentuate her brown eyes and wearing some very attractive earrings. Looking at Natalie’s white, well manicured hands Fiona felt compelled to pose the question, “May I ask why, in particular, you want to show dogs?”

Natalie Bennett looked slightly embarrassed, “Well, it's a bit of a long story. Do you have the time?" Fiona nodded her head and Natalie continued, “My husband died two years ago after a long illness and a year ago my daughter got married and went to live in New Zealand. She was so worried about leaving me here but I told her that I would be fine because I was going to take up a brand new hobby of breeding dogs. I’d bought my Cumbrian from you just after my husband died for companionship; with absolutely no intention of breeding. The idea came to me out of the blue and I said it to put her mind at rest. That was why I mated her.”

“How did you cope with the birth?”

“Fine, you see I was a nursing sister before my marriage. A long time ago now but, as they say, old habits die hard.”

Fiona nodded, “Yes, I see. So you want to know how to go about starting to show dogs. Well, it's not everyone's cup of tea you know. It's time-consuming, very expensive, wears your car out, gives you massive phone bills and is full of disappointments. Having said all that, it is an all the year round, compulsive and absorbing hobby. Look, you'd better bring the dogs over for me to see them first and then, if they have any promise in them, we'll proceed from there."

"That is so kind of you. My time is pretty well my own so you tell me when would be most convenient."

Later, as she was shutting up the dogs for the night, she again thought of Natalie Bennett. What a bloody nuisance it was that she had chosen to ask her about dog-showing. Look at what it had done to her own life so far. The woman was obviously pleasant, kind, educated and had had some traumatic happenings in her life. Did she really need dog-showing? It would certainly give her a purpose for living. It would give her an all the year round interest. She might even make one or two new friends. She would spend a lot of money, have no opportunity to wear her lovely clothes, make-up and nail varnish and all for a few pieces of paper! "Oh, what the hell," Fiona said to Sally as they walked back to the cottage, "I'll tell her what to do and then it's up to her."

Natalie brought the two youngsters to the cottage for Fiona to look at with a judge's eye. She said nothing as Fiona carefully went over them in the stripping shed and when Fiona put the second one down on the floor, she could contain herself no longer, "Well, what do you think?"

"I want you to walk them up and down for me so that I can assess their movement to see if it is correct."

They went out into the yard and Natalie duly walked up and down, first with the dog and then the bitch. She looked at Fiona somewhat apprehensively, "Well?" Fiona realised from the tense way in which Natalie was looking at her that her answer meant a lot to her and that her decision to show had not been just a random idea. Natalie was certainly far more lonely than she was letting on, and her assessment of the dogs was important.

"I liked them both. You could show both of them if you wished. Having said that, I think that the dog is the better one. The other one, the bitch, you could show for a while but I think that she will get a bit too big. She should make an ideal brood bitch though. Of course, that is only my opinion."

“Oh, I accept your opinion entirely. I'm so pleased that you like them. Now, what do I have to do first?”

“Look, why don't you put them in the car, we'll have another cup of tea and talk about it”.

The kettle was just boiling as Natalie Bennett gave a little knock on the door and came into the kitchen. “This is so kind of you Fiona and I do so appreciate you giving up your time to...”

Fiona interjected, “If the truth be known, I'm pleased to have the company. I've even made a cake and I certainly wouldn't have bothered if you hadn't been coming.” They both smiled and Natalie sat down at the kitchen table. The time passed quickly with Fiona getting quite enthusiastic when explaining the finer points of the breed. It was only when Natalie’s dogs in the car started to bark that Natalie looked at her watch, “Is that the time, I do apologise, I’ve kept you from your work. I must go. Thank you very much.”

After Natalie had gone she had to hurry around to catch up on the work.

Fiona picked up the phone and dialled Beryl's number, “Hello Beryl, how are you? How is Peter?”

“We're just fine. How are you. Everything alright?”

Fiona told her about Natalie's visit and how much she had enjoyed the company.

“She was only here for a couple of hours but she was so easy to talk to. We had quite a lot in common, she even likes reading similar books. She wants to start showing her dogs and I have sort of said that I would help her and...”

“But I thought that you didn’t want to show any more.”

“Well I don’t but I thought that if I just got her started... and I do miss the anticipation and the excitement a bit and... well you know.”

After she had put the phone down Beryl walked back into the lounge biting her lip.

“Who was that love?”

She told Peter about the conversation that she had just had with Fiona.

“Oh, that's good then isn't it?”

“I don't know. She has obviously been feeling very lonely, far more than she has said. She seemed so pleased to have the company. It's months since Simon went. I should have gone over a lot more.”

"Perhaps she didn't want you to."
"Um, perhaps. There was that man who answered the phone that time. I couldn't find out......"
"Now look Beryl, don't go adding two and two and making five. She told you who it was. Anyway, although she is still the wife of my brother, we don't have any right to interfere in what she does."
"Perhaps I'll give Simon a ring and see how he is getting on."
"Call him by all means, he hasn't called us for a week or two but please Beryl, don't you dare mention Fiona unless he does."

As Fiona lay reading in bed that night, although her eyes were on the page her thoughts were on the events of the afternoon and how much she had enjoyed the company of Natalie. When she had moved here with Simon she had had no need of anyone else. She had thought of her old friend Laura now and again but her love for Simon had been so overwhelming and the business of dog showing and breeding had taken up so much of their time, that everyone and everything else had been subsidiary to that. Tears welled up in her eyes. She had been so very happy. Blast bloody dog showing. How could she advise this poor woman to enter into that complex world. She would be doing her a disservice. Or would she? She'd be alright if she stuck to the open shows. They were friendly, mostly near home and they gave rosettes. If I went with her to just a couple of shows I could help her. Yes, I'll do that. I'll show with her. Saxon was too good not to be shown. Yes, we could share the driving expenses and... Simon.... suppose she ran into Simon. Well, damnation to Simon. He stopped me going to shows before; he won't now. Happy with her decision, she put the book down, turned out the light and promptly fell asleep.
Fiona awoke to a light room and the birds singing. Looking at the clock, she threw the bedcovers off and jumped out of bed. Good heavens, it was seven-fortyfive. She'd slept right through the night. When she had finished her kennel chores and a little bit of housework, she decided to phone Natalie before she went to the book shop for the afternoon.
"Hello Natalie? This is Fiona Philips. Had a thought after you had gone yesterday. How about I come with you to the dog training classes and, later, the Open shows? It's time that I got Saxon into the ring."
"Oh, that it so kind of you. I'd be most grateful for any help."

“That’s settled then.”

Before she went to the book shop that afternoon, she called in on the newsagents and asked them to start delivering the weekly dog magazine again. She must tell Natalie to do the same, only get the other one, and then they could swap. Yes, they could decide on which shows to go to and keep abreast of all the news. Smiling, she made her way to the book shop.

“Hi Fiona, you’re looking chirpy this afternoon,” Alison, who managed the shop smiled at her.

“Do I? I expect that’s because I had a good night’s sleep. I must admit, I feel marvellous. I think I’ll buy myself some new make-up on the way home.”

“Good for you.” Just at that moment a customer came into the shop and, smiling, Fiona asked if any help was required.

CHAPTER THREE

Simon put his knife and fork down on the plate, not a bad lunch he thought. Not a patch on Fiona's steak and kidney pie but, not bad. Better than some of the lunches dog societies provided. He looked around at some of the other judges sitting at various tables. One of them looked up and nodded in Simon's direction and Simon nodded back. Can't remember who he is or what breed he judges so he can’t be of any importance. Not worth engaging in conversation anyway.

He looked at his watch. Only two o’clock! Can't go home yet, I’ve still got the Terrier Group to do. Hope that it's not one of those shows where the show manager wants all the groups done separately for effect. Effect! Usually most of the bloody exhibitors have gone home by then and the place is echoing. God, I'm fed up today, must have been that Indian takeaway I had last night, must have upset my digestion or something. He got up and wandered back into the hall where the show was being held.

“Hello Simon, long time no see.” He turned around to see Joan Skipton's smiling face, “Hello Joan, what are you doing in this neck of the woods?”

“I'm desperately trying to get the last points for my Junior Warrant with this bitch.”

“How have you done today?”

“I'm just waiting to go in now so wish me luck.”

God, he thought as he watched her retreating back, haven't seen her since Fee got her third CC with Sapphire. Damn, I don't want to think about that. God, what a bloody day. I'll go up to the other end of the hall. She'll only want to quiz me on my break-up with Fee. He walked up to the far side and sat down to watch the Newfoundlands being judged but, he couldn't seem to concentrate. What the hell, my wife cheated on me and here I am with no bloody home of my own, no money and all I can do is think about her at every turn. I shouldn't have walked out but I thought that she'd want me to go back - on my terms. I suppose that it's time that I saw a solicitor and started proceedings. Bloody Hell, two divorces. His thoughts were interrupted,

"Ah, there you are Simon. I got the two points that I wanted. Isn't that marvellous."

"What! Oh did you. Congratulations Joan. It takes some doing with these new KC regs. Bring back the old ones I say. At least they kept entries up at these Open shows"

"Now, how are you and Fiona? Haven't seen her for a while. Is she alright?"

"Yes thanks. Good Heavens, is that the time? Must be going. They'll be calling me for the Group soon. Good to see you again Joan."

"Yes you too, well give my regards to Fiona."

"Will do, bye," he pushed his fingers through his thick black hair as he walked away, he'd got off lightly there. She obviously didn't know.

It was late afternoon when he let himself into the house that he had rented. It wasn't much of a house and it was damned expensive to rent, but they had not objected to his dogs. The dogs greeted him rapturously, "Hello, all right, down, down, lets get those leads on and go for a good, long walk." Smiling, he stroked their heads and put on their leads, "Let's brush those cobwebs away, come on." As he left the house, the door to the neighbouring one opened, "Ah, there you are at last. Do you know that those bloody dogs have been barking all day? Your landlord is a friend of mine and, if this goes on, I shall see that he knows about it." Simon apologised to the man and said that he would see that it didn't happen again but, inside he was fuming. What a bloody awful day, roll on tomorrow! Later that evening, when he was watching the football match on the TV the phone rang, "Hello Simon it's me Peter. How are you?"

"Fine, just got back from judging a show. Had a good time. I was just watching Match of the Day. Everything OK?"

"Yes, both Beryl and I are well. Beryl was wondering if you would like to come to Sunday dinner tomorrow?"

"Great, especially if it's a roast. How about I come around 12 o'clock and we can then go for a pint. Haven't done that for a while. Do you mind if I bring the dogs? Get left a lot on their own these days."

"No, I'm sure Beryl won't mind. See you then. Bye."

Peter put down the phone and went back into the lounge, "Yes, he said that he'd like to come and before you ask, no, I don't think that we should invite Fiona as well. I did say that he could bring his dogs though."

"What!"

"Well, he asked and what could I say?"

"Oh, Peter! Anyway, I wouldn't dream of inviting Fiona as well. It might be better if we don't even mention her name. It always seems to create an awful atmosphere with Simon. Remember now Peter, don't mention Fiona."

"Fine by me."

Peter was finding any conversation difficult in the pub where they had been dispatched by Beryl. He had told Simon what had been going on in his office, he had told him his plans for the garden that summer and where they were going for their summer holiday, he had asked Simon what he thought of the match between Arsenal and Tottenham the previous day but, apart from a non-commital yes, no, or um, Simon had had nothing to say about anything. Peter put his glass down on the table, "Simon, is there something wrong only you're very quiet." Simon let out a sigh, "Is there something wrong! No, nothing's wrong, nothing much except that I haven't got a bloody garden to plan, I'm not booking a holiday to Portugal with my wife, in fact I'm not doing a bloody thing. Here I am approaching fifty without a home of my own and with a wife and an ex wife living in the lap of luxury. No prospects at work either unless someone bloody well pops their clogs. No, nothing's wrong Pete." He picked up his glass, "Ready for another?"

As they came through the front door Beryl glanced at Peter who frowned and shook his head slightly. Beryl sighed, it was going to be the same as when Simon and Fiona had first split up. Simon had been a pain to live with then, she sighed as she took the roast potatoes out of the roasting tin, she had nobody to blame but herself, she shouldn't have asked him but she just felt so sorry for him, well for them both.

"Have you had any good wins lately Simon," she asked as she passed him the gravy. "Several firsts with my youngster but it's early in the season. I'm hopeful of better things later in the year." He knew that he was lying but he wasn't going to tell them that his wins were beginning to dry up along with his cash. No pressies, no parties, no wins, it was as plain as the nose on your face. He'd somehow have to have a litter in order to get some cash.

"Oh good," said Beryl, "I went to see Fiona the other day." Peter nearly choked on the food that he had just put into his mouth.

"Peter don't eat so quickly. As I was saying, I went to see Fiona the other day. She was looking very well although a little thin I thought."

"Was she."

"Yes, she told me that the young dog that she had, I believe she called it Saxon, is growing up to be very nice indeed."

"Yes, I remember, he looked promising as a puppy."

Peter tried to catch Beryl's attention, but failed.

"Did you know that she works in a book shop three afternoons a week now?"

"No, I didn't. Who looks after the dogs?"

"The lady who used to be your kennelmaid, she pops in I think just to see all is well, and did you know..."

Simon interrupted her, "Peter tells me that you are going to Portugal for your holiday."

Beryl opened her mouth to speak but this time Peter managed to silence her with a glance.

"What's for pudding Beryl?"

"You know what's for pudding Peter."

"Well, could we have it then?"

As he drove home from Peter's house, Simon suddenly decided to look at the cottage just out of curiosity. He knew that, if he parked slightly up the hill and about sixty yards from the entrance to the cottage he could see the kennels from across the adjoining field. My God, she's at it again, anger welled up in him, there was a bloody car parked up near the kitchen. Hold on though, he'd seen that car somewhere before. Just at that moment two women came out of one of the kennels. One was Fiona and the other was, he couldn't quite make her out. Feeling a bit guilty at his initial reaction, he watched as the other woman got into the car and drove out. He ducked down as she drove past. Bloody Hell, look what she's brought me to, he thought as he drove off, I'm behaving like a bloody private detective.

He still hadn't got over that business with Alan Burgess. It had been the devil's own job not to smash his face in at the first championship show he had attended after breaking up with Fee. He knew in his heart that what she had told him had been the truth but, even the thought of Alan seeing her naked and laying on a bed nearly drove him crazy. He hadn't spoken to him since but merely nodded if their paths had crossed at a show. The only thing in Alan's favour was that, it would appear that he had not mentioned that afternoon to anyone else. There had been no snide remarks or knowing looks from anyone. He had managed to keep going to the shows and was actually doing a little bit of winning so Fiona's dreadful judging had not completely tarnished his reputation as a judge who could be relied upon to do the correct thing.

As he stopped the car in front of his house he sat there for some time looking at it's grubby exterior. He should have been driving into the drive of the cottage, going into the warm kitchen and kissing Fiona. Feeling her warm, willing body beside him in bed, holding her in his arms and.... he groaned and hastily got out of the car. As he took the dogs into the house the curtains twitched in the downstairs window next door.

CHAPTER FOUR

As Fiona walked into the church hall no-one would have known that she was nervous. Smiling broadly, her face made-up and wearing a pink jumper and a reasonably decent pair of trousers, she led Natalie into the brightly lit church hall where the local dog society held their ring-training classes. Several people smiled and waved as they made their way towards some empty chairs at the side of the hall. Fiona had decided before coming that no-one was going to commiserate with her about her break-up with Simon, she was going to look vivacious and happy. She had reasoned with herself that enough time had passed for the gossips to have latched onto some other poor devil and she would be left in peace. However, she had hardly walked halfway across the hall when Viv Butcher sidled up to her with false sympathy written all over her face, "Fiona, lovely to see you again. How are you managing now? I mean it must seem very lonely without that gorgeous hunk to help you. I did hear though that you have already found a replacement. Is that true? Naughty, Naughty." She waggled a finger at her and smiled.

Oh God, someone must have seen Paul going in and out. Fiona had been hoping that that little episode had gone unnoticed. Too much to ask I suppose in the dog world she thought where everyone made everybody's business their business. Damn, how the hell did she know about Paul? Viv had always had her big brown eyes on Simon but she must have been watching her as well. Nosey devil! I wonder if she's already told Simon? No she couldn't have Simon would either have come round or, at least phoned her.

Fiona looked at the attractive woman in front of her, small, neat with beautiful black hair she looked like that film star who played Cleopatra, "Heavens no Viv. Twice bitten, even more shy. You ought to know Viv." Fiona smiled at her and walking across the hall with Saxon on his lead, sat down. After a while, Natalie came and sat beside her, "I think that I did a little better that time Fiona, when she asked me to walk straight up and down, Jamie actually walked beside me both ways."

"Yes, I noticed. Good, I'm sure that you'll soon get the hang of it. We'll have you at an Open show in no time."

"Just the thought of that makes me nervous. Fiona, I can't thank you enough for coming with me this evening. I was dreading that Jamie or I might do something silly. Everyone seems so friendly though and the dogs are all well behaved aren't they."

"Yes of course, all show dogs are well behaved. It's the owners that you've got to watch!" She and Natalie both laughed, "I wanted to get Saxon out anyway and it's good for me to get out too. I'm really enjoying myself. Off you go and stack him on the table for practice."

Laying in bed that night and unable to sleep, Fiona remembered Viv Butcher's remarks. The cheek of the woman! She had been married and divorced and that fellow from the Afghans had lived with her. She had an awful reputation in the breed for tale-telling and gossip. A real trouble-maker. How dare she criticise her!

Fiona sighed deeply, Paul, what a fiasco that had been! When she had invited him to stay with her she had felt so sorry for him. Injured in a ski-ing accident and trying to cope on his own. Fiona had thrown caution to the winds and bundled him and his dogs into the estate car and brought them back to the cottage.

Poor Paul, he had told her that he was in love with her and shouldn't come, why hadn't she thought of the consequences first It was just like the Alan Burgess episode, she didn't look ahead enough at the possible result of her actions. Talk about out of the frying pan and into the fire. Had she perhaps hoped that romance would develop from it? She didn't know. Perhaps a silly bit of her had hoped it would, he was a very nice person. Was she perhaps making yet another mistake in helping Natalie and going back into dog showing?

"Sally, this is silly. Let's go down and have a cup of tea and a biscuit." At the word 'biscuit' Sally raced down the stairs ahead of Fiona.

Sitting by the Aga in the warm kitchen, Sally at her feet, she again thought about the month that Paul had come to stay. At the time she was still so angry with Simon for his treatment of her, so upset that another marriage had failed that Paul seemed an oasis of peace and tranquillity in a troubled world. Dear Paul, he'd always been so kind, especially when he had come to see her in hospital after she lost the baby. His first marriage had been a failure. She had often wondered why, she thought that perhaps now, having shared a house with him, that she had some idea.

It had all started so well, she had made him up a bed on the sofa-bed in the lounge and had cooked meals for him. He had been so attentive and grateful, so complimentary about everything that she did. It had been good for her to have someone to care for again and to talk to in the evenings. It had certainly eased the pain of the separation. He had held her hand when she sat beside him and he told her how he had loved her since their first meeting.

She giggled as she remembered how, after two days, he had hesitatingly asked if there was someway that he could take a bath. After much deliberation, they had decided that a stand-up bath was the only answer. Fiona had brought a large plastic bowl into the kitchen in which she and Simon had sometimes bathed a dog. This was placed on the floor by the Aga and filled with hot water the idea being that Paul could stand and sponge himself down. In reality, he had found it almost impossible to bend sufficiently to reach the water. On hearing Sally's demented barking Fiona, after a moment or two's hesitation, had knocked on the door. The barking continued but there was no reply from Paul. She knocked again and called his name but there was still no reply so she had opened the door a little and looked in, "Paul is everything al......." She had burst out laughing at the sight that met her eyes. The tiled floor was awash with water, Sally was racing round and round Paul, who still had one foot in the bowl, she was excitedly barking and trying to grab the towel thoroughly enjoying this new game. Paul, after one desperate look at Fiona, tried to put the towel around his body but, in his haste, it slipped out of his hand and onto the floor, as Paul made a desperate bid to grab it he almost overbalanced sending even more water sloshing onto the tiles. With his bright red face, his windmilling arms and his bobbing penis Fiona went into fresh gales of laughter, while Sally, thoroughly enjoying the new game, grabbed the towel and delightedly ran around the kitchen with it.

"Fiona, would you please get the towel from that dog. I'm very sorry about the mess, it hasn't worked out terribly well. Now, would you please hand me the towel and take Sally out into the garden." With tears streaming down her face and nearly choking with suppressed laughter, Fiona handed the towel to a very embarrassed looking Paul and took Sally outside.

When she managed to control her mirth, she went back indoors. Paul was still standing by the Aga now draped in the towel and was looking very cross. He apologised for being such a nuisance but, could he please bother her for some more hot water. Fiona got him some more hot water and left the kitchen.

She lay on her bed and thought of Paul's naked body. How very white his skin was compared with Simon's lovely skin, perhaps it was because he had red hair. How solid he looked too with his thick waist and big thighs. On reflection though, the rest of him hadn't been so big! Fiona giggled and rolled onto her side, Simon's body was beautiful, she sighed, she hadn't realised before how much a man's physical looks meant to her. She had always thought that mind compatibility was everything. She sighed again, looked at her watch, got up and went to the mirror to comb her hair.

As the days went by Paul, having got the bathing routine sorted out, continued to be his courteous and attentive self. He, in fact, often reminded her of Duncan which made her feel a little uncomfortable. She liked Paul very much, he was kind and always respected her views and opinions. He was good for her damaged ego but she had to admit that he was rather fastidious and particular over small details when it came to his comfort; a pedant in fact. Perhaps it was the result of living on his own for so long. Perhaps it made you selfish and fussy. She felt that they could be very good friends but that was all. Just as well she had thought, no problems.

One evening, when Paul was obviously feeling more comfortable and in less pain, he asked Fiona to come and sit beside him while they watched the late night film. The film had some passionate bedroom scenes in it and Fiona found that she was thinking of Simon and the wonderful nights of love-making they had spent together, her thoughts were interrupted by Paul's hand on her thigh, she turned towards him and he, taking this as acceptance, drew her towards him with his arm and kissed her. She pulled away, "Oh Paul, you startled me."

"Fiona, my love, if you only knew how long I have wanted to kiss you like that. It was wonderful."

Fiona's mind was racing, that was awful. Simon's kisses made her mind disintegrate and her body melt. Paul's kiss had just been pleasant, a bit soft and wet; it had done nothing for her. Perhaps it was because she wasn't prepared for it.

"Kiss me again Paul and slowly this time."

He drew her towards him once again and kissed her. She closed her eyes and told herself that this was great, just what she wanted a loving friendship; but it wasn't what she wanted. It was so tame, so ordinary, so unexciting. Curse Simon he was even now ruining her life. She pulled away from Paul's moist lips, "I don't know about you Paul but I'm absolutely shattered. Shall I make a cup of tea or would you prefer hot chocolate again?"

During the next week and a half, Paul kissed her on several occasions and told her he loved her. Each time she kissed him willingly hoping that the magic would be there but it never was, he often told her that he loved her but she never said that she loved him. She enjoyed his company, they had a lot in common but he was just a good friend, set in his ways and finicky perhaps, but, what the hell, she was twice married and almost fifty. Who did she think she was? Certainly not the catch of the year. She'd found love and passion and excitement with Simon and look what that had done. She had never told Paul about the episode with Alan Burgess because she felt that he too, would not have approved any more than Simon had. What double-standards men had. The next day she drove him to the hospital. His leg had so improved that the plaster was removed and heavy strapping put on instead. He was smiling broadly as he came out into the corridor, "That feels much better. It's good to be a bit more mobile again."

As they drove back to the cottage, he was making plans for them. They could go on the steam railway again, they would soon be able to go to shows again. "You won't mind will you Fiona if we see Simon? I know that it will be a little awkward at first but, in time. I mean, I've never asked you about the reasons for your separating; I never would. If you want to tell me I know that you will. Good Lord, I'm drivelling on, I'm so pleased to get that damned plaster off."

Fiona had said nothing but tried to concentrate on the road ahead. Showing again, but with Paul instead of Simon. She had deliberately not spoken about the reasons for her and Simon separating, never even spoken about dog showing in any detail. The various times that showing had come up in conversation, Paul had always seemed to change the subject almost as if he wasn't very interested. Fiona parked the car and went into the kitchen to make a cup of tea for them, as she placed the kettle on the Aga, Paul's hands slipped around her waist and he kissed the back of her neck, "My sweet Fiona, what a wonderful time we are going to have together". She turned around, "Paul there's something that..." He kissed her drawing her close to him and she felt his body harden against her, she pulled away, "But Paul I really must tell...."

"Later, later my sweet love, kiss me again it's feels so good to be able to hold you. Wait until I get this blasted bandage off altogether and I'll show you how much you mean to me my dearest. You know how I feel about you." He was fully aroused now and he was holding her tightly against him. It's no good she thought, I can't do this, as much as I don't want to be lonely, I can't make love to him. She pulled away from him.

"Paul, I'm sorry, I'm so terribly sorry, it's all my fault, I persuaded you to come here I know. I'm very fond of you. You've been very kind to me. You're so nice, far too nice for me to lie to you Paul, I don't love you. I don't want to go to dog shows with you. It was the shows that ruined my marriage to Simon. Paul, I like you, I've always liked you and on that basis you are welcome to stay but, as a friend, a very dear friend." Frowning, Paul dropped his arms and stepped back a pace. "Fiona, what are you saying. I thought that we were getting on so well together, I... you seemed happy. Is it this damned leg or something.... it was lovely kissing you. Did I come on a bit too strong? If so, I aplogise, I don't understand, what has any of this got to do with us showing the dogs?"

"Oh Paul, it's all to do with showing dogs I'm afraid, and Simon of course. I can't explain. I'm so sorry."

For the next few days their easy, pleasant relationship was rather strained, it was obvious that Paul did not understand what had gone wrong. He was very courteous and polite and made no attempt to kiss her again. A few days later and by mutual agreement, she drove Paul back to his house. He was very quiet on the journey but, as they stopped in his drive, he turned to her, Look Fiona, I can't say that I understand all this I still .... but..... don't let's stop being friends. I'll give you a call when I can manage the dogs and I'll come and collect them. Thank you so much for all your help." He swung one leg and then the other out of the car and stood up, "I haven't given up all hope Fiona. Please keep in touch and call me if you want anything. Perhaps we could go out together some time."

She nodded and waited until he opened the front door before driving away. She felt absolutely awful. How was it men always managed to make her feel guilty?

Fiona was just having a hurried lunch next day when a van drove up to the kitchen door. She opened the door and was confronted with an enormous bunch of roses all wrapped in cellophane and tied with a large, red bow of ribbon.

"Fiona Philips?" The florist questioned.

"Yes."

"These are for you."

Her heart leapt, were they from Simon. "Who are they from?"

"There is a card inside."

Fiona laid the large bunch on the kitchen table wondering if she had enough vases to hold them and quickly looked for the card. It must be from Simon saying that he is sorry, she opened the little envelope, 'My love and my grateful thanks. Paul.'

CHAPTER FIVE

"Um," Paul rubbed his, as yet, unshaven chin. "Um," he shook his head. The house had a decidedly dowdy appearance this morning. Must be the sunlight he thought because it hadn't looked too bad when Fiona had brought him home the other week. He'd been so busy catching up on some of his work and the dog scene that he hadn't, until this moment, noticed just how neglected it looked. Mrs. Benson did her best, she had been cleaning for him for years now. How old was she? Perhaps it was getting too much for her. Damn it. The trouble was that he'd got used to being looked after by Fiona; he'd enjoyed her company too. He couldn't leave things as they were, that was obvious, he didn't trust Simon not to try to patch things up. Now, as he had on several previous occasions, he wondered what exactly had gone wrong between those two, from one or two of Fiona's remarks he felt that it had something to do with showing the dogs. Fiona had been very reluctant to discuss anything to do with Simon. He went up to the bathroom to shave, "I shall have to work on this, the sooner he is off the scene the better." he said to his reflection and applied the shaver to his face.

"Hello Fiona, isn't this nice, just like old times," Ruth was standing in the doorway of the kitchen, "so you're off to a show again. Knew you wouldn't be able to resist it for long."

"I know, old habits die hard. I'm taking Natalie Bennett to her first show as well."

"Natalie Bennett, wait a minute. Wasn't she the lady who found you when...."

“Yes, that's her. She wants to start showing her Cumbrians so we’re going together. I’m taking Saxon.”

“Well enjoy yourselves. Anything special that I need to know?”

“No, I've put the answerphone on for any calls and the rest is routine.”

“Right, have a good time and bring home a red rosette.” Fiona laughed and went out to the car. Just like old times she thought yes, I’m quite excited. Her stomach knotted up though when she thought that Simon might be at the show. Oh, well, it was a bridge that she’d have to cross. Just then she turned into the drive of Natalie’s house. Good heavens, she thought as she stopped the car. She had assumed that Natalie’s husband had left her comfortably off but this! Before her, nestled into a beautifully tended garden, was a Tudor manor house. The small mellowed red handmade bricks, the roof tiles and tall, ornate chimneys, everything told her that this was an old house which had stood the test of centuries. Natalie opened the heavy, oak, front door, “Hello Fiona, I shan’t be a moment.” She reappeared with the dog, a new travelling box and her bag. As they drove the short distance to where the show was being held Fiona could contain her curiosity no longer, “Natalie, your house is gorgeous, however do you manage such a big house and garden on your own?”

“Well, there is only me now. Jessie, who has helped me since I had the children still comes in every day and of course, Brian keeps the gardens neat and does any odd jobs. Most of the major alterations and repairs were done years ago. There is very little for me to do. I suppose I ought to sell it and buy something smaller but, I haven’t been able to think about that yet.”

As they walked into the equestrian centre where the show was being held, Fiona was distractedly looking around. She saw one or two familiar faces but not Simon's.

“How do we know where to go Fiona?”

“Oh sorry Natalie, there's a board over there. It will tell us which ring the Cumbrians will be judged in and whether we are in first or not. I wish that all societies would put approximate show times in their schedules. It would save so much worry and stress, especially if you get held up in traffic.”

“Fiona, I am so excited. I’ve been awake since five o’clock. At last, I'm a dog shower. No, I am showing dogs, that sounds better. I must remember every detail so that I can tell my daughter all about it when I next write to her."

A little of Natalie's excitement got through to Fiona as they walked to the appropriate ring. Once there, they both set up their tables. Several people waved to Fiona and smiled. As their breed was first in the ring, everyone was brushing and grooming the dogs. Soon the judge and steward appeared in the ring and shortly afterwards the first class was called.

"Fiona, I'm petrified. I'm shaking. Supposing Jamie won't walk?"

"He'll be fine. Just relax and do exactly what you were taught at the ring training classes. Good Luck."

There were only three puppies entered in the class. Fiona watched carefully as Natalie showed her dog in case there was something needed correcting or improving. The judge gave Jamie a second in the class and a red-faced, beaming Natalie came rushing out of the ring towards her, "Fiona, did you see. He got a second. Look, his first rosette! I shall treasure it. I've brought my camera, would you please take a photo of Jamie, me and the rosette so that I can send it to my daughter."

"Of course, I will but I'm in the next class."

"Oh, I am stupid. Do go, you might miss it. We can do this later. Hurry Fiona, I'd hate you to miss it."

The judge smiled at Fiona as she walked into the ring. She had known him for several years now and he certainly knew how well she and Simon had done in recent years. She looked around at the other exhibitors. No, there was no-one of importance. She should win this class and get BOB.

Later, having won her class and BOB she was tidying her grooming tools away, "Well done Fiona, although it was a pretty foregone conclusion wasn't it. I knew as soon as I saw you come." She looked around to see Bob Adams. He was one who had never quite made the big time and was astute enough to know why, but too hard up or too honest to do much about it and too proud to lick boots, she admired him for it really but wondered why he kept going, "Hello Bob how are you and how is Annie?" After a brief conversation she excused herself and went back to Natalie.

"What did that man mean Fiona, it seemed an odd thing to say."

"Just ignore it. Simon and I have known Bob for years."

She had made her mind up not to indoctrinate Natalie into the unpleasant side of showing if possible. She felt that, with Simon telling her the ins and outs of the system early on, it had removed a lot of the pleasure from her showing. Natalie was quite astute and observant, she might find it out for herself in time.

"What do we do now?"

"Well, there are several trade stands we can look at. We can watch other breeds being judged if you are interested or we can just sit until they call for the group judging."

"You choose, I'm so enjoying myself that I don't mind."

Just at that moment a woman came up to Fiona, "Hello, Fiona Philips?"

"Yes."

"Wasn't sure which one of you it was. I'm the secretary of this society and your name has been put forward to judge Cumbrians at our next show in September."

"That's a nice surprise. What date exactly?"

"The 14th. Could you do the Group as well? Yes. Oh that's a load off my mind. I'll send you the paper work."

"Fiona, how marvellous."

"Yes, it is nice to be asked to judge. Any chance of another cup of coffee?"

Fiona and Saxon came second in the group judging and they then packed up and drove home. She dropped off the still elated Natalie and went back to the cottage. Ruth told her that all was in order and, having seen to Saxon and unloaded her gear from the car, she finally went into the kitchen and flopped into a chair. She had quite forgotten just how tiring showing could be but, she had to admit, it had been nice winning again. As the kettle heated up for a cup of tea, she wandered out into the hall to play back any messages on the answerphone. There were four messages, the first was an enquiry about a stud dog for the person's bitch, she made a note of the number, the second was a puppy enquiry, again she noted the number, the third was from Laura asking how she was and would she please phone her back and the last call was from Beryl. She seemed quite lively and was eager to tell her that they had had Simon come to lunch on the previous Sunday and, during the course of conversation, he had said that he might pop in to see how you were managing. "Did he?"

Fiona cancelled the calls and was just about to return to the kitchen when the phone rang again, "Blast, I'll never get that cup of tea," she exclaimed as she picked up the phone, "Simfell K..."

"Ah, you're there, where have you been? Have you seen Simon?"

"I'm sorry to disappoint you Beryl but I've only just come in. I took Natalie Bennett to a show today. Ruth looked after the kennel and she didn't say that Simon had called. I'm sure she wouldn't forget something like that."

"Oh, Fiona, I'm so sor..."

"Anyway, how are you and Peter?"

"Fine, Simon did say that he was fed up with the house that he's renting at the moment and is looking for something else. He mentioned a place in a village, fairly near you I think, called Auberton. that he was going to look at the weekend. That was when he said that he might pop in. Perhaps he changed his mind."

"Yes, well let's hope so. As long as he doesn't think that he can come back here because it's more comfortable and cheaper."

"I know that you're hurting Fiona but so is he, I'm sure, although he hasn't said anything about why you broke up. I'm sure that he misses you very much."

"I'm tired Beryl and forgive me but I really don't want to go over the past any more. I've started showing again and building my life again without him."

"Of course, I do understand Fiona. Look, how's about I come up for the day. One day next week perhaps?"

"Yes, do, I'll look forward to it."

She turned the light off in the hall and went back to the kitchen. Parked just up the hill from the cottage, Simon saw the hall light extinguished and guessed that Fiona had been on the phone. He had been to look at a little terraced house in a village about ten miles away. He had agreed to rent it with an option to buy in a year's time. Well, he shrugged his shoulders, who knows what can happen in a year's time. There was that bloody show in Germany for starters. He had received a letter from a well-known club in Germany asking if he would judge a certain terrier breed and Fiona would judge the Cumbrians. It was his foot into judging abroad, something he had wanted for a long time. Who knows where it could lead if he played his cards right. He had wondered what to do for several days but had, in the end, returned the slip agreeing to do the judging both for him and Fiona. He might be able to persuade her to do it. She might have seen sense by then. If the worst came to the worst, she could perhaps be suddenly taken ill and he might be able to judge both the breeds. Now that would be a feather in his cap. No, best to leave well alone just now. They'd got the appointment and that was enough. He didn't want to rock the boat at the moment because it would be best if he could get back with Fee first, on his terms of course. He started up the car and went home.

CHAPTER SIX

Fiona woke up and turned over in bed feeling for Simon's warm, hard body. She had gone to bed feeling pleasantly tired and relaxed after the show and had gone to sleep fairly quickly for once. She had been dreaming that Simon was making love to her and awoke with her whole body aching for him. Damn the man she thought. Why, oh why couldn't I have felt like this over Paul. It must have been a combination of the showing and of Beryl telling her that Simon might be moving to Auberton that had prompted the dream. Why was he doing that? It was obvious that Beryl thought that he was trying to be nearer to her and that they might get back together again. Dear Beryl, what was more likely was that the dogs were proving to be a problem and he was trying to get them back in the kennels. Hard Luck.

Since he had gone she had begun to get a little of her self esteem back. There was no way that he was going to get near enough to make her feel so bad about herself again. His unwillingness to be seen with her at dog shows because she had been 'blacked' had made her feel leprous and a failure. Who the hell did these unknown people who were supposed to organise who won and who didn't, think they were? Little tin gods ruining peoples lives for a bit of glory and causing untold harm in peoples private lives as well. Simon had never said how they were supposed to organise such a vast system only that, as far as he knew, it was all done by word of mouth, nothing was written. To hell with all that anyway, she had decided to decorate the lounge and she was making a start today. Throwing off the covers she got up and went into the bathroom for a shower.

After the morning rounds and chores in the kennel, Fiona grabbed a cup of coffee and dashed out to the nearby town for some emulsion paint for the walls and some gloss for the woodwork. She had also decided that, when she was satisfied with the colour of the paint etc., she would have some curtains made and re-cover the two armchairs in the same material She might even have lampshades made as well. She hadn't tackled anything like this since the early days of her marriage to Duncan. It would be fun and a new challenge, if it was successful she might tackle another room, the bathroom was looking decidedly tatty. She had just returned from the store, where she had wandered round the various aisles getting masses of new ideas for decorating, when the phone rang.

"Hello Fiona, it's Natalie. I just wanted to thank you for a marvellous and exciting day. I really feel that I can look forward to the future with interest and purpose. When I wrote to Candida last night I was able to write so much about the show. I can't wait for our next show in two weeks time."

"I'm glad that you enjoyed it so much."

"Well, I know that it can't be as exciting for you but you did enjoy it too. Didn't you?"

"Of course I did. As I said, old habits die hard."

"Would you think me a nuisance if I were to come over some time for a bit more advice on trimming and stripping? I'm determined to show Jamie as best as I can."

"Of course not, pleased to help. Why don't you come round on Thursday afternoon."

She was frowning when she put the phone down a few minutes later. If Simon took that place in Auberton. Would he start going to the local shows round here again. No, now that he thought that he was 'in', he was getting like a lot of other people, too high and mighty to go to Open shows unless it was to bring out a new puppy. Like most of the 'in' crowd nowadays he only went to Champ Shows because that's where you could make up a Champion. Rubbish, what percentage of Champ show exhibitors made up a Champion, not many! Well, she thought, I think the Open shows are more fun, cheaper and you can see more breeds which made it so much more interesting. You could learn so much more about other breeds, get rosettes and not travel so far and she intended to continue to go to them.

As she gradually cleared all the movable furniture out of the lounge and covered the rest with old sheets, she started singing to the music on the radio. Some three hours later, after covering the parquet floor with newspaper, she had washed the walls down and the woodwork and filled a couple of small cracks with Polyfilla. Standing back to look at her handiwork, she felt tired but really satisfied. Going out to see to the dogs, she looked around at the kennels and the adjoining field and wood. This really was a lovely cottage and it was ideal for the kennels, no near neighbours but close enough to main roads for easy access; smiling she went back to the kitchen to cook herself a meal. She had just started eating when the phone rang, "Hi Fiona, how are you?"

"Laura! It's lovely to hear from you, I'm so sorry, I meant to phone you but I've started decorating the lounge and I forgot the time. I was going to phone you this evening."

"Decorating!, you're brave. Look, say if it's not convenient but the boys have got a holiday soon, you know, Easter, and they are pestering me to ask if they can come and stay again. I wasn't sure how you were managing and if you would want then without, well... without Simon there to halve the burden."

"I'm managing very well indeed and I'd love to have the boys, they are such a help round the kennel and exercising the dogs. Yes, when do you want them to come?"

"Can't remember the exact date but I'll ring you again with the details and thanks again Fiona. You are a good friend to me and, I think you're much braver than I could ever be."

Returning to her meal, Fiona reflected that her life seemed to suddenly have speeded up a bit. A new friend in Natalie, going to the shows again and now Laura's three boys coming to stay at Easter. Things were definitely looking up.

Two weeks later, with the decorating finished to her satisfaction and another successful show behind her, Fiona opened the door to Laura and the boys.

"Good heavens Laura what have you been feeding them on? They have grown inches since I last saw them." The boys all smiled and stretched up a bit taller. Tom's voice was even beginning to change slightly.

Laura greatly admired the new decor in the lounge, "You really do have an eye for colour Fiona and the whole scheme is just perfect for the cottage. It has such a relaxed, mellow feel to it."

"You wait until I get my new curtains and covers that I've ordered." Fiona looked at Laura as she was speaking and noticed that Laura still did not look her usual rosy, chubby self. She hadn't since that spell in hospital.

"How are you feeling now Laura?"

"OK, my last check-up was alright. I'm just a bit tired that's all, the children keep me so busy these days. I know that it must sound awful to you but I'll be glad when Amanda is a bit older and can go to school all day. I really do appreciate you having the boys here for a few days Fiona."

"Heavens Laura, what are friends for, anyway, I love having them here. I've cooked loads of cakes and planned trips out. They are such good company and make me laugh. They take quite a bit of the work off my shoulders too."

The boarding part of the kennel was full for the Easter holidays and Fiona was very pleased to have the extra help. After dinner, they got down to the serious business of playing Monopoly. Just for a moment Fiona felt miserable when she heard the echoes in her head of Simon and Tom laughing as they managed to skip over Mayfair once again, much to the annoyance of Richard. She soon forgot though as the excitement of the present game built up.

Over the next few days, they went to the pictures, found some frog spawn on one of their walks and, amidst much laughter and dropping of flour, tried to make some chocolate gingerbread men for Amanda and their Mum and Dad.

Fiona awoke to sunshine on Easter Sunday morning having slept right through to seven o'clock. Scrambling out of bed and hurriedly showering, she raced downstairs and, grabbing her anorak, hurried out to let the dogs out. She got the usual rapturous welcome from her own dogs and friendly greetings from all but one of the boarders. He was an old dog and obviously set in his ways. Being in a kennel environment did not please him too much. She stroked him and felt that he was warm enough, although he had the heating on, she had also given him extra blankets to make the old joints comfortable.

"Not for long now old chap, you'll soon be back to the comforts of home." His owners had brought his own blanket and some toys but they lay around untouched, "I'll get Tom to come and talk to you and play with you for a bit shall I old fella."
She hurried back to get breakfast for herself and the boys as she was taking them home that morning and Laura had invited her to stay for dinner. It had been arranged for Ruth's eldest daughter to come to look after the kennels for the three hours that she would be away. She was just having a last look round to see that the boys hadn't left anything when the phone rang, "Hello, Simfell kennels."

"Hello Fee, Simon here. Just wanted to wish you a Happy Easter. How are you? Are you busy?"

"What do you want? And yes, I am busy. I've had Tom and the twins here for a few days and am just about to take them home."

"Oh, then I won't keep you. Are you alright for someone to look after the dogs?"

"Yes, Hannah, Ruth's daughter will be here. Everything is under control."

"I see. Well, Happy Easter to you and the boys and my regards to Laura and Michael."
She put the phone down, damn the man, why had he phoned her? What was he up to now? I won't let him spoil my day. When Hannah arrived she impressed on her not to let anyone into the cottage or the kennels and to spend a bit of time with the old dog. In the company of Laura's family and the fun of giving Easter eggs to the children, and the laughter when the boys produced the rather weird gingerbread men, she put Simon to the back of her mind until she got back to the cottage. She arrived back at the kennels late afternoon, "Hello Hannah, everything OK?"

"Yes, the dogs are fine. There are a couple of messages on your answerphone and..."

"And what?"

"I wasn't sure what to do. Mr Philips called in and I didn't know if you meant that he couldn't come in or not. He said that it would be alright. He had spoken to you this morning."

"Yes he did. OK Hannah don't worry about it. Did he come in here?"

"Oh yes. He said to tell you that he liked the colours in the lounge."

"Oh did he. Well here's your money Hannah and thank you very much for helping out."
She could hardly wait for her to go before going into every room to see if he had changed or taken anything. Satisfied that all appeared to be as she had left it, she then checked on the kennels. Nothing had altered. She wasn't going to leave this intrusion of her privacy and once again indoors she phoned Beryl.
"Is Simon there with you?"
"Fiona? No, Simon isn't here. Is anything wrong. You sound upset."
"I'll say there's something wrong. If he is there. I want to speak to him. Now"
"No he isn't here. We did invite him but he has only just moved into his new place and he said that he had too much to do. What's the matter Fiona? You sound very angry. Can we help at all?"
"Thank you Beryl that is kind of you but it's nothing for you to worry about. Do you have his new phone number then?"
"As a matter of fact we do. He gave it to us the other day. I'll get it for you."
The phone rang for some time and she was just about to replace the receiver when Simon's voice answered. Even as angry as she was her wretched heart beat a bit faster when she heard his deep tones, "Hello, Simon Philips."
"How dare you come round here snooping. You have no right at all to come here uninvited. This is my property and nothing to do with you any more. Who do you think you are?"
"Fee? Yes, you're quite right Fee. It is your property as you have always made abundantly clear and I was not snooping. One of my boys has a sore foot and I popped in to see if I could have a bit of the special cream that we always used. As to the question, who I am, as far as I know, unless you have instigated divorce proceedings without my knowledge, I am your husband."
"Oh, don't twist my words. You're good at that. Always making me feel that I am in the wrong. That it's me who is unreasonable. Men are good at that sort of thing. The fact remains you came here uninvited."
"Fee, what the hell are you talking about. If you had been there, I thought that you would just let me have a bit of cream until I could get to the Vets. Is that so bloody unreasonable. For God's sake the dog's in pain. Have you declared war on my dogs as well?"

"Oh, don't be ridiculous. You're trying to get at me through the dogs now. You knew that I was going out. You knew that I would not be here. Why didn't you ask when you phoned me?"

"Because I hadn't noticed it then."

"So, it's me whose in the wrong again as usual. Well, don't try to tell me that you had to go into my house then for the cream? What's your excuse for that?"

"Fee, let's end this conversation here shall we. I'm sorry that I came and I shall bloody well send you a tube of cream in the post as soon as I can get to a Vet OK? By the way, changing the subject, that was a damn good effort on the lounge. Well done."

Fiona, speechless with anger, slammed the phone down. Of all the bloody cheek. Had he only come for some cream? Was she reading it all wrongly? Why had he come into the cottage then? It was too much of a coincidence surely that he should have phoned her that morning. Her thoughts were interrupted by the phone ringing, "Yes." she snapped.

"Fiona, are you alright? Peter and I were so worried about you. Did you manage to get hold of Simon?"

"Yes, I did."

"Was he able to help?"

"Yes and no. Look, I must go and shut the dogs in and do the rounds. I'll ring you later Beryl and tell you all about it. Thanks for being concerned."

She went upstairs to change into her working clothes. It was as she laid her skirt on the bed that she noticed that the duvet was slightly rucked up. She pulled it down and there, on her pillow, was a box of her favourite chocolates with a little, toy fluffy chick sitting on it. Tears pricked her eyes as she looked at them, "Damn the man!" she said as she stroked the yellow fluff on the chick.

Viv Butcher opened the box of chocolates and picked a coffee cream from the selection. It had been so kind of dear old Mrs Lampton to bring them to the surgery for her. She called to the dogs and gave them a little piece of chocolate each.

CHAPTER SEVEN

"Do you want anything else?"

"No thanks, just the bill."

Simon was putting his jacket on just as the young boy came back with the bill. He was getting sick of motorway meals but, at least, it meant he didn't have to get himself anything when he got home. Wearily, he walked back to the car. The two dogs he had taken to the championship show raised their heads to see who it was and then laid down again and closed their eyes. Funny, he thought, when we win, even they seem to know and are brighter. He had gone today knowing that he wasn't going to get top honours. In fact he knew that he wasn't going to get much more than a first for some time. He did have a championship show to judge this year. Thank God it was in the bag before Fee had judged that bloody show. He should be able to organise something from that but, the presents, bottles of whisky etc., had to be put on hold for now. It would mean a bit of a lean time next year.

All the past couple of years work, thrown away on one bloody Champ show. All that work, all that careful breeding, making all the right contacts, smarming up to some of those bastards, all gone, well nearly, and for what, just so that she could put up the dogs she liked. He thought it had sunk in that a lot of judges didn't judge the dogs! He thought it had sunk in that all the bloody judging seminars, lectures and certificates in the world didn't make the slightest difference to how most people judged.

He sighed as he turned off the motorway, soon be home now. She'd certainly learned how to smarm up to bloody Alan Burgess. He had seen him at several shows recently but had always managed to avoid him. Every time he saw him now he could see Fee. laying naked on a bed and knew that that bastard could too. The thought still nearly drove him mad, he had believed her when she had told him what had taken place. Had it happened to anyone else, he'd have thought it bloody funny but Fee... No, too bloody honest for her own good, he frowned as he turned into the front of the house he had recently rented.

That evening, watching the ten o'clock news, an item came up about a librarian who had found a letter, reputedly written by Lord Byron, in an old book. This made him think of Fiona again. Blast the woman, he tried to keep her out of his mind but she still came back in a hundred ways. He wondered what she had done when she found the chocolates under her pillow, he presumed she hadn't found them when she phoned him. He hadn't stayed long. It had been bloody agony to go into that room, smelling her perfume, smelling her hair, her body when he picked up the pillow He got up quickly, just the thought of her was having a very uncomfortable effect on him. He smiled, Mary, his first wife had always said that he was a randy bugger. He had just gone out into the kitchen to make a cup of coffee when the phone rang.

"Hello Simon, Paul Aston, hope I've not rung at an inconvenient time."

"No, just making myself a cup of coffee. How did you get this phone number. I haven't long moved in here."

"Ah, well I phoned Fiona and she gave it to me. She said that she had spoken with you. I didn't realise that you had made it up with her."

"Haven't. Just called in to be friendly and get something for one of the dogs and got my head bitten off in the process."

"I see. Well I just phoned for the results of today's show. I presume that you did go?"

"Yes, I went and a fat lot of good it did me. You know who the judge was so you must have a good idea who won."

"Ken Oldham?"

"Of course. Made the bloody dog up now. Have you looked at it's mouth?"

"Um, not recently."

"It's overshot and that's an understatement. Oh, well that's how the cookie crumbles. You got anything in the pipeline for next year? Perhaps we could get together and..."

"Yes, in the first part of the year. Thank goodness that my leg is fully healed now".

"Look Paul, I'll give you my new address and you must come round for a couple of jars."

"Yes, fine. I'd like that. I'll let you know when."

Paul heaved a sigh of relief when he hung up, it sounded as if Simon's visit had been a spur of the moment thing. He had phoned Fiona previously that evening to ask if she would agree to go to the theatre with him next week. It had been obvious from the way that she answered the phone that something was wrong. She had positively snapped at him. After hearing her account of Simon's visit, she had not found the chocolates at that time, he commiserated with her and then asked her if she would like to go to the local theatre with him. She had readily agreed. This was promising; she had already been out for a drink with him and a meal, things were improving. He felt a little uneasy about Simon's visit, he certainly didn't want him queering his pitch with Fiona. He had thought long and hard about the time they had spent together at her cottage. They had got on so well, if it hadn't been for his damned leg he would have been more passionate, more romantic. He decided that a friendly call on Simon for that drink might be advantageous, just to see how he felt about his separation from Fiona.

Simon finished his coffee and went up to bed wondering what Paul had really phoned him about. Bloody hell, what would dog showers do without the phone! He had known Paul long enough to know that he never did anything without a very good reason. Was it because he was judging later in the year? No, he'd never bothered before and he didn't drop any hints about how well his dog was doing. There was something he was missing. When he and Fee were together they often used to sit down and work these connections through. With hindsight, when they read the show reports in the dog papers, often little happenings, puppy sales, committee members, previous wins, studs, all seemed to have a bearing on who had won later. God, he missed those talks. He missed Fee. Damn it, he really loved that woman. He'd have to get back with her without losing his pride, but how? No-one but no-one would ever know how much that Alan Burgess business had hurt. He was just drifting off to sleep when a thought entered his mind. Good God, could Paul Aston be sniffing round Fee? If so, he was going to have to move quicker than he intended. Could that have been the reason for the call? Finding out just what the situation was between them? Wide awake now, he sat up in bed and turned the light on. He was going to get Fee. back and soon.

"Um, not too bad. Could be worse." Paul ran a comb through his thinning hair. "Wonder if she'll like this aftershave." He was talking to himself again. He had started doing it when he had come home after staying with Fiona because the house had seemed so quiet. Adjusting his tie and straightening the jacket of his suit, he left the house for his date with Fiona. She too had taken care with her appearance and, as he led her to their seats in the theatre, he felt very proud to be in her company. "May I say Fiona that you look lovely in that dress?"

"Thank you Paul, I'm glad you like it. It is a favourite of mine."

As the house lights dimmed, he took her hand in his and she did not try to withdraw it. The play was a 'whodunnit' and when they went out in the interval for a drink, they chatted away happily about their theories as to which of the many characters was the murderer. In the event neither of them was right. Paul drove them home and she invited him in for a coffee but Paul declined. He had already decided that he was going to take things slowly, she had enjoyed the evening and that was enough for now.

During the next few weeks he took her to York to see the railway museum and to Crick to see the tram museum. Fiona was delighted with both outings and, as they rode on the top of a tram, she turned to him and kissed him on the cheek, "Paul, I have had such a pleasant day. We do seem to like the same things don't we."

As he gave her hand a squeeze, Paul smiled and nodded in agreement. His plan was working.

Simon was looking at his bank statement. Bloody Hell, buying that bitch from Geoff had crippled him. Worth it though, it meant another CC in the bag at a future date because he'd certainly paid over the odds for her. He would have to mate her up when she next came in season. According to Geoff she'd had one litter and was a good whelper. She was due in season about next month, if he used that young dog of Fee's that she was showing, it would kill two birds with one stone. Help his depleted finances and give him the best possible excuse to see Fee again. She'd then want to see the puppies and.....

Well, it might sort out a lot of his problems. He had been slightly surprised when he first saw her name in a show critique but, thanks to good old Bob and Annie, he had found out that she was going to shows with that Bennett woman. Saxon had been doing quite well at the Open shows so it wouldn't look too bad if he used him.

"Hi Fiona, Simon here. How are you?"
"I'm fine thank you."
"Fee, I bought a lovely bitch from Geoff Richards a while ago and she's due in season shortly. I'd like to mate her to Saxon if you wouldn't mind."
"Why did you buy a bitch from him and why do you want to use Saxon?"
"Why? Well because she is partly our lines and it should be a damned good mating."
"And that's the only reason?"
"Yes."
"OK. Let me know when."
"I'll do that and, thanks Fee."
Whistling up the dogs, he put their leads on and took them out for a good, long walk.

Fiona had been short with Simon because she was angry, she and Natalie had been to a show and, although the judge was in another terrier breed, she knew Fiona quite well by sight so there was no excuse. Natalie's Jamie had won his class, Viv Butcher had won the next class and Saxon had won the Open class and then, in the challenge the damned judge had given BOB to Viv Butcher's dog. She was so angry that it had been very hard to congratulate her. Viv had looked so damned pleased with herself. Natalie had been very surprised at Fiona's reaction.
"I'm sorry Natalie to go on but I can't stand that woman. She is very unpopular generally."
"But why? She is a receptionist at my doctor's surgery and she is so kind and helpful."
"Well, she isn't in dogs. No-one has a good word to say about her. She is a most terrible gossip and trouble-maker so be careful what you

say to her. In fact, say as little as possible. That's what most people do. Don't ever think of using her dogs either. The stories I've heard!"

"I don't understand Fiona, what do you mean about her being a troublemaker and what's wrong with her dogs? The dog today looked very nice I thought."

"Just take my word for it Natalie, she causes trouble and her dogs have, well, in the past, there have been lots of problems."

As Viv walked out of the Group ring having come second no-one came up to congratulate her but then, she didn't expect it anymore. She had been labelled as bad and that was that.

CHAPTER EIGHT

Viv sat at the side of the ring. She tried to do this nowadays at the few Champ Shows that she attended because it didn't look as if she was on her own with nobody to talk to. If she sat near her bench she felt very isolated because nearly everyone passed by without speaking to her. Some nodded in her direction, a few enquired whether she was, 'alright', as they quickly passed by. The odd newcomer to showing would recognise that she was an 'old hand' and stop to speak and ask advice on some matter or another. She always spoke to them and gave advice freely but found that, once they were established and had sufficient information to know that she was a nobody and unable to advance their career, they also started to ignore her. She sighed and tried to concentrate on the judging but the line-ups were such a mixture of type and size that it was obviously fixed or the judge hadn't a clue what he was doing, in either case it was not possible to try to guess in advance what the judge would pick out. Well, it was, but not from the dog but from the face of the exhibitor. She sighed deeply and settled herself more comfortably into the chair.

"Hello Viv. Didn't expect to see you here today." She turned round in surprise and saw Bob Adams standing behind her chair, "Hello Bob. No, I'm sitting here wondering why I bothered. I suppose that I am stupid really to still live in hope. This showing lark is like a drug isn't it, you can't give it up. Who have you brought?"

"Nobody. I thought that it would be a complete waste of time. No, I've only come here today to pick up a bitch puppy from Lily Gregson."

"Oh, Are you branching out then?"

"Yes and no, Annie and I have decided that we'll never win with our own dogs so we thought we buy one of Lily's, after all she is always winning with her dogs isn't she. If it doesn't work out then we'll finish with showing altogether."
Poor Bob, thought Viv, as she looked at his honest, kindly face, he and Annie are such nice people and they adore their dogs and yet they don't stand a hope in hell of doing well, even with one of Lily's dogs. It was a shame because they didn't even realise why they didn't do well. "Don't say that Bob, I should miss your face at the shows, you and Annie always cheer me up."

Just at that moment the exhibitors for the next class came into the ring. One of them was Simon Philips and Viv lost interest in talking to Bob. It was in the hopes that Simon had entered the show that she had actually made an entry and come. With Fiona seemingly out of the running, she was going to see what she could do. She had thought that he was a gorgeous hunk when she first saw him but he had always been so absorbed in the dogs, and then in Fiona and the dogs, that she had never dreamed that there was a chance for her, but now..... It was certainly worth a try.
Simon won the class as she expected he would, he and Fiona had made some useful contacts recently, she watched as he spoke to one of his many friends and then followed him back to his bench, "Hello Simon, that was a nice win. Well-deserved too."

"Hello Viv, thanks. Are you showing today?"

"Yes, later, just brought a bitch. I'm not in 'til Post Graduate."

"Oh, well, Good Luck." He walked off towards the ring.

Not an auspicious start she thought but, it's a beginning. She also went back to the ring so that she could watch the challenge later. When Simon came into the ring for the challenge he was looking fairly confident, over the years Viv had come to recognise that look, it usually meant that it was the CC or the Res CC , he was also judging a champ show later in the year. Simon's dog did end up with the Res CC. She applauded loudly and then quickly got out of her chair to congratulate him, "Well done Simon, that was richly deserved. How's about we have a drink to celebrate. My shout. Only I'd like to ask your advice about something."
Simon seemed to consider his reply for a second, "Yeah, OK why not, I'll see you in the tent."

Viv felt warm inside, this was a good. In the crowded, noisy tent they had to stand up as all the seats were taken but, undaunted, Viv got the drinks and then. launched into her rehearsed speech, "Simon, I've long admired your stock and, at the moment, I think that you've some outstanding dogs and I was thinking of using one of them on one of my bitches. Could you have a look at the bitch I've got here today and perhaps recommend one of your studs for her?"

Simon looked at her attractive face. What's she up to? She's never asked to use my dogs before. He shrugged his shoulders, he could certainly do with the cash, "I can if you like."

"Oh good, that would be lovely. I see from the catalogue that you have moved again. Auberton isn't it. That's quite near to me."

"Um," Simon looked at his watch, "All right if I look at the bitch now? I want to be off fairly sharpish."

They walked back to the tent where the Cumbrians were benched. Viv noted that one or two heads turned in their direction as they walked by. Good, she thought. That'll set the tongues wagging, the phones will be hot tonight. Simon recommended that she use one of his younger dogs to which Viv readily agreed. She couldn't care less which one he suggested it just gave her the excuse to be with him.

During the afternoon, she went into the ring with her bitch and, as was expected came nowhere, well fifth out of seven which was in effect the same thing. No write-up in the dog papers, so most people wouldn't even know that she had been there and, of course, it didn't reinforce her prefix in people's minds. Those that were at the show would just see her lose again as she invariably did so there must obviously be something wrong with the bitch, even though she looked nice, would be the general conclusion. Viv sighed and packed up her gear ready for the long journey home. There was so much psychology went into all this. Did people realise this or did they not want to?

Once she was on the motor-way it was a long, boring stretch to her junction, the car was warm and as she relaxed her thoughts went back to when she had first started showing. She pulled a face, that was a long time ago now. She had married Chris when she was only twenty-two. It had been a whirlwind romance. Chris was twenty-five, a university graduate, good looking, ambitious and fun to be with. She had been a secretary to one of the managers in a pet food manufacturing plant. Chris was into computers and was certain that it was an up and coming business, "Viv the sky's the limit," was his favourite saying in those days.

Sexually demanding, it took all her energies to do her job, they needed her salary to live on, and to satisfy his sexual demands. He also insisted that they both needed to entertain his potential clients and they spent long hours at restaurants and pubs. He had such drive and never seemed to tire and after a couple of years of this hectic rush his business took off and became very successful. The trouble was that, for her, life was not so successful. Chris started to find fault with her dress sense, to criticise her lack of knowledge with regard to the computer world and worst of all, if she wasn't wildly enthusiastic and innovative with regard to their long, sexual playtimes, he would either hit her or storm out of the house and not return till the early hours of the morning. She could only guess where he went.

Their marriage ended when, one night, after an evening of drinking and entertaining a prospective client, Chris suggested that it would be fun if she did the dance of the seven veils for the man. She declined at first thinking that it was a joke but Chris took her into the bedroom and threatened to beat hell out of her if she didn't; a lot of money was riding on this he told her angrily. It was only a bit of fun he kept saying. He had bought her the revealing outfit to wear to a party once but she had been too embarrassed to wear it. Knowing what would happen if she refused this time, she finally put on the skimpy outfit and went back into the lounge. The client ogled her body as she entered the room and totally embarrassed, she started to dance to the music, when she got down to the last two veils she stopped and turned to go back to the bedroom. Chris shouted angrily at her and she hesitated and then turned back. Chris invited the client to remove the last two veils himself.

Horrified at this turn of events and frightened, she stood still as the man came up to her and, removing the veil from the breasts, started to fondle them. She tried to move away from him and threw an agonised glance at Chris for help, he was laughing and egging the man on to remove the last veil. Now really terrified, she pulled away and ran crying into the bedroom. Furious, Chris ran after her and grabbed the last veil so that she was completely naked. He then grabbed her arm and forced her back into the other room laughing as he did so. The other man was unzipping his trousers. She felt so utterly humiliated and in despair she broke away from Chris's grasp and ran to the bathroom where she locked herself in.

About an hour later, she heard the client go and came out. Chris immediately grabbed her and beat her nearly unconscious. When he sobered up in the morning and saw the extent of the bruises on her face and body, he begged her not to go to the hospital because it would ruin his business. In pain, disillusioned and desperately tired having lain awake all night, she agreed on condition that he gave her a divorce. She insisted that she be allowed to move into a hotel straight away and that he would put enough money into her bank account to enable her to buy a house. He readily agreed to all her demands and..... her reminiscences were halted there as she saw the sign for her junction coming up.

CHAPTER NINE

Picking up the phone Natalie dialled Fiona's number and got her answerphone, “Hello Fiona it's me Natalie. I know you must be very busy but how would you like to come over this evening for a meal if you’re free. It saves us both cooking doesn’t it?” Putting the phone down Natalie went into the kitchen to see what was in the freezer. “Yes,” she said to the dogs, “Chicken pieces it shall be. Easy to cook something grand or, if Fiona can’t come, you can have a feast tomorrow.” She looked out of the window and saw that it was still pouring with rain, “Do you know Jamie, I think it was a good thing that we didn’t have a show today after all.”

Fiona phoned her back about lunch time, “Hello Natalie. Thanks for the invitation. I should love to come. I’ll bring some chocolates and a bottle of wine.”

Fiona hadn't eaten the chocolates that Simon had left but had kept them by her bedside while telling herself every day to throw them away. She would take them over to Natalie’s and they could both enjoy them. She must remember to talk to Natalie tonight about entering for a Champ Show. She had been doing quite well with Saxon at the little Open shows and it was now time for him to be launched into the Championship show scene. Natalie and Jamie should be seen as well, it reinforced the Simfell name. It had been a stroke of luck meeting up with Natalie like that, and, it had certainly been mutually beneficial.

“Have another chocolate Natalie, blow the calories. Now, how about we enter for one of the Welsh Championship shows? They are good shows to go to and, if we leave pretty early, the journey is no bother."

"Oh, I don't know Fiona. Do you think that Jamie and I are ready for Championship shows? I should be a bag of nerves and my trimming isn't good enough yet."

"Yes, of course it is. I'll help you with the trimming, you know that. Look upon it as an adventure. I very much want to go to see how Saxon fares against other dogs of his age and I'd love you to come as well."

"All right I'll come, but you must help me get him ready."

"Are you OK for the show next Saturday? As this is quite a big Open show, we ought to leave a bit earlier than we have previously. If I pick you up at say eight 'o' clock, will that be alright? Good, see you then and thanks for the lovely dinner. Don't forget to send for that schedule for Wales."

As she left the cottage to go to the Open show the following Saturday, Fiona was quite excited. The judge was an old friend who had been to one of their Christmas parties and had also used one of their stud dogs in the past. As he was also judging the Terrier Group she was more than hopeful of doing quite well. You never know she thought, I've never had BIS; perhaps this could be the show. She was in good spirits when she arrived at Natalie's house to pick her up.

"Morning Natalie, it's going to be a lovely day."

Natalie too was hopeful of perhaps getting a first but, as this show was tented and being held outside, she was a little concerned that Jamie would get too excited. As they drove into the large field and showed their car pass, Natalie was getting rather nervous, "Do you think that Jamie will be OK. Fiona? Perhaps it would be better if you could show him for me?" Fiona did not reply, she seemed to be anxiously looking at the rows of cars lined up in the car park, "Sorry Natalie what did you say?"

"Oh, nothing important. It can wait a while."

Fiona opened up the back of the estate car and together they started to get the trolley, cages and gear out. The dogs were eager to get out of the car. It was obvious that they loved the excitement of the show and the noise of other dogs giving voice to their feelings. Pulling the loaded trolley together over the slightly rough grass, they made their way towards the ring in which they were to be judged.

"As we're the first breed in the ring Natalie, I think it might be best if we don't go in the tent but stay by the ringside and get the dogs ready." They put up their tables and started grooming the dogs. Out of the corner of her eye she saw the judge and the steward walk into the ring, she turned and smiled and the judge smiled back. Oh good, she thought, today is going to be a good day Natalie was in the second class of the day and as she walked into the ring, Fiona stopped grooming Saxon to watch how Jamie behaved and looked straight into Simon's brown eyes! He smiled and waved a hand. She nodded quickly and turned back to Saxon. Why hadn't she seen his car in the car park? He must have arrived late. She looked up again but he'd disappeared.. She hurriedly looked at the schedule, surely he wasn't judging here today. Perhaps she missed it, no he wasn't. He must have come to spy on her. No, don't be silly, you're getting paranoid she told herself.

"Fiona wasn't that... Are you alright Fiona. You've gone rather pale?"

"Yes, I'm fine just fine. How did you do?." She looked at the red card in Natalie's hand, "First, well done. I must go now." She put the show lead on Saxon and walked into the ring. There were already four other exhibitors in the ring and as she placed Saxon on the ground ready for the judge to look at the line-up, someone hurried into the ring to stand next to her, it was Simon with Sara the litter sister to Saxon.

"Hello Fee. May the best man win," he grinned at her.
She ignored his remark and tried to stay calm, she didn't want her feelings running down the lead and getting Saxon excited.

When the judge had gone over the six dogs and when he had pulled out the first, which was Simon, the second, third and fourth, Fiona was still trying to bravely smile and show Saxon, but when he pulled the other dog out for fifth place and she was asked to leave the ring by the steward, she was so mortified that she felt physically sick. Hurrying out of the ring with her head down she bumped into Natalie who was full of concern, "Fiona, what happened I just don't understand?" Fiona was so close to tears that she could only miserably shake her head. The steward was calling for unbeaten dogs and she nodded in the direction of the ring, "Go on Natalie, they're calling for you." The judge gave Simon and Sara BOB and Jamie got RBOB smiling he shook their

hands and asked them to do a lap of honour. As this same judge would be doing the Terrier Group she had a pretty good idea who would be winning it. Now, she knew why Simon had turned up.
Natalie came out of the ring elated and bemused at the same time. She was at a complete loss to understand her placing over Fiona. She found that she actually felt a bit embarrassed as she went up to the white-faced Fiona.

"I'm so sorry Fiona but, at least it was your breeding wasn't it. If.... if you want to have a word with Simon don't mind me, I'm so excited that I need a cup of coffee."

"No, I don't." It was all she could trust herself to say. She was choked with emotion. Anger and humiliation mostly. Her chaotic thoughts whirled around as she stood beside the ring, "Must go Natalie. Absolutely bursting and there's sure to be a queue." She hurried away to the other side of the field where the portable lavatories were. Once inside the little cabin, she put her hand to her aching head and sighed deeply. What a fool I was to think that I could win! Of course, he was part of the system, he knew that she didn't play the game so she had to be taught a lesson. Just as Simon had prophesied. Did she have to be so humiliated though; after all it wasn't a Champ show. He must have seen that Saxon was a good dog. Perhaps that was it. The better the dog the greater the humiliation. She relieved herself, washed her hands and started to walk back across the field to the rings all the pleasure of the day had gone.

"Fiona wait," someone shouted behind her it was Simon.

"If you've come to gloat. Don't bother and don't worry, I've got the message loud and clear. Did you enjoy arranging it with him just to prove that you were right all along"

"Now, just hold on there." He grabbed her arm and swung her to face him, "I didn't even know that you were bloody well going to be here today."

"Oh no, so what was this, 'May the best man win' then."

"You know I always say that to other people in the ring."

"No I don't. You knew that you were going to win."

"Yes, I had a pretty good idea but I honestly didn't think that he would do that to you. Third or fourth maybe but not chuck you out. Saxon's turned out to be a bloody nice dog."

"Thank you and that makes it better does it?"

"No, but.. I did warn you didn't I Fee. I tried to bloody well tell you but you wouldn't have it would you."
Tears were beginning to well up in her eyes, she pulled her arm free and started to run,

"Fee, come back, Fee wait...."
The day she had so looked forward to was ruined, in ashes, she walked around the other rings until she could get herself under control and then went back to a worried Natalie.

"Fiona, you look terrible. Are you alright?"

"Yes, I'm OK now. Think I must have eaten something that disagreed with me. Do you mind if we don't stay? I'd like to get back home."

They quickly packed up and left the show. Fiona kept her eyes on the ground as they walked out. She couldn't bear any commiserations from anyone. She was so grateful to Natalie when, on the journey home, she didn't ask her any questions about the happenings at the show although she must have had so many.

"Hello Simon, poor Fiona, didn't do too well today did she. Glad to see than you won with that lovely bitch of yours."
He knew that voice. Turning round he looked at Viv Butcher, "Hello Viv didn't see you in the ring."

"No, I just came for a look round today. Congratulations on the BOB. You should do well in the Group too."

"Yes, well I'm hopeful. I know that Ian likes this bitch."

"Fiona seems to have left you all on your own. Thought she might have stayed. How about going for a cup of tea, or perhaps you fancy something stronger? I've always had you down for the strong, silent type."

My God thought Simon, this is a come on. Bloody Hell! Viv Butcher!. She had had a fairly successful kennel in the past with two or three breeds and everyone knew exactly how she did so well. God, she must be into her fifties by now surely. Mind you, you wouldn't know it, standing there in front of him she looked quite appetising. She's offering it on a plate so she must be after getting something when I judge. "Thanks Viv, but I need to get some dog food and I must get the bitch ready for the Group. See you."

She looked at his retreating back. It was going to be a bit more difficult than she had thought to get to know him. Never mind, there was always the mating with his dog.

That evening, too upset to want to eat, Fiona sat in the lounge watching some rubbish or other on the TV. Although she was looking at it, nothing was registering in her brain. She just kept reliving that awful moment when she had to walk Saxon out of the ring. How could Ian McNally do that to her. He and his wife Moira had sat in this very room laughing and talking at their parties. They were friends! Perhaps he had really thought Saxon was a poor specimen. No, she knew that couldn't be true. No, it must be this 'black' that Simon had spoken about when she had judged that championship show, but, surely it didn't extend to showing at Open shows. Surely not. It was true that she had not been approached to judge another Championship show since and only one Open show, but to be this vindictive! Had Simon meant all this when he had warned her of the consequences?

Did it mean that she was completely finished. That she would never win very much again! She would certainly never be able to make up another champion, even if she wanted to! How could these people have so much power. How did they organise it? It was like the Mafia not dog showing.

Her thoughts were interrupted by the phone ringing. She had put the answerphone on because she was worried that Simon would phone. Walking out to the hall, she could hear Simon's voice, "Come on Fee, pick up the phone, Come on Fee. I know you're there. Fee, look, I had absolutely nothing to do with today's events. You know that. For God's sake, you surely don't think that I would willingly allow that to happen to you. Please Fee, talk to me........ Oh well, I tried for God's sake. Anyway, perhaps now you'll believe what I warned you about before. You thought that I was exaggerating didn't you... Fee, will you bloody well pick up the phone, I'm worried about you. Look, if you don't pick up the phone, I'm coming round."

She quickly picked up the phone, "Don't you dare come round here. I hate you. I don't ever want to see you again. You or your rotten, vicious cronies." She slammed the phone down and burst into tears.

The following evening she phoned Natalie, "Hello Natalie. Everything alright?"

"Yes, I'm fine. How are you? I've been so worried. You were obviously terribly upset."

"I'm OK now. Must have eaten something," she had made her mind up not to burden Natalie with the sordid details because she wanted her to enjoy her showing as much as possible. She looked a different person now and it was obviously important to her well-being and happiness.

"The judge just didn't like Saxon for some reason. It happens."

"But Fiona, he liked Jamie and your husband's dog and they are all so similar."

"Oh, well don't let it worry you. It's just all part of showing, you know, win some lose some."

"But you were so upset."

"Oh, well, let's say that it was more to do with an upset tummy and to Simon being there than anything else. Let's leave it at that shall we. We'll look forward to our next show instead."

Natalie realised that Fiona did not wish to discuss it and respected her wishes but spent odd moments during the day mulling over the events of that show. She felt sure that there was something she was missing. She accepted that it had something to do with Simon, perhaps it was because his dog won over her dog but surely not. She felt that she knew Fiona well enough now to know that she wasn't a bad sport. No, there must be something else. Why, for instance did that judge think that Saxon was so poor? At the other shows that they had attended everyone had said how good he was. She would have to watch things more carefully at the shows to see if she could get a clue.

She didn't know that, at the same time, Fiona was making up her mind never to go to another show again No, she would do something else. She had been toying with the idea of applying to the council to enlarge her boarding facilities She had also considered whether to take up Agility or Obedience training with the dogs or there was this new thing, Flyball. She had always enjoyed watching the dogs doing the Agility tests. Yes, perhaps she would look into that. She was determined not to let these unknown dictators ruin her life.

CHAPTER TEN

Nearly two weeks had passed since the show but still the humiliation of her 'blacking' kept floating into Fiona's mind. She just wasn't able to reconcile the fact that the result of one Championship show would be able to affect her whole life! It just didn't make sense, "For goodness sake Fiona, take a hold of yourself. They can't beat you unless you let them." She had got into the habit of talking to herself or Sally lately, "You can cope with it. Remember what Simon was always saying, 'Don't let the buggers grind you down', " she smiled and stroked Sally's head, "D'know Sally, that's it. I must find a way round it."

Just then the phone rang, "Hello Fiona, it's Natalie. How are you? Have you remembered that we have a show at the weekend? I wondered if you were OK as I haven't heard from you."

Oh God, she'd forgotten all about it. Well there was absolutely no way that she was taking Saxon into that ring until she had sorted this problem out. Natalie would have to start getting used to going on her own for a while.

"Hello Natalie, look I'm sorry I haven't been in touch, but I've had a lot to do this week; and I'm sorry but I won't be able to make it on Sunday either, but do let me know how you get on and good luck."

Natalie was frowning as she returned the phone to its' cradle. She knew now that she should have listened to her conscious and gone round to see Fiona days ago. She felt sure that something was wrong and that it was to do with the last show but, not having known her for that long she didn't feel that she had the right to intrude. Going to her writing desk, she looked at the schedule for the show in question. Good, it wasn't too far away, and she wasn't first in the ring so it shouldn't be a problem. As it happened, she managed to find the venue quite easily on the Sunday morning. The traffic had been light and she had had no problems with the directions. Feeling very strange on her own she pulled her trolley to the side of the ring, set it up and started to groom Jamie and Juno.

"Hello, Mrs. Bennett?"

She looked up to see the tall figure of Simon Philips smiling down at her.

"Yes, that's right."

"On your own today?"

"Yes, Fiona was too busy to come to the show."

" I see, um. Has she got a new litter or something?"

"No, I don't think so. She hasn't said anything about a litter. Are you showing your dog today?"

"No, just thought I'd look in. See what was around. Well, nice to see you again. Good luck."

"Oh, before you go Mr Philips, could you please explain something to me."

"If I can."

"Why did Saxon do so badly at that last show? He has always, well nearly always done very well at all the shows I've been to with Fiona. I just don't understand why that judge didn't like him."

"Didn't Fee say anything to you?"

"No, I don't think she was feeling too well at the time and later all she said was something like 'you win some you lose some', but I can't help but feel that there was more to it than that."

"Well these things can happen in showing and sometimes it does surprise you what a judge will do, but thanks for telling me, I'll have a word with Fiona."

She watched him as he walked away to the car park. Such a handsome man, she wondered as she had often done before, what had caused the rift in their marriage, he and Fiona seemed to be so suited. She shrugged her shoulders, sighed and returned to her grooming.

"Hello, Mrs Bennett isn't it? I've seen you before at the shows with Fiona Philips haven't I. By yourself today?"

She stopped grooming and looked up, a woman was standing beside her. She had noticed her at the previous shows and at the training classes. She thought her name was Viv something or other. She too had Cumbrian terriers. She must be around her age or perhaps a bit younger, slim and smartly dressed., "Yes, Fiona couldn't come today. Please do call me Natalie."

"I'm Viv, Viv Butcher. Didn't I just see you talking to Simon?"

"Yes, he was asking where Fiona was."

"Oh, I see. Still not together then. Well, have a good day." Natalie watched her walk away. I wonder why she is so interested in Simon? Heavens, she would have such a lot to write about in her next letter to Candida in New Zealand.

"Hi, Natalie, on your own today?"

Again, she stopped grooming and looked up. This time it was Caroline Amery. She was always a friendly person and she knew that Fiona quite liked her too.

"Yes, I am on my own today and it's a bit daunting so it's nice to see a friendly face. Which class are you in today?"

"Open."

"Oh, I'm in Junior. We should soon be in shouldn't we."

"Yes, after the Norfolks, let's hope the judge isn't late. Not that I'm too hopeful today."

"Why?"

"Oh you know, it's one of those shows where the committee show their dogs."

"Does that matter?"

"What! you're very new to this aren't you. I'd have thought Fiona would have put you wise to a few things."

Natalie frowned as she watched Caroline walk away with her dog, so the committee showing their dogs was detrimental then, could that have had a bearing on Fiona not winning at that previous show?

As it happened Caroline won BOB that day and Natalie went over to congratulate her, "Hello again, I'm so glad that you won. He is a lovely dog. Are you on this committee then?"

Caroline burst out laughing, "I like it. I like it. No, I'm not on the committee. Look, ask Fiona when you see her next. She'll put you in the picture." Viv walked past them both and looked the other way.

"She didn't congratulate you."

"Take no notice Natalie. She's always like that when she doesn't win."

Natalie, decided not to wait on as she was on her own. I could call on Fiona she thought and show her the catalogue, she'd like to know who has won. As she neared the kennels, she saw a car in the drive. She wasn't certain but it looked like Simon Philips car. She would just knock and see if Fiona was all right and give her the catalogue.

When he had discovered from Natalie Bennett that Fiona was at home, Simon had gone straight to the kennels. Fiona had just returned from walking some of the dogs and was putting them back in their kennels as he drove in. He stood by the kitchen door and, as she walked towards the cottage, she looked up and saw him standing there. She stopped suddenly and, after a moment or two, carried on towards him.

"Fee, I just had to come round to see how you are."

"Well, as you can see I'm fine and I'm very busy too so don't hinder me."

Stepping aside from the door he said, "Please Fee, I know how upset you were. Please just let me come in for a cuppa and we can talk things over. Just let me explain."

"There is nothing to talk over. You made your position quite clear months ago and as far as...."

"Bloody Hell Fee, don't go all snooty on me. I...."

"Just go will you Simon. Go back to all your sleazy, conniving, cheating, miserable pals. I want no part of it or you."

"Come off it Fee, you were perfectly happy when we were winning and others were losing, you knew the score then, I hadn't kept anything from you, but, of course, Miss High Moral Mighty had to judge fairly didn't she. You brought it all on yourself and you bloody well know it and that's what really hurts isn't it. You know now that I was right all along. Anyway, what about us?"

"What about us! What about us! Go away, just go away will you," tears were forming in her eyes as Simon stepped forward and took her in his arms. She struggled for a second or two but the chemistry was still there, the familiar feel and smell of him, the warmth of him, she put her head against his chest.

"Fee, don't let's be like this. I love you. Can't we go in, and talk about this. I want to talk to you. I want to sort this all out once and for all. I'm sorry Fee, I'm sorry for everything. He gently, brushed a bit of hair from her face and, as she looked up, he bent his head and kissed her. She closed her eyes and the feel of his lips was exactly as she remembered them in her dreams. He walked her unresisting, into the kitchen and shut the door.

He kissed her again and again holding her tightly against him. He kissed the lids of her closed eyes, the tip of her nose, her mouth, her neck and she felt him hardening against her, "God Fee, you've no idea how much I've missed you, wanted you, wanted this." He went to kiss her again but she broke away.

"I'll put the kettle on shall I. Then we can talk", she walked towards the Aga.

"Fee don't bloody well tease me, come back here and let me kiss you until it boils - the kettle that is!"

He grinned and following her to the Aga, grabbed her from behind and, running his hands round and round her breasts until her nipples hardened, he kissed the back of her neck sending goose-pimples down her back, she sighed and putting her hands behind her grasped his buttocks and pulled him even harder to her. How much she had missed this too, the feel of him, the warmth of him, the fun of him and that smell that was so uniquely him. He tightened his arms round her and kissed her ears. After a few moments he released her, turned her to face him and putting a hand on either side of her face, he looked at her for a second and murmured, "God Fee I love you," she opened her mouth and they kissed deeply and for a long time with his body pressed hard against her. Her mind was lost, incapable of thought, every fibre of her body alive to his touch, her whole being merged with his. The kettle boiled on unregarded until Sally started to bark and it was only then that they saw that the kitchen was full of steam.

Fiona broke away from his arms, "Simon, the kettle, it must have nearly boiled dry."

"Who bloody cares, I don't want the tea anyway, I want you, now." He was breathing hard and his face looked tense.

Fiona refilled the kettle and tried to control her emotions, she turned to face Simon, "You said that you wanted to talk."

"Good God woman, I'm flesh and blood. Can't it wait."

"No, I want to talk first. Please Simon we must sort things out first, it's important to me."

Simon looked at her for a moment or two and then sighed, "OK, let's talk."

"Firstly, I want to know why you came round here today."

"To see you of course. I went to the show at Headsworth, thought that you might be there and when...."

"You really didn't expect me to go to that show after being humiliated like that did you?"

"Why not. A lot of the Open shows would be OK. You were just unlucky the other day. You know that Ian is a boot-licker. Mind you the word will get round a bit more now but..."

"I don't want to hear any more."

"But Fee. If you stop altogether, you're the loser not them. They don't care a damn now as long as you don't win or judge at the Champ Shows. As long as you keep your head down."

"But it's so unfair. So few are allowed to do really well. The rest have to be content with the crumbs."

"You knew all this almost from the start Fee."

"I know, but I didn't really think that it was so cut and dried, so restricted to the chosen few. I really thought that, if I bred a really good dog, that it would have to win. After all, what about the breed standards that they all go on about?"

"Oh my darling wench, what about the breed standards? How can you have got to this age and be so innocent of life?"

"But everyone is always going on about conformation etc., articles are always appearing in the dog papers. The Kennel Club maintain, quite rightly, that all the showing and breeding is to improve the breeds, so how can you be right."

"Oh Fee what can I say, have you never heard the expression, don't do as I do, do as I say. Look, why don't we go to a few Open shows together that might help."

"What be seen with me! Won't that jeopardise your chances? I couldn't live with that."

The conversation was getting out of hand, Simon got up and went over to kiss her again but before he could do so there was a knock on the back door of the cottage.

They stood still. Fiona felt too emotional to talk to anyone. Sally barked and ran to the door. Natalie knocked again, Sally barked again. Natalie reddened as a thought struck her. Heavens, of course, she had seen Simon's car in the drive, they must be upstairs making love. It had been such a long time since she had made love that she hadn't thought of the possibility. How silly of me. Poor Richard had had to take things so easy with his heart long before he died. She sighed and hurried back to her car. She felt embarrassed and very lonely. Simon and Fiona heard her walk away and relaxed.

"Now, where were we when we were so rudely interrupted?"

"I was making some t...."

Before she could finish the sentence, he was kissing her with such force that it took her breath away. She couldn't stop her body longing, aching for him, her whole body was melting, together with her will to resist him. All that her mind told her was that she wanted him to enter her, to love her passionately, now, this minute, to take away that ache deep inside her. Her knees were buckling and Simon lifted her up into his arms and started to walk to the stairs, Sally, thinking that this was obviously a good game, barked. Fiona's mind was jolted out of it's sexual torpor.

"Simon no, Simon, no, no. We can't, we mustn't, not till I'm sure. Not till I'm ready."

"Ready, My God, you're bloody bursting for it, same as I am." He tried to carry her up the stairs but she wriggled and insisted that he put her down, "Simon please, I'm not ready for this."

Simon stood there and the excitement of the moment gradually dissipated.

"Simon, I mean it. It's too quick, I'm still not sure. I'm sorry."

"God Fee," he put her down and went outside. When he came back into the kitchen he was quiet and serious.

"I've made a cup of tea Simon."

"No thanks, I'd best be off. See you week after next. I did tell you that the bitch has just come in didn't I. OK for the Wednesday evening?"

"Yes, that'll be fine."

When she heard his car leave the drive, Fiona sat down at the table and sipped the hot tea, "Oh, Sally, why did you have to bark."

Sally wagged her tail but she wasn't quite sure if she had been good or bad.

CHAPTER ELEVEN

Natalie felt very pleased when she came out of the hairdressers. She had changed her hair style to something shorter and more modern. Richard had always liked her hair long. She had met Richard at a Christmas ball in aid of the hospital. One of the doctor's had called her over to meet 'his good friend' Richard Bennett, "Richard this is Sister Allardyce a friend and colleague." She had looked at Richard and smiled, not very tall but fair-haired and blue eyed, he was exactly the sort of man she liked. He had asked her to dance and, from then on they had danced and chatted all night. Their romance had taken it's prescribed course from then on. They were married a year and a half later in the parish church in which she and her family had worshipped for many years. He was a barrister and already carving out a good career for himself. They honeymooned abroad and then settled down in a house near enough to London for Richard to commute daily. As they were both in their early thirties, they had decided to start a family straight away and Candida had been born just after their first wedding anniversary.

That summer, whilst out for a drive, they had seen the manor house with a For Sale sign outside and had immediately fallen in love with it. They had lived happily there until Richard's fatal illness. She had kept her hair long and rolled into a bun at the nape of her neck ever since, it was time for a change. Tonight she was going to a charity dinner organised by the Masons. Richard had been a Mason and they had always supported these charity events. Dear old Frank, her escort for the evening, had been a senior partner in the same chambers as Richard. Looking at her new, younger looking image she reflccted that it would have been rather nice to have been going with a handsome, younger partner too.

Paul stopped outside Fiona's cottage and sounded the horn, Sally and two other Cumbrians came rushing out of the kitchen door barking loudly. Fiona appeared in the doorway. She was wearing an evening dress in some blue silky material and looked slim and elegant, "Hello Paul, won't be a second. Come on you three, indoors, now!" As she got into the car he smelled a drift of some flowery perfume, "Fiona, you look absolutely lovely."

"Thank you Paul. How is the leg now?"

"Fine, I shall glide over the floor tonight. I've also just about caught up with all the backlog of work so, I'm going to the East of England show next week, My first show since the accident. Are you going?"

"Oh, no, I've been too busy rearranging everything at the kennels. I got permission for those extra boarders and for a cattery but I haven't got that underway yet. Showing will have to take a back seat."

"Pity, Saxon is really turning into a grand dog and people need to see him. You should do well with him. I would like to use Saxon at some time in the future if I may."

"Please do. Simon has recently used him so you could have a look at that litter."

"Has he. I didn't know that you had seen him. When was this?"

"Last week."

"Did he stay long?"

"No, I made him a cup of tea and we had a 'doggy' chat but that's about all. Why do you ask?"

"No reason, just wondered how the mating went and how he was settling into his new house."

After they had had a drink they were shown to their places at the table. Fiona was loving every minute, she had taken a lot of care with her appearance and felt attractive. She had decided after the episode with Simon in the kitchen, when she had almost let him make love to her, that she must be sensible, divorce Simon and marry Paul. He was kind, loving, dependable and most of all, trustworthy. He didn't thrill her like Simon did but, well, sex wasn't the be-all and end-all of life. She wasn't getting any younger and she had to be practical. She had organised the business to provide more money. She had a circle of friends and now she had to organise a companion. With this in mind, she set out to charm Paul that evening. Looking up and laughing at one of Paul's jokes she saw, across the room, a familiar face. It was Natalie, but she looked different she'd changed her hair style, it was short and seemed more curly and it made her look years younger. Catching her eye, she gave a little wave.

"Who have you seen?"

"It's Natalie Bennett, you know, I've told you about her. She shows Cumbrians now."

"Oh yes, you have mentioned her."

There was dancing afterwards and Paul held her close as they danced round the floor and he kissed her hair and whispered in her ear that she was beautiful. He tightened his hold on her and spun her round as the tune ended, " Thank you, you dance divinely."

"Thank you Paul, that was most flattering."

"But true."

As they left the floor they met Natalie with her partner, "Hello Fiona, I didn't know that you were coming here."

"Hello Natalie, have you met Paul? He is an old friend and a Cumbrian exhibitor too. Natalie Bennett this is Paul Aston."

"Bennett, not Richard Bennett's wife?"

"Why yes, did you know him?"

"Only met him a couple of times and that was several years ago. It was to do with my work. I'm an accountant. I think I saw you at several do's though. How is he?"

"He died a couple of years ago now."

"Oh, I'm sorry to hear that. He was damned good at his job."

"Thank you."

Natalie's partner was introduced and they all chatted for a few moments before going back to their tables. Paul was attentive and amusing, Fiona found that the evening went all too quickly.

When he stopped the car at the cottage she invited him in for a coffee but he declined saying that he had to meet a client fairly early the next morning, "Anyway, with the way you look tonight I don't think that I should come in."

"Oh Paul." Fiona laughed and then leaned across and kissed him.

"Um."

"What do you mean. Um."

"I was trying to remember when we found out that we were related."
"Related?"
"Yes, it seems that I am your brother."
"My brother?"
"Let's start again shall we."
Taking her face in his hands he kissed her several times each kiss lasting longer than the one before. "Now that is a goodnight kiss. Don't you agree?"
Fiona who found that she had been pleasantly surprised by his kisses nodded and smiled, "Yes, I agree." Putting her fingers to her lips and then touching his lips she said, "Thank you Paul for a wonderful evening."

The phone was ringing when she came back from exercising some of the dogs the next afternoon and she hurried into the hall, "Hello Fiona Philips speaking."
"Hello Fiona it's Natalie. Did you have a pleasant evening?"
"Oh yes thank you. I didn't know that you knew Paul."
"Well I don't really. He met Richard through his work and I believe that they were in the same lodge at one time."
"Lodge? Oh, I see. Yes. I didn't know."
"He seems a very pleasant man."
"Yes, he is."
"I feel in need of a little company so I'm ringing to ask you round for a cup of tea. I've made your favourite coffee cake. Does that tempt you?"
"I'll say. How about if I come over around four o'clock. I should be finished here by then."
Natalie poured their second cup of tea and looked up, "Have you known Paul long?"
"Yes, ever since I first started showing. He is a good friend of Simon's and he had a puppy from my first litter."
"I see," Natalie smiled and drank her tea.
It was the East of England show on the Thursday, Paul, she knew had entered but she didn't know if Simon was going, he hadn't said when he last came round. If she went she might find out if all this 'blacking' was true or not. She would ask Paul about it. It seemed very strange to pay at the gate as a member of the public not as an exhibitor

and she hurriedly looked at the boards displaying where the breeds could be located. As she passed by other breed rings one or two people recognised her and gave a friendly wave and her heart lifted. Simon had been wrong. She had thought so. Nobody would 'black' her just because of one show. People weren't that horrible. Finding the ring where the Cumbrians were being judged she bumped into Joan Skipton, "Hi, Fiona, long time no see. Are you entered today? Didn't see your name in the catalogue."

"No, too busy at the kennels. Have you been in yet?"

"No, he's still on dogs. I've got my JW bitch here today. Where's Simon, is he here?"

"Must fly Joan. Just bursting to go to the loo. See you later. Good Luck," she hurried away into the crowds of visitors and exhibitors..

Locating the tent in which Paul was benched she hurried in, he was chatting to Caroline Amery who was benched next to him, "Hello Paul. Hello Caroline."

"Fiona, how nice to see you," Caroline gave her a peck on the cheek.

"I didn't expect to see you here today Fiona." Paul smiled and turned to Caroline, "Nice talking to you Caroline but if you will excuse me." Taking Fiona's arm, he led her away. "That was opportune, a little of Caroline goes a long way. She is such a moaner."

"Have you been in yet Paul?"

"No, class after this though."

"I'll go and find a seat then," she squeezed his arm, "Good Luck."

Fiona found a seat by the ring and sat down. One or two people round the ring waved and smiled. She watched as Paul's class came in. It was quite a large class but, after some deliberation, he was finally placed first. She was just about to get up and congratulate him when she saw Ian Jones go over to him and start talking. He seemed to nod in her direction as he spoke. What was he saying? Paul seemed to excuse himself and move away towards the tent where he was benched so she quickly followed him.

"That was a good win Paul in such a large class. He really looked the part.."

"Thank you Fiona. I'd better get ready for the challenge though now."

Fiona went back to the ring to watch, when Paul was handed the big green card, she applauded and cheered loudly.

"Well, I was rather pleased about that," he said as he came out of the ring, "it makes him up. Their progress back to the bench was hindered by well-wishers but finally, when Paul had put the dog back on the bench he turned to her, "By the way, is Ian Jones a particular friend of Simon's?"

"He's known him a long time and, as you know, he and Moira used to come to some of our parties Why do you ask?" Here it comes she thought, he must have told Paul about the show.

"No reason really, just wondered how good a friend he was. Are we still going to the cinema on Thursday?"

Fiona's anxious face broke into a smile, "Most definitely, wouldn't miss it for the world."

That evening, as he ate the dinner which he had cooked in the microwave, he thought over the day's events. He was pleased that the dog was made up at last. He could now send him to Gunter in Germany. He frowned, what the devil had Ian been talking about and why had he not been told about this blacking. It must have been decided when he had that accident and they'd forgotten to tell him. Fiona had slightly messed up on her show but that was just a bit of nerves. He would have to have a word or two in the right ear and sort it out, he could then see that she was all right on her next show. Fiona being blacked did not fit in with his future plans at all. She may even have to eat a bit of humble pie in certain quarters for a while but - in time. Pouring himself another glass of wine, he sat down and picked up the phone.

CHAPTER TWELVE

As she opened the back door her attention was immediately drawn to the cages of the kennels. Every one seemed to have a balloon or something on it. Fiona hurried towards the kennels, yes, from every door fluttered a brightly coloured Helium balloon. Some said, Happy Birthday, some had a big number Fifty on them while others said, I love you, Congratulations or You're Gorgeous. Fiona burst out laughing, this just had to be the work of Ruth and her family. What a wonderful start to her birthday. Hurrying to the door as the postman pushed several envelopes through the letter box, Fiona excitedly called, "Sally, Sally look at this, lots and lots of cards."

What a birthday I'm having she thought as she opened first one and then another and here I was dreading today and being fifty. Everyone seems to have remembered, Beryl and Peter, Laura and Michael, Duncan, Barbara and little Donald, that's Paul's writing. that's Simon's, there's Ruth, Natalie, even Alison from the book shop. She gradually stood them all up on the kitchen table and stood back to admire them.

Just then the phone rang, it was Laura, "Happy Birthday Fiona, Michael, Amanda and all the boys send their love and we hope that you have a lovely day. Are you doing anything special?"

"Yes, I'm going out to lunch with my doggy friend, Natalie and this evening I'm going out to dinner with Paul Aston."

"Paul Aston? Whose he?"

"Another doggy friend who has been very kind and helpful to me."

"Oh. Well, it seems that you are going to have a lovely birthday. I'm really pleased. Enjoy yourself and I'll be in touch. Bye."

The phone rang again almost immediately, "Hello Fiona, Happy Birthday from us both." It was Beryl, "Did you get my card? I only caught the second post."

"Yes, I did thank you. It's a lovely card Beryl."

"We thought that we'd come over at the weekend and bring your present if that's OK."

"Oh, that would be good. Why don't you come early on Sunday. I'll do something interesting for lunch."

"That would be lovely. Are you doing anything special today."

Fiona repeated for Beryl what she had just told Laura but got a very different response.

"Whose this Paul then, is he the man that I spoke to that day?"

"Possibly, he is a very good friend."

"Oh Fiona, I hope you know what you're doing."

"Yes I do. I'm sorry Beryl, I must cut you short, I still have a lot to do before I go out. See you both on Sunday."

She was just about to shower when the phone rang again, "Damn I forgot to put the answerphone on," nearly tripping over Sally, she raced downstairs. The conversation didn't last for very long but, as she put the phone down she smiled broadly and did a little war-dance, what a birthday she was having. Wait 'til she told Paul.

Already late meeting Natalie, she was just getting into her car when a florist's van drove up.

"Mrs Simon Philips?"

"Yes," she looked at the enormous bunch of mixed pink and white flowers the florist was holding. Good heavens she thought, they must have cost a fortune, they were wrapped in cellophane and tied with bows of pink and white ribbon. "Who are they from?" she asked the driver as he put them in her arms.

"The card is inside."

She bent her head and smelled the delicate perfume, they must be from Paul, it was just the sort of thing he would do.

Unlocking the kitchen door, she part-filled the sink with cold water and gently laid the stems of the bouquet in the water, that would have to do until she got back she thought as she hurried out to the car.

As they sat over an excellent lunch, Natalie handed her a small gift, "Happy Birthday Fiona." On opening it Fiona gasped at the beautiful pendant necklace laying on blue velvet, "Natalie, this is so lovely. It must have cost a small fortune."

"Do you like it."

"Like it, I love it. Thank you so much."

"Fiona, it's just a small token of my gratitude for your valued friendship and advice."

Her excitement seemed to be transmitted to the dogs because when she exercised them that afternoon, they ran around the field, barking and chasing each other and she had quite a job to get them back into the kennels. As she entered the cottage she suddenly remembered the flowers, as she picked them up a card fell onto the floor, picking it up she read, "Guess who." She arranged them in vases and placed them around the house. She must ring Paul.

"Paul, you will never guess what has happened."

"Hello Fiona, you sound very excited."

"Paul, firstly, the secretary of the Farlingham Champ show phoned this morning to ask me to judge the show. You did know that George Fairbrother had had a car accident a while ago?"

"Yes, I had heard about it."

"Well, he has told the secretary that he will not be fit enough to take on the engagement now and she has asked me to do it instead."

"Good choice if I might say so. By the way, Happy Birthday. See you at seven."

"Oh Paul thank you for the flo..." he had hung up. She had hardly put the phone down before it rang, "Hello Simfell Kennels."

"Hello Fiona how are you. You have had a busy day. I have called several times."

It was Duncan. Ever since her miscarriage, he had regularly phoned her about once a month and now he had remembered her birthday. Knowing him, she rather suspected that he had kept a note in his Filofax. He was always methodical and so kind.

"Hello Duncan, I'm fine Thank you for the card. How are you and Barbara? What has Donald been up to lately?"

At the mention of Donald, Duncan was in full flow. He told her every small detail of what his young son had been doing in the two weeks since he last phoned her. Fiona, listening intently, smiled to herself. Duncan was so very proud of that little boy; it made her heart ache. "How are your mother and father Duncan."

"I think I told you when I last phoned that my father wasn't too great. He is, unfortunately not any better."

"Oh, I'm sorry to hear that, your mother must be very worried. Do give them my regards."

"We're planning a little holiday at the beginning of February next year. I did some work for a client a while ago and he has invited us all to his chalet in Switzerland."

"That sounds absolutely marvellous."

"I'm sure that young Donald will enjoy the snow and Barbara says that she has never been skiing so she is looking forward to it as well."

"I know that you will all enjoy it."

"Must be off, now don't overdo it with all those dogs Fiona and, by the way, our dog is fine. Barbara sends her regards. Goodbye."

"Is everything to your liking Fiona?"

"Yes Paul, you know how much I enjoy Chinese food and this is an especially good restaurant you have found. Why do your ask?"

"You seem a little down. You were so excited when you phoned this morning."

"Oh Paul, I'm not at all down. I've had a wonderful day. As for getting the appointment, that was great, You see that proves that Simon was absolutely wrong and I've been worrying about nothing."

"Simon? Wrong about what?"

"He said that I was blacked as far as dog showing was concerned."

"Simon said that. What did he mean?"

"There you are you see, you don't even know what I'm talking about do you. It was just some bee that Simon had in his bonnet and it caused so much trouble."

"Well, I hope that he doesn't go round saying such things, it could harm him in the ring if he did. Anyway, let's forget about all that, let me fill your glass. Now my dear, I have had an idea for your birthday present but I thought that perhaps I should ask you first."

"This sounds fascinating."

"A client of mine has a cottage in Devon. It is, apparently, a beautiful spot quite near to the coast and we could have it for a weekend."

Fiona sat twisting the stem of her wine glass while thoughts raced through her head. A cottage, together. That meant sharing a bed and sex, or did it? She had thought about this so many times in recent months. If she could have contemplated having sex with Alan Burgess for a CC, then surely she could manage sex with Paul for love and security. If she did go, that would be a watershed; there would be no going back. She would divorce Simon and marry Paul. It did make sense, she looked up, "Paul, it is a wonderful surprise but, you have rather sprung it on me. Could I let you know in a couple of days?"

When she got home there was a message on her answerphone from Simon, "Fee I came round to see you but you were out. Did you like the balloons and did you get my flowers? You know Fee I don't care a damn how old you are, you're beautiful and I love you. Happy Birthday."

CHAPTER THIRTEEN

Laura's boys came to stay at the cottage for part of their half-term holiday. Michael brought them and thanked her profusely for having them.

"Nonsense, I look forward to having them. They are a great help."

"You just make sure that they are. You know they'll get out of doing anything if they can at home." He tousled the head of the nearest twin, "That's true isn't it." All the boys laughed and shook their heads.

"No honestly Michael, they are a great help, especially Tom and they are all marvellous company for me."

"I feel that I ought to warn you Fiona, they insisted on bringing an old metal detector that my father gave them and...."

He was interrupted by all the boys trying to talk at once, telling Fiona of all the wonderful finds they hoped to make. As soon as their father had left they begged Fiona to let them start their hunt for the gold torques and jewelled daggers hidden under the soil, laughing and beginning to feel some of their excitement, she agreed. It was just before lunchtime when she was preparing some man-sized sandwiches that she heard voices shouting, she hurried outside to see the three boys hurtling down the field, setting all the dogs barking, "Fiona, Fiona, look at this. Look what we've found." They raced up to her rosy-cheeked and with their eyes shining, in Tom's outstretched hand was a silver coin, "Look Fiona look, I think there's a horde up in the woods." Excitedly Fiona inspected the coin, "Oh Tom, it's an old sixpence."

Tom's face fell, "Isn't it Roman?"

"No, but it is an old one and I'm pretty sure that that means it's made of silver."

"Yippee, it is a silver coin. We'll go back with a spade and dig. I'm sure there's a secret horde up there."

"Maybe, but before you do that I think that you'll need something to eat so come on in and wash your hands."

The following Saturday, Simon's car drew up and the boys rushed out to see him, "Hi, Simon, we've been metal detecting in the woods and found a silver sixpence"

"Have you, that's something I've always wanted to do. Can I have a go?"

"Yes, you might find a horde of Roman coins, we're pretty certain that there must be some up there."

"Right you're on."

They all came into the kitchen together laughing. Simon came over to her and kissed her quickly on the mouth, "Hi Fee. Everything alright?" That was a neat move she thought, "Yes, fine. Did you know that the boys were here; or was there something else?"

"No to both questions. Just popped over, that's all right isn't it?" This wasn't strictly true. The previous evening when he had stopped the car up at the top of the hill, as usual, he had seen Tom shutting up the dogs for the night.

"We're just about to have a sandwich, would you like one?"

"Yeah, fine."

As promised Simon went off with the boys; they were gone for about an hour and when they returned it was with two rather rusty nails and an old horseshoe. The boys were over the moon with the horseshoe.

"How would you three like to go to the shop for some sweets? My treat."

"Yes please Simon."

They went off together with instructions from Fiona to stay together and to come straight back.

"Now Simon, why did you come over?"

He took her in his arms and kissed her soundly, "That's why. Bloody Hell Fee, if you only knew how much I miss just being with you and as for chasing you all round the house and taking one piece of your clothing off at a time and kissing you until........"

"Well you can't and the tea is going cold."

"Bugger the tea."

Fiona laughed, it pleased her tremendously to feel that she had the upper hand now and could call the shots, "Sit down, I've got something to tell you."

"That sounds ominous."

"No, quite the opposite, but you will be surprised."

"Well come on, what gives?"

"I have a Champ Show appointment."

"What! Where!"

She told him of the phone call she had received on her birthday.

"I was as surprised as you when she said that she was the Secretary for the Farlingham Champ Show and wanted me to judge it. Apparently, George Fairbrother has had to turn down his appointment because he is still poorly after his car crash and the Secretary picked my name from the A list.

"I'd heard that poor old George had had a car crash. He must be worse than I thought if he has said that he can't do the show. Bloody Hell. I've entered for that show. Now I shan't be able to go." Suddenly he stiffened, "Fee, for God's sake, tell me that you didn't do anything...."

"Didn't what?. Oh, Simon, how could you think that. I was asked fair and square."

"But Fee, you're blacked. That means that the old whispering campaign comes into force, you know, a whisper in the Secretary's ear to the effect that, if you are chosen then you won't get much of an entry. The Sec of course, wants a good entry for the show to be a success and to pay so.... You don't get the appointment. Simple but effective, so, how did you get the appointment?"

"I've told you. You just don't want to admit that you got it all wrong. I'm not 'blacked' as you call it. I can't be. You've just got it all wrong."

"Oh, no I haven't. There's more to this than meets the eye, a lot more. Anyway, I've got to go. Only came round to see that you were OK. See you soon Fee. I'll say goodbye to the boys if I see them on the way. Thanks for the tea."

Over the course of the next few days, their conversation kept floating into her head at odd times. In the past Simon had always been right about dog matters, why was he still so sure that she was 'blacked' when she had patently proved to him that she was not. It was just pig-headedness. When Paul rang to ask her if she would like to go for a meal on the following Thursday, she accepted readily. The boys had gone back home and the cottage seemed very quiet. Paul would be expecting her answer concerning their weekend together. She had put it to the back of her mind while the boys had been with her but now......

It was an unexpectedly warm day on the Thursday and when she had finished all the cleaning and exercising of her dogs and the boarders, she was feeling a bit jaded but a shower revived her and she took quite a bit of time with her hair and make-up. She looked at her image in the mirror. Mm, not too bad. A spray of perfume and some earrings and she would be ready. She had made her decision. Paul, as usual was punctual and looked very smart in a dark suit. His red hair gleamed in the evening sunlight as he smilingly opened the door of the car for her. As they drove along he looked at her once or twice and smiled, "You look a bit pensive tonight Fiona. Are you worried about something?"

"No nothing at all"

He took her to an Italian restaurant that she had never heard of, "You do like Italian food I hope Fiona. I must apologise for not having asked you before."

"Yes, I love it."

"Good."

The restaurant was tastefully furnished and the glassware on the tables gleamed in the soft light, a dark-haired waiter smiled and escorted them to their table. Fiona drew herself up to her full height, tucked her tummy in and felt quite special as the waiter held her chair for her.

"Paul, this food is excellent."

"Yes, I've been here once or twice and it has always been very good. I'm glad that you are enjoying it.Would you like some more wine?"

"Paul, may I ask you something?"

"Fire away."

"Well, it's about this being 'blacked' in dog showing, you have been in showing so long, surely you must have heard of it."

As I said before, no. But, why do you ask? I thought that this had all been settled."

"Because I was asked to do Farlingham."

"I still don't understand your question though."

"Well, I presume that I wouldn't have been asked to do it if I had been 'blacked'."

"Let me guess. This is Simon again isn't it? You told him about the appointment."

"Yes. He popped over when the boys were staying with me."

"Look Fiona, Simon is a charming man and a good friend but he does have a vivid imagination. I don't think that you are 'blacked' as you call it for one minute. As you say, you wouldn't have got the appointment. Now let's talk about more pleasant things. Have you given our weekend any more thought?"

"Yes, Paul I have and yes I would very much like to come."

He leaned across the table and held her hand, "Wonderful, this calls for another bottle of wine. Now, may I suggest that we go the weekend after your judging appointment."

"That's a lovely idea," her stomach flipped as she said the words. Oh, she thought, I do hope that I've made the right decision. I do hope that I can make love to him. An image of Simon arose in her mind stark naked and aroused coming towards her in their bedroom. She avoided Paul's eyes and tried to erase the image from her mind. She relaxed and smiled at Paul as the waiter brought their coffee to the table.

The drive home was a little quiet with Fiona's thoughts totally focused on the problem. Should she perhaps invite him in now and get it over with. She had drunk quite a bit of wine and, at least, she'd know if she could and what it was like before she committed to a whole weekend of it. When they arrived at the cottage, shc invited him in for a nightcap. He got out and opened the door of the car for her and taking her in his arms, kissed her, in no time his tongue was exploring her mouth. The wine had made her a bit giddy and she found herself responding. She could feel that he was very hard through the thin material of her dress and was just about to place her hand on him when, she stopped.

"No, no Paul, not like this. Let's wait for Devon shall we. Let's make it special."

"Fiona, that's not fair. Can't you feel how much I want you."
"Yes, I can Paul."
"Well then," he started to lead her to the door of the cottage, "let's make tonight truly special."
Fiona looked at him for a second and then nodded her head. As they took their outer garments off in the warm kitchen, she suddenly felt very awkward, shy and nervous. He looked at her and then took her hand, "Shall we go up?"

In the bedroom she suddenly felt guilty as she quickly undressed, dropping her clothes on the floor; she felt that Simon was there. She shook her head, silly thoughts, it was just the wine, she had made her decision. She looked across the room to see Paul still looking at her, he had watched her take her clothes off and, as she slipped shivering into bed, he started to undress. As he removed each garment, he laid them neatly on a chair. As he turned towards the bed, naked, Fiona noted that, although he was a much heavier man than Simon, he was not quite so well endowed in other ways. He got into the bed and, taking her in his arms, started to kiss her. His body was hot and hard against her and she responded to his kisses putting one hand behind his head and one hand on one of his buttocks in order to pull him even closer to her but, as she did so he stopped kissing her for a moment to gasp in her ear, "Oh, my darling, gently, gently, I want this moment to last for ever."
She stopped pulling him close to her and lay quite passively while he, gasping and groaning, ran his hands over her breasts, "Oh, my dearest, now, now." He slid into her and ejaculated almost immediately. Fiona just lay there, his weight pinning her to the bed. Oh dear, she thought, what an anti-climax! After a while, Paul stirred, rolled away and turning, looked at her, "My darling, that was wonderful. Thank you so much. You are very beautiful to love." He started to get out of the bed, "I'll use the bathroom first if you don't mind and then I'll have to go home and see to the dogs." She watched as his white buttocks moved towards the bathroom and then quickly slipped on her dressing gown and ran down stairs. Could she cope with that in the years ahead. Yes, she could but, how boring!

Later, after a shower, Fiona fell asleep almost as soon as her head touched the pillow only to wake up at five o'clock. Well, she thought as she snuggled down under the blanket, I can't go on like this, I'll have to make up my mind which one I really want to spend my declining years with. Do I want Paul or Simon or, should I keep my independence and have them both. Now, there was a thought.

Viv lay awake thinking of Simon Philips, she had always been attracted to him, he was so alive, so energetic. He must be feeling lonely all on his own, perhaps now was the time to do something about it. She finally fell asleep trying to imagine herself making love to him.

CHAPTER FOURTEEN

Viv looked at her watch and breathed a sigh of relief as the marshals waved her into a parking space at the Birmingham Champ Show. The traffic had been very heavy and she had been worried that she would arrive too late for her class. It cost so much now to enter these shows that to not even take part seemed a terrible waste of her precious money. She entered the showground and found that the terriers were benched in tent A. Smiling and acknowledging everyone as she made her way across the ground to the tent and then to her numbered bench she only drew only a few nods from fellow exhibitors Having settled the dog she stood on the bench and looked around to see if she could see Simon. He was the real reason for her being there, she knew that she stood no chance of being placed. Ah, there he was talking to Ted Roberts.

"Hello Viv," she looked behind her to see Caroline Amery bearing down on her. "Didn't expect to see you here today. Taking a day off from work?"

"Hello Caroline, no, I've managed to swap with another receptionist for today. Who have you brought?"

"Oh, my new hopeful. He's still only eight months old but he's done well at the Open shows recently that I thought I'd give it a try."

"Oh well, good luck," you'll need it she thought knowing that Caroline wasn't in the top league or ever likely to be. She knew that this judge was in a certain clique and, if the dog wasn't bred or bought from someone in that clique you'd had it as far as winning was concerned, Caroline was not in that category. God, here I go again she thought, I really ought to get out of this sleazy business, it makes you

sour. I used to think nice things about people. She poured herself a coffee from her Thermos and sat down to watch all the goings on, "Hello there Fiona. Hello Natalie."
Fiona stopped pulling the trolley with their cages on it. "Hello Viv didn't expect to see you."

Having unloaded Natalie's stuff, Fiona moved on to find her bench. What a damned nuisance it was that Natalie was benched next to that bloody woman. What was worse, Natalie seemed to like her!.

Simon was already installed on his bench next to her and he smiled as she again stopped the trolley, "Hi Fee. Here, I'll give you a hand to unload." As he came close to her he put his arm around her and kissed her on the cheek saying, "Good for you, as I always say, don't let the buggers grind you down."
She smiled at him. Now that she had committed to Paul, she could afford to be kind and forgiving, she was master of her own fate. Simon intuitively noticed the slight change in her attitude towards him and his spirits soared. At last, she's got over it, I'll be out of those bloody digs and back home soon.

"Hello Fiona," Simon looked up to see Paul standing there, "I'm so glad that you took my advice and came."

"Hello Paul, I'll see you later."

"Hey. What's this, 'I'll see you later' and what's this, 'So glad you took my advice' business?"

"Just that Simon. I will see him later and I did take his advice. He said that Saxon was too good to not be seen at Champ shows."

"I've bloody told you that and you didn't take my advice."

Just then a steward announced that judging of Cumbrians was commencing, "Sorry Simon, I must go. I promised to watch Caroline's puppy in the ring to see how he goes. She's so proud of him."

Out of interest Viv too had gone to watch the puppy dog class judged. Caroline came into the ring with her puppy. Mm, Viv thought, not bad at all, nicely put together, pity. The pup walked well and Caroline looked so hopefully at the judge but, unfortunately only came fifth. Viv turned to go back to the tent and bumped into Fiona, "Pity wasn't it, nice pup."

"Yes, I thought that it looked quite promising, but, there you are." Fiona shrugged her shoulders and a look of understanding passed between them.

Later, in the Open Dog class with five entries, Fiona with Saxon got the first place while Simon only managed to come fifth with his dog. When all unbeaten dogs were called into the ring Fiona's heart was pounding, the judge was an all-rounder and she didn't really know him so wasn't sure what he would pick out. When he walked over to give her the Res CC, she was breathless with excitement.

"Oh, Fiona, Fiona how marvellous. I'm so, so pleased," Natalie flung her arms around her as she left the ring, tears were running down Natalie's face, "You so deserved it. Saxon looked magnificent." Others came up to pat her on the back, shake hands or kiss her on the cheek. It was just like old times except - where was Simon? And Paul?

"I'm so pleased for you my dear," it was Mrs. Emsworth, "He is a credit to your breeding."

"And to yours Mrs. Emsworth, don't forget that."

Finally arriving at her bench she could see that Simon had benched his dog but, of him, there was no sign. She settled Saxon down, asked someone to keep an eye on him for her, and hurried off to look for Simon.

"Natalie, have you seen Simon?" Natalie shook her head but Viv chirped up, "Yes, saw him going to the beer tent to drown his sorrows. I was just off to join him. Incidentally, congratulations. You certainly know how to pick your men."

"What do you mean by that! I hardly know this judge."

"Who's talking about the judge," Viv walked off in the direction of the refreshment tent.

Simon downed his second whisky, his brain hurt, damn the drink driving laws. He got up to get another.

"Hold on there chum. Remember what you always said to me." Fred Wilson was looking at him. A no-hoper but a good sort.

"Sorry Fred but you just don't understand." How could he tell him that the whole sordid Burgess business had come straight back into his mind when he saw Fee win. She was blacked for God's sake. How could she bloody well get the Res CC? Unless..... He needed another drink!

It had proved to be fascinating walking round the showground with Natalie. They hadn't found Simon but Natalie had found several old friends from years back. She seemed to know a lot of the big-wigs, the Chairman of the show, a member of the Kennel Club, a big all-rounder, all greeted her warmly and asked her the same question, "What are you doing here? How lovely to see you again." What with this grand procession and the fact that Natalie was entranced with so many stalls and bought several things, it was a couple of hours before they could pack up and go home.

Fiona was relating this to Paul that evening as they sat eating a celebratory meal, "Apparently they were all friendly when her husband was alive. The masonic do's mostly. It must have been about the time that you knew them."

"How interesting. Now my dear, I thought that it would be rather nice if I came to see you on Saturday evening. You were so beautiful when we made love that I can't get you out of my mind. Shall we say eight o'clock?"

Viv's heart was banging so hard it hurt her throat as she knocked on the door of Simon's house, she had found his address in the catalogue. She heard barking and then a voice shouting to the dogs to be quiet. She had panicked and started to go back down the path when the door opened and a decidedly drunk Simon stood there, "Who's there? Oh, Viv it's you. Come in."

She hesitated for a second, was she about to make a third big mistake where men were concerned.? First her husband and then Shaun, weak, plausible Shaun, who had moved in with her and taken almost every penny she had before moving on, "Hello Simon, I thought that you might like a bit of company."

"Yeah, come on in," he followed her into the one big room downstairs, "What do you want to drink? Whisky do you?"

"Oh, yes, just a small one please."

Simon poured a generous helping of whisky into two glasses, "Cheers."

Viv took a small sip of her whisky and watched while Simon sank his glass in one go.

"Come on Viv drink up. I know that you like your booze."

"Sorry Simon but I'm not too fond of drinking."

"S'not what I've heard," Simon sniggered, "well I'm having another anyway."

Viv tried to talk about dogs and about using his dogs for the matings. Simon drank more and gradually said less and less until, finally he fell asleep.

Viv sighed and looked at his sleeping form. Well, the evening had not gone as she had hoped but, she smiled, perhaps she could enjoy some of it. She managed to rouse Simon from his drunken stupor sufficiently to get him on his feet. He draped his arms around her and walking backwards, she managed to get him to the stairs. Pushing him up them and into the bedroom took some time, but then she put her arms around him and walked him to the bed. He immediately crashed onto it and was sound asleep again. Smiling, she proceeded to undress him until he was naked. Yes, she thought, I have often wondered what you would look like naked and now I know, very sexy. Still smiling, she bent and kissed his lips then she ran her warm hands over his hair, his face and down over the warm skin of his body, he stirred slightly as her hands slid down either side of his groin but did not wake. Viv tucked the covers around his sleeping form, kissed him again and turned out the light. She went back downstairs, saw to the dogs, locked up for the night, got her coat and just as she was going out of the front door she stopped, returning to the room, she found a piece of paper and wrote, 'Thank you Simon for a wonderful evening. Love Viv'. As she shut the front door she reflected that it had been a successful evening after all.

Simon opened his eyes and closed them again quickly. God the light was bright. He licked his dry lips. My mouth tastes bloody awful he thought., I need a cup of tea. Trying to sit up he groaned, and put his hand up to his forehead. God, I hung one on last night. After a few minutes, and desperately needing the lavatory, he pulled the bedcovers back and swung his legs out of the bed. He shivered and, still holding his head made for the lavatory. Feeling much relieved and on his way back to bed he stopped, didn't Viv Butcher come round sometime..... Oh God no! He hurried back to the bed and looked at it. Looked pretty tidy really, nothing could have happened. Surely he would remember if.... but how did he get to bed?...... where were his clothes?....... there they were all neatly folded on the chair... Oh God No! Nearly falling down the stairs in his haste, he went into the big room and looked around. No sign of her thank God, she must have gone. Better let the dogs out he thought and, as he opened the back door, a piece of paper blew onto the floor, he picked it up grabbing his pounding forehead at the same time and read it. A groan escaped his dry mouth.

CHAPTER FIFTEEN

It was only two weeks now to the Farlingham Championship Show; the summer suddenly seemed to be racing away, the boarding kennels had been full for weeks and Fiona had been very glad of the help she was getting from two girls on holiday from University. With so much going on she hadn't even had time to buy herself something new to wear for her judging appointment but what did it matter, the sun was shining, all the dogs were well and life was good.

The phone was ringing when she entered the kitchen. It turned out to be the first of what. no doubt, would be several pre-judging calls. How strange she thought that Simon should have been so right about some things and so wrong about others. He hadn't called her or popped over recently, not since Birmingham in fact. Perhaps he was still sulking. The phone rang again.

"Hello Fiona, it's Viv, Viv Butcher. Didn't really get a chance to talk to you at Birmingham but then, with two men dancing attendance upon you it's hard to find a slot, and you got the Res CC didn't you, but that was only to be expected. Anyway...."

"Wait a minute Viv. Why was it to be expected?"

"Oh, you know. Anyway as I was saying, I got a second in Graduate today with my young boy at Richmond. Pity you weren't there. It was very hot competition too. I'm hoping that, with a little bit of luck, he'll make it to the top. Should do if there are any other judges left out there who still judge conformation. He has fantastic conformation, every judge who has gone over him has said the same. Don't you agree?"

"I can't say Viv. I haven't had that pleasure."

"Ah well, must go and feed these brutes. Never a dull moment. By the way, have you heard from Simon lately? See you soon. Bye."

"What......", Fiona got no further because Viv had rung off. What is that bitch cooking up now Fiona wondered. Viv had never phoned her before, she must be coming under me at Farlingham. Why did she ask if Simon had phoned me? Natalie had phoned last night terribly excited and a bit apprehensive at going on her own to Richmond. Fiona cursed, I should have asked Viv how Natalie got on, she hoped that, at least, Jamie had been pulled out. Paul had gone as well, he had been very disappointed that she had not entered but, with Ruth and her family away on holiday, she had felt obliged to stay at the kennels. The rest of the day passed swiftly for Fiona, the students helped her lock up and went home, she prepared a bit of salad for her dinner and it was 8 o'clock when the phone rang again, "Hello Simfell Kennels."

"Fiona, Fiona, it's me Natalie. Fiona I got a first. I got a first. I'm so excited. Over the moon in fact. He's qualified for Crufts."

"Natalie, that's marvellous news. Congratulations."

"Oh Fiona, I've had such a wonderful day. Everyone has been so kind. Paul was effusive in his congratulations. He bought me a cup of tea to quieten me down and, do you know, he seems to know so many people as well as all my old friends that we met at Birmingham. Isn't that a coincidence."

"Yes, it is."

"And I've had a letter from Candida and she and her husband are coming over for Christmas. I shan't sleep tonight for excitement. How has your day been?"

"Busy, I'm just having a rest, and I think I'll go to bed early and read."

Tomorrow night, Saturday, Paul was coming over as arranged. Her stomach flipped a bit when she thought about it. Last time had been quite easy. He hadn't asked much from her, in fact, if she admitted it, it had been very dull and ordinary, rather like Duncan's love-making. Perhaps, if she took the lead this time, it might be better.

The following evening she dressed to attract and anticipated the evening with a bit of excitement, when Paul arrived at eight o'clock, punctual as ever, she kissed him warmly, and poured him a generous glass of wine,

"There's a film that I've been wanting to see Paul and it's on at the local cinema this week. Would you mind if we went to see it?"

"Not at all. I'm flattered that you should ask me."

"Shall we say Wednesday evening then," she was pouring another glass of wine when she felt one of his arms go round her waist. He lifted her hair with his other hand and kissed the back of her neck, "You are looking very attractive tonight Fiona. That black dress is..." Slowly turning her round he kissed her on her lips and, taking the bottle out of her hand and putting it on the table, he put his hands on either side of her face, he looked at her for a second and then, bending his head, kissed her again with rising passion. She quickly responded, parting her mouth and exploring his mouth with her tongue. He raised his head and regarded her for a moment or two, she slowly undid the buttons on the front of her dress and slid his hand inside. He immediately responded by kissing her again. Breaking away from his mouth Fiona gasped, "Let's go upstairs." Paul nodded silently and bent his head to kiss her again,. "Please Paul now, here, now! She grabbed his hand and pulled him into the sitting-room, she flung her clothes off and helped him undo the buttons on his shirt, she was a little surprised to see that he wore a vest but helped him off with it, undid his trousers but then, Paul held her hand, "I'll finish Fiona," his face was red and he was sweating a little, and nearly fell over in his haste to remove his trousers and pants. She draped herself round him and kissed him pulling him to her as close as she could.

"Paul, Paul, love me here, now, on the floor." He picked her up in his arms to carry her to the settee when the phone rang.

"Leave it," he gasped, his face red and strained.

"It might be important. It's late." She said panting for breath and holding him with her hands.

"Leave it." He started to lay on top of her and then stopped, "Fiona, stop please or you will ruin everything," he got up and looked for his jacket, "we're not prepared."

Visions of Alan Burgess floated into her mind, Oh God! but this was different; wasn't it? She knew that Paul loved her and was being kind and considerate. The phone stopped ringing.

"Oh good, come on then Paul, I'll race you up the stairs," he stared at her retreating buttocks for a moment and then followed.

This time she didn't lay on the bed but flirted and played with him until he begged her to lay down his face red with exertion and passion, he swiftly entered her and, before she could say anything, it was over. She lay there with Paul beside her, she sighed, well you couldn't have everything in life. She turned and smiled at him.

"Whatever got into you tonight, you minx, I didn't think that I was going to make it that time."

"It must have been the wine."

Paul put a hand up to stroke her hair, "You are a dark horse, I had no idea that you were so...."

"So... sexy?"

"Well, passionate."

"Listen, is that the phone again?"

"Leave it."

"Oh Paul, I'm sorry I can't, it must be urgent it's nearly midnight," she slipped on her white towelling dressing gown and ran down the stairs.

"Is it bloody true that you had Paul Aston staying with you in January?" It was Simon.

"Good heavens do you know what the time is?"

"Bugger the time. This is important"

"Yes, if you must know now, it's perfectly true. And, before you say anything else, he had his leg in plaster so don't go reading anything into it."

"God Fee. First Alan Burgess and now him. What the bloody hell are you playing at."

"Nothing, absolutely nothing. I was helping a kind friend and that was all."

"Just as I thought we were getting back together, just as I thought that I could trust you, you....."

"Look, I'm tired Simon and it's very late. Can we talk about this another day?"

"We certainly can. I'll be round tomorrow after work and you had better be there."

When she went into the bedroom, Paul was asleep. She smiled to herself, poor chap, I've worn him out. She gently shook him awake, "Oh, I'm so sorry Fiona, must have dropped off. Was the call important."

"Yes, I'm afraid it was. I'm so sorry about that Paul. Would you..... I mean do you still want.... shall we try again? I'll pour us some more wine shall I or would you prefer coffee?"

They drank the coffee in silence sitting at the kitchen table, both wrapped in their own thoughts. Suddenly Paul stood up, he had dressed in the sitting-room, "Well, I'd better be going Fiona, the dogs you know."

"Yes, Paul of course and thank you for a lovely evening and for the flowers. You know Paul you are such a lovely person."

He smiled, gave her a gentle kiss on the lips and left. Fiona sat down and sighed, "Oh, Sally, what have I done. He was almost speechless." She giggled and stroked Sally's head. "It must have looked very funny to you."

The following evening Fiona had to smile to herself again. She was sitting at the same table in the kitchen only, she was drinking tea this time and it was Simon opposite her. Her life was getting very complicated.

"Well Fee. I'm waiting."

"For what?"

"Come on, you know bloody well what. It's been driving me mad ever since Joan told me."

"Joan? Not Viv?"

He flushed, "Viv? What do you mean Viv Butcher, what's she been saying? No, I said Joan. Joan Skipton. She was very upset when she told me, she thinks the world of you."

"Ah, I see. Well I know where she'd have got that piece of information, from dear Viv. Well, as I told you on the phone last night. It is true. I was at the dentist's when I saw in a dog paper that Paul had broken his leg. When I went round there he was in quite a fix with the dogs and everything. I invited him to stay with me and brought his dogs over as well. He stayed until he had the plaster off and could manage. Does that satisfy you?"

"No, it bloody doesn't. What went on?"

" Nothing went on Simon, he had his leg heavily plastered."

"It wouldn't have bloody stopped me. We'd have managed somehow. There must be some position that allows.... Let me think" There was a moment's silence and then they both burst out laughing.

"Yes, and I bet you would have found one," Fiona said wiping tears of laughter from her eyes.

"And what's more you'd have helped." they both laughed again and Sally, sitting by the Aga, wagged her tail. Simon stood up, came round the table and looked down at her, "Fee we had so much, don't let's throw it all away."

Fiona looked up at his handsome face and nodded knowing what he said to be true. "Yes, we did and, if only I felt that I could trust you......" There was a moment of complete silence while they just looked at each other and some sort of understanding passed between them without a word spoken.

Very quietly Simon said, "I tell you what Fee. I haven't got any plaster on at the moment"

She looked at his face, "No, you haven't have you."

Neither said a word as he locked the door and followed her upstairs holding her hand. She lent over the bed to pull the duvet down but before she could do so, Simon had pulled her pants down and entered her, grasping her breasts with his hands and pulling her close to him. Keeping her hands on the bed she moved with him and they soon climaxed together and fell in a heap on the bed laughing.

"God I needed that Fee."

"So did I," she sighed, "so did I, but could we take a bit more time, next time? Even perhaps go mad and take our clothes off?"

They both got up, tore their clothes off and strewed them on the floor. He went to grab her and she ran downstairs with him in hot pursuit, she evaded his grasping hands and ran upstairs again, cornered in the bathroom, she screamed as he caught her and kissed her, pulled her onto the bed and began to stroke and kiss and tease her until she cried out aloud for him to love her.

"Wench, you'll wear me out, but what a bloody marvellous way to go but, not yet, not yet." He kissed her and then started to gently caress and lick the inside of her thighs starting at the knee and working upwards.

He explored all of her well-remembered body, kissing and caressing all the areas that he knew pleased her the most. She groaned as he kissed and licked her nipples and then licked her navel as his fingers played with her nipples, she begged him to stop as he gently parted her legs and licked the inside of each thigh and with rising passion she grabbed him and pulled him close to her screaming, "Oh, Simon, please please." He kissed her but kept on caressing her until, with a loud cry, she shouted, "I can't bear this agony any longer. Now, please now", and raised her body to meet his, wrapping her arms and legs around him and straining to pull him as close to her as was humanly possible. Large wheals appeared on his back as she clawed him with her passion. She screamed and he shouted as they climaxed together and then falling back onto the bed they burst out laughing with complete satisfaction. Later, Fiona lay in the dark, all passion spent and gently traced the features of his face with her forefinger. She still loved him so much, only he made her feel so beautiful, powerful, young, lithe, svelte and female.. the rest of the world no longer existed. She studied the outlines of his face, why did he have to do things behind her back, like the Masons and the wedding? Had it really been, as he said, a lovely surprise? She lay there with many happy memories floating in and out of her mind, why was she even considering a life with Paul?

During the night she woke up feeling cold, Simon was sound asleep beside her, they were both naked and all the bedclothes were on the floor. She smiled in the dark as she remembered their love-making, "Simon, Simon wake up. What about your dogs?"

"Uh, what. Oh, God, the dogs. I forgot the dogs."

Getting up. He pulled his clothes on and kissed her on the lips. "You'd better come down and lock the door behind me. God, it feels cold, it would be better if I were to move back Fee. Wouldn't it? Let's put it all behind us and start afresh. Love you Fee," he bent and kissed her.

"I don't want to rush anything Simon. Let's wait a bit." she said as Simon hurried away down the stairs.

CHAPTER SIXTEEN

Paul was due any minute now, Ruth was here already and out seeing to the dogs, she had got her car park pass and her pen in her handbag, a change of shoes, her raincoat, was there anything else. Fiona stood there thinking, it was the day of the Farlingham show at last, her stomach was tied in knots and she was dying to go to the lavatory again. Coming back into the kitchen she remembered to put the answerphone on, she smoothed her hands over her hips, on a whim yesterday, she had rushed out and bought a new, dark blue trouser suit to wear today. Should she have worn something old and comfortable? Paul's car stopped in the drive and Fiona took a deep breath and went out. After a few exchanges, Paul drove in companionable silence which pleased Fiona, she was far too nervous to think of polite things to say. Both Natalie and Simon had offered to drive her to the show but she had declined, she needed to relax and concentrate on the day ahead.

As the signs for the show started to appear at junctions on the road Paul started to tell her not to be worried, he knew for a fact that several people, who he named, would be there and their dogs were doing so well that she would have no problems in picking some of her winners. Fiona smiled and nodded hardly taking in what he was saying. her stomach was so tight with nerves that it was all she could do to try relaxing techniques and to control her breathing.

As Cumbrians weren't first in the ring, she decided to sign in, have a coffee and then wander around the show and the stalls. She saw several Cumbrian exhibitors as she walked around, some pretended that they hadn't seen her, while others nodded and smiled. Suddenly she saw Simon, he came hurrying up to her, "Been looking for you. Now, Fee, you are going to be sensible today aren't you. So much depends on it."

"What do you mean."

"Come on Fee. Surely you've been dropped a few hints about how nice certain people's dogs are and how well they have been doing lately? Don't try to tell me that you haven't had the pre-show phone calls? Even the threatening ones."

"Yes, I did get one or two."

"Well, take the hint this time for God's sake. Only the important ones mind you."

"Why did you say that so much depends on it?"

"Well, I wasn't going to tell you 'til afterwards but we have both been asked to judge in Germany next year and, well I accepted for you too, so you need to do well here today. Don't want to turn up under a cloud do we. Or, worse still, lose it in some way. Get the picture."

"Wait a minute Simon. Did I hear right? You have already accepted this appointment for me?"

"Yes, I signed the form for you, well, things weren't right between us at the time and...."

She was suddenly so angry that she couldn't find the words to say, it was just like their wedding day all over again. How dare he do this to her all over again. She glared at him and walked away just as the tannoy called for her to go to her ring.

She didn't go straight to the ring but took a circuitous route to it in order to calm down. She'd show him, she would put all the little people up and then get out of showing altogether. Yes, that would teach him to put the showing before her, she'd ruin him too! Paul was standing beside the ring, "Good Luck Fiona," he said and lightly touched her arm, "Are you alright?"

"Yes, I'm fine thanks. Just fine."

She remembered then that he had been telling her how well certain people's dogs were doing in the ring, was he the same as all the others. No, surely not. He was far too decent and kind. He was just helping her knowing that she was a bit nervous and, as he had said, she was a bit out of touch with the current winners. She spent a little time calming down by getting her pen out, re-arranging the mat on the table and taking off her jacket. As the day progressed she found that she did, in some classes, put up the few names that Paul had mentioned. The one, in fact, that she gave the dog CC to made him into a champion They were quite good dogs on the whole no better than several others though, had she been influenced by Paul? One had a very poor mouth and, as this dog was already a champion, she was quite taken aback at this discovery. Surely the other judges must have noticed such an obvious fault. Did this confirm perhaps what Simon said? She was still able to give the odd first or second here and there for some who did not often feature in the placings at Champ Shows which pleased her. When she finally awarded the BOB to the bitch CC winner, one that Paul had also mentioned favourably, Fiona was met with a round of clapping and cheering. She looked round for Paul and Simon, Paul was clapping and smiling but she couldn't see Simon anywhere. He should be the one clapping, hadn't she done what she was told, well mostly.

"Your very quiet Fiona. You've hardly spoken all the way home. Is everything alright?"

"Oh, Paul, I'm so sorry. I was thinking about the show. There were some very good dogs there today and some I couldn't put above fourth."

"No need to worry, on the whole I think you did a creditable job. Pleased quite a few people who matter. That's the point."

"Mm, yes, I suppose so."

"Now, I know that you're tired but, shall we go out for a meal this evening. It'll help you to unwind."

Fiona did the rounds of the dogs checking that all were settled for the night. I hope that he doesn't want to come back after the meal she thought, I'm far too tired. Considerate as ever, when they had had a very pleasant meal at a local hotel, he brought her home, kissed her goodnight and left.

"Sally, I'm shattered, I'll write my critique in the morning." Fiona had just made a hot drink when the phone rang. She heard Simon's voice, "Pick up the phone Fee. It's me Simon. I want to explain about Germany. Where the hell have you been all evening?"

She definitely did not wish to speak to him at the moment. She needed to do a lot of thinking about Simon and about Paul, about Germany, and about the years ahead. Sighing, she picked up the mug and, followed by Sally, started to go upstairs to bed. "Goodnight girls, sleep well," she said to Sapphire and Silver, Sally's daughters, who now slept in the kitchen. Sapphire raised a sleepy head, gave one wag of the tail and closing her eyes, laid her head down again.

Simon phoned twice the next day and left messages on the answerphone. Fiona ignored them. Knowing what his next move would be, she went out in the evening to see Natalie.

"I'm so glad that you came round Fiona. I was coming over to congratulate you on your successful judging on Saturday."

"Thank you. I was lucky enough to have some very nice dogs to go over."

"Paul said that you made a good job of it. He was singing your praises Fiona to several people, telling them what a competent judge you were."

"Was he. Who?"

"I don't really know who they were but they all seemed to know him well. I was having tea in the judges tent with Audrey, she kindly invited me, and he was at the next table with several other people. Most of them seemed to be judges."

"Oh, well Paul has been showing for quite some time and he has been rather successful. He must know tons of people. Fancy you hob-nobbing it in the judges tent."

A couple of days later, Fiona was letting the dogs out into their runs in the morning when she noticed that one of her young dogs was laying on it's bed and did not race out to greet her. Inspecting him, she noticed that his nose was a bit runny and, just as she was standing up, he gave a dry, hoarse cough.

"Oh, no." she said out loud. Hurrying back indoors, she checked that the dog's vaccination for Kennel Cough was still valid. Yes, it was. Well, he shouldn't get it too badly. She quickly put him in her isolation kennel away from the other dogs. She then changed her clothes and washed her hands so that she could feed the other dogs first. They all seemed to be well at the moment anyway. Thank goodness, Silver, who was pregnant was indoors. She had better get in touch with the Vet after breakfast and then she would.... Fiona stopped, she would have to phone round and stop people from coming to the kennel if the Vet confirmed that it was kennel cough.

The Vet came in the afternoon and agreed that it was kennel cough and told her to keep an eye on the others. She had already checked that the others were up to date with their injections.

"Well Mrs Philips, we've caught it early and you've done all the right things so, with any luck, there won't be any more. Let's hope so anyway."

She had taken Sammy to training classes for the last couple of weeks, perhaps he had picked it up there.

"....so Paul, I think it's best if you don't come round next Saturday don't you?. I'm so sorry."

"Well, these things happen, it can't be helped. We can still go out for a drink or something."

"Yes, I'll miss you Paul on Saturday."

She left the call to Simon until the evening, " Simon, it's Fiona. I'm ringing to let you know that Sammy has kennel cough so don't come round here. Goodbye."

"Hey, wait a minute. Did you say Sammy? How bad is he?"

"Not too bad at all but he is still infectious."

"Sorry about that Fee. I've been meaning to phone you anyway Fee about Farlingham. You passed with flying colours. I'm glad you've seen sense at last."

"If you mean that I can now judge in Germany, forget it, and if you think that I did it for you, forget it In fact, just forget everything, including me." she put the phone down. As she expected, it rang again almost straight away but she ignored it.

Simon stood looking at the phone, should he try to ring again or not. She was furious about something, surely she couldn't be that mad about Germany. God, a thought struck him, had Viv been talking to her? What a bloody mess that all was! He had phoned Viv the morning he woke up naked in bed and asked her what had happened. The bloody bitch had laughed down the phone and asked him what he could remember of their evening together. When he had said not a bloody thing she had replied that she could remember every little detail. It had all been so wonderful. He had accused her of making the whole thing up, he'd have remembered if he had done something like that but she just laughed again and reminded him of the mole that he had on his belly half hidden with hair. Since the phone call, he'd tried and tried to recall the slightest detail of making love to her but, for the life of him, he could remember nothing. Of course, the bitch could be making it up but, he could still see his clothes all neatly piled on the chair. She'd phoned him several times recently about mating her bitches, would she have been so nice if he had rejected her.

CHAPTER SEVENTEEN

"It's no good Peter I'm going to see Fiona and find out what's going on."
Peter started to say something but before any sound came out of his mouth Beryl said, "I know what you're going to say but I just can't 'stay out of it'."

"If I can get a word in edgeways, I was going to say that, with the quarantine, I'm sure that Fiona would appreciate a visit from you."

"That's just what I thought. It's obvious that something else is very wrong besides the dogs. Fiona seems a bit quiet and Simon is not his usual self at all. Just as I thought that things were getting better between them. If I go, I might be able to find out....."

"There you go Beryl; look he's my brother but do you see me interfering?"

"I'm not interfering."

"No, well what do you call it then?"

"Concern! I'm very fond of both of them, yes, even bad-tempered old Simon. Those two belong together, they're meant for each other Peter, I've always said so."
Peter sighed, "Oh Beryl, you've been reading too many romances. They are both sensible adults. They will know if they are meant for each other, as you put it, and will do something about it."

"Rubbish," Beryl went out into the hall to phone Fiona leaving her husband to shake his head and sigh.

It was Fiona's day for trimming nails, she tried to have set days for things like nails, cleaning teeth or clearing anal glands. Today it had been nails, she was just finishing when she saw Beryl walking up the path to the kennels, "Oh Beryl," Fiona said as she put her arms around her, "it was lovely to get your call yesterday. I'm so glad to see you and I do so appreciate the effort you make to come out here to see me."

"Nonsense. It's good to get away from the house for a while. I love Peter dearly but he's not the best conversationalist in the world."

As they sat at the kitchen table, they chatted away for some time with Beryl telling Fiona about the new lounge carpet that she and Peter had just bought and the trials and tribulations of getting it fitted. Fiona, for her part, showed Beryl the now finished lounge complete with new curtains and covers.

"It looks lovely Fiona, you do have such a good eye for colour. I love those ornaments they match beautifully. Where did you get them?"

"In an antique shop, we just happened to see them and I knew that they would be perfect for here. They weren't expensive either."

"We! Did you go with Simon?"

"No, it was Natalie actually. We'd been out for a lunch and saw this little Antique shop on the way home and called in." Fiona frowned, she hated lying to Beryl but, until she had made up her mind about Paul, she didn't want Beryl telling Simon anything."

"Anyway, I'm absolutely furious with Simon at the moment and I'll never trust him again."

Beryl sat forward, "Oh, why?"

Fiona proceeded to tell her all about the judging in Germany and how Simon, once again, had forged her signature. Beryl listened in silence, biting her lower lip occasionally and frowning. When Fiona stopped speaking, she placed her hand over Fiona's hand, "Oh my dear, I am so very sorry. What a stupid thing to do. What is the matter with him?"

"He's just so obsessed with 'getting on' as he puts it in the dog show scene, everything else, including me, are just pawns in the game. He's not alone you know, loads of women too are like that in showing; children, family, friends, often have to come second."

"You make it sound like one of these religious cults that takes people away from their families."

"Well, showing is certainly a powerful drug, I know that. I went along with it at first for Simon's sake but I can't now. Not everybody's like Simon of course. Some people do keep the showing in

perspective, but enough of that. What have you been doing in the garden lately?"
They went on drinking coffee and chatting about inconsequentials for another half hour or so until it was time for Beryl's bus.

That evening she told Peter what Fiona had said.

"What a bloody conniving idiot that brother of mine is, you didn't tell me that he had forged her signature on the wedding application. Why not?"

"Fiona asked me not to, she felt embarrassed about it."
Peter put his newspaper down and got up.

"Where are you going?"

"To phone Simon of course, the bloody fool, someone's got to talk some sense into him." He deliberately shut the door, so Beryl had to strain her ears to hear anything at all. When he came back Peter's face was red and his eyes were glinting, she had never seen him so angry, "What did he say?"

"I don't want to talk about it. I'm ashamed that he's my brother."

"But you must tell me, I'm involved."

"Yes, that's the trouble, if you hadn't poked your nose in we wouldn't be in this situation now."

"If I.....," she decided that discretion was the better part of valour and quietly got up, "I'll just go and sort some washing out to put in the machine ready for tomorrow." That was the nearest that they had ever got to a quarrel. Peter was so equable normally, heaven knows what Simon must have said to him.

Simon put the phone down, the dogs hearing a raised voice, had all lain down in various places and were looking at him with sad eyes, "Bloody hell!" The shout echoed around the room and the dogs all looked away, "Bloody nosey bastard," first one dog and then another slunk off into their beds in the kitchen uncertain as to what they had done to displease him. "Damnation," he banged his hand on the phone book and the rest of the dogs slunk off to the kitchen. It had to be Fiona blabbing to them, no one else knew about Germany. He poured himself a stiff whisky and sat staring into space. What the hell was happening to his life, if only he hadn't met that bloody woman. If only he hadn't bought that puppy from her. No, that's not true, it was that bloody Alan Burgess, damn his eyes; he'd ruined everything. Lately, if he didn't know better, he'd have said that it was he who was blacked not Fee. Fee! Why the hell had she told Beryl and Peter? It was nothing to do with them, it was between him and her. Who the hell did Pete think he was anyway talking to him like that! He'd get to the bottom of this right now. He dialled Fiona's number.

"Hello Simfell kennels."

"Why the hell did you have to blab to Beryl and Peter about Germany?"

"What, what are you talking about?"

"It's simple enough, why did you tell Beryl about Germany? I've just had Peter on the phone slamming me into the bloody ground about Germany and the wedding, you, the baby, in fact every bloody thing he could think of!"

Although the conversation didn't last very long and ended with Fiona banging the phone down, it was very heated, with both of them shouting at each other and a lot of resentment being aired on both sides. Accusations flew between them and a lot of hurtful things were said. Crying, Fiona went into the kitchen and the dogs came up and put their heads on her lap as she sat down. How he hated her, where had all that love gone? Why did Beryl tell Peter? Could you trust anybody these days. Well yes, Natalie and Paul. Yes, Paul, he was reliable.

"Come on Sally, let's do the rounds."

It was now October and there was a cool wind blowing the leaves from the trees in the wood as Fiona settled Sapphire down in the kitchen. She had been up since two o'clock with Sapphire and the birth had gone without a hitch, one pup had looked a bit weak, but she had stimulated it and had fed it with some special puppy drops and now it seemed to have turned the corner. All three pups, two bitches and a dog, looked as if they would do well now. It was the first litter she had had for some time and she felt that, as she was on her own, it would be easier to manage them indoors. It was a lovely feeling to have babies again. Fiona hurried through the daily rounds in the kennels. There were no boarders in at present so things were quite easy. It had been such a relief when none of the other dogs had gone down with the kennel cough.

She was going out with Paul at the weekend to a concert being held locally, she would need the next few days to do her hair and make herself look good. She hadn't seen or heard from Simon since that last phone call, although his litter must have been born some time ago. He should have let her know about that at least and, as far as she knew, he hadn't even been to any dog shows since then either. She wasn't going to get in touch with him though, Germany had been the last straw. She had told Paul about it on one of the evenings they had spent together. He hadn't said anything for a minute or two and appeared to be thinking deeply, "I think my dear that, on the whole, it might be a good thing for you to go out there and judge that show. I know the odd exhibitor out there with some good stock, it would enhance your experience, broaden your knowledge. Make a good job of it and I'm sure that there might be more overseas appointments in the future. Who knows we might be able to go together somewhere. You'd like that wouldn't you? You could go out there quite separately and need have nothing to do with Simon."

Paul collected her on the night of the concert and commented on how very beautiful she looked. As she had spent some time at the hairdressers that afternoon having highlights put in her hair and was very pleased with the result. She supposed that Paul would be coming back afterwards to make love to her, he had been over several Saturday evenings now and she was getting used to his brief love making and no longer tried to infuse a lot of passion into it. It was a small price to pay for happiness.

Lost in the spell of the music, she started when Paul touched her hand, "I can see that you really enjoyed that."

"Paul, it was divine. I adore Tchaikovsky."

"And I adore you, we have so much in common don't we."

"Yes, we do Paul. You will be coming in for coffee won't you." He helped her on with her coat and his hand lingered on her shoulder, " Of course my dear, need you ask? You haven't forgotten that we are going on our favourite steam train tomorrow as well have you?"

"No, course not, I'm really looking forward to it."

Their love-making that night was just as she had expected with Paul saying very little and then falling asleep almost straight away. Laying beside him unable to sleep, she hoped that he wasn't getting tired of her, not now when she had finally decided that she would live with him and forget Simon. Perhaps she shouldn't have eased up on the sexy bits, perhaps he had liked them. She pressed herself against him and started to caress him. He woke up, smiled at her and removed her

hand, "I take that as a great compliment my dear but I really am snowed under with work at the moment and, although the spirit is willing....."
Fiona frowned, was she right? Was he going off her? Oh! please no.

"Look Paul, it will soon be Christmas. You are going to come and spend Christmas here as you did last year aren't you and perhaps stay until the New Year? I would very much like to see this New Year in with you." She had planned to do this because she thought that it might be the right setting to prompt him to ask her to marry him. In view of her decision, she had already been to her solicitor in order to start divorce proceedings against Simon. It had taken all her courage and a stiff whisky before she could do this but, the deed was done. She looked at Paul as he got out of bed and started to dress, "That sounds a lovely arrangement Fiona but I must look at my work diary first. I'll let you know."

As Paul came out of the drive and turned right, he did not see the car parked half-way up the hill. Simon looked at his watch, yawned and shivered, it was twelve forty-five. He let Paul get well away before he started his engine. Neither Fiona nor Paul knew that Simon sat there most Saturday evenings at a spot where he could see the cottage. He let in the clutch and drove home utterly despondent.

At two o'clock, with the idea of sleep totally abandoned, Fiona sat in the kitchen beside the warm Aga. Sapphire had stopped her maternal duties to wag her tail at her but had then laid her head down to clean her small family and keep them warm. It was worrying Fiona that Paul had not seemed too eager to stay for Christmas. Perhaps it was all in her imagination. Now that she had committed to the divorce it was more important than ever that Paul should ask her to marry him. She knew that she still loved Simon, always would whatever he did, but did she love Paul as well? She remembered how staid he had been when he had lived in the cottage. She put a hand to her aching head, would he drive her mad with his fussy little ways? Good question, only she didn't have the answer at the moment.

CHAPTER EIGHTEEN

The doorbell rang, the bloody woman was dead on time Simon thought as he made his way to the door, this was the moment he had been dreading for days, ever since Viv had informed him that her bitch was in season. The bell trilled again and all his dogs started to bark as he opened the door, "Hello Viv brought the bitch I see."
Viv smiled and walked into the small hallway, "Yes," she replied, "and she's absolutely ready," She had been in a fever of anticipation about the outcome of today and had taken particular care with her appearance. She had even gone to the lengths of asking her next door neighbour to look in on the dogs if she wasn't able to get home that evening.

"Right, well I'll get the dog, Sacha wasn't it. Come on through, I've got a shed out the back which I generally use for matings." It was a bit of a lie because he hadn't had any matings for the dogs since he had moved in there and had had to spend all the previous evening cleaning it out and getting it ready. Sacha was an experienced stud dog and he quickly coupled with the bitch and tied. I hope he doesn't tie for long Simon thought, I don't want to be too near this woman any longer than I have to be or she'll be wanting a repeat performance! He covertly looked at her breasts showing through her tight jumper. No, no way, he had absolutely no recollection of what they looked like or felt like, surely to God he couldn't have been that drunk. If he had have been he wouldn't have been able to perform anyway! No, she was trying to put one over on him. The dog moved slightly but remained tied, Simon eased his back.

"Come on Sacha tell the lady to let you go, my back's killing me."

"Well, it looks like a good mating Simon."
" Yeah."
Viv looked at his handsome face, it wasn't going quite as she had hoped, she had tried to talk to him while the dogs were tied but he wasn't being as friendly as he could have been. Perhaps it would be better when we got back into the house. After another ten minutes the dogs parted and having seen to the dog and the bitch, Simon suggested that she put the bitch back in the car. Locking the car door she returned to the house, it must go right now, something in her life had to go right for her, she'd make it go right she had to, she was so desperately lonely.
"Thank you Simon, I shall look forward to having a lovely litter. Now, how much do I owe you?"
He told her the price and wrote out a stud receipt, "Usual terms of course."
"Thanks Simon," she wrote out the cheque and handed it to him. There followed a few minutes silence, "Simon, is there any chance of a cup of tea. These things seem to make me very thirsty."
"Well, I've got to go out shortly but, OK. I'll make you a cup."
Her stomach was churning, what could she say to put this right. He came back into the room with one cup of tea, "Oh Simon aren't you having one?"
"No, I don't think so."
"Please Simon, I always drink alone, it is so nice to have a cup of tea with someone. If it's about that night, if your worried about that other night, then don't worry. I promise I won't mention it. I'm talking too much aren't I. It's being on my own so much."
He looked at her for a minute sitting at the table and holding her cup of tea and saw, instead of a pretty vamp, an anxious, nervous woman, strange really, he'd seen Viv for years at the shows and had never really looked at her at all. She was a troublemaker and she was to be avoided at all costs. Seen talking to her and you were lumped in as a troublemaker too. He shrugged his shoulders, what the hell did it matter now, he poured a cup of tea for himself and sat down.
"Isn't it funny Simon, I've known you for about fifteen years and yet we've hardly spoken in all that time have we. Well not really spoken, if you know what I mean."
"That's dog showing for you."

“Yes, but other people seem to make friends, I never have. No, that’s not quite true, I did at first. Everything was fine until I went onto the Cumbrian committee.”
That woke a spark of interest in Simon, he had never known the real story about that, lots of rumours had flown around at the time, all getting embellished with the telling, he’d never heard her version though, “Yeah, I’ve sometimes wondered about that, exactly why did you come off that committee?”
“Oh, it’s a long story, do you have time to hear it?”
“Well, I’m not going out immediately.”
She proceeded to tell him how, having office skills, she had been asked to join the committee and, at first, all had been well, she had done her job of being Cup Secretary and everyone had been very co-operative and friendly. They had then suggested that she apply for the retiring secretary’s post. She had been so surprised when she got it on a vote. She found the job quite easy and was able to cope with all the pressures involved. After a year, she was persuaded to put herself forward for the club judging list, she again got a good percentage of the votes. Her dogs were doing well in the ring, her stud dog was in demand and she was getting quite a few appointments to judge at other shows and........
“So, what went wrong?”
“Nothing specific, well nothing that I was aware of at the time, I just gradually noticed that the committee members didn’t chat so much, weren’t so friendly. Then I noticed.....”
“Would you like another cup of tea?”
“Yes please.” When Simon returned with two cups of tea, Viv continued her narrative, “Well as I was saying, it was some time before I fully accepted that people weren’t so friendly, I kept telling myself that I was imagining things but little things were said, there were little slights and snubs and sometimes I was completely avoided. In the end I had to accept that something was wrong, so I decided to ask the then Chairman if I was doing the work well enough and....”
“Go on, what did he say?” Simon was sitting forward in his chair, “I bet I can guess.”
“He said that my work was excellent but that, when I had been in dog showing longer, I would realise that the older members knew better how to run a club. He also suggested that, in my role I should

also be aware that sometimes it was in my power to help other members of committee. They too could accept appointments and liked to breed their dogs. I kicked myself for being so naive, I had just given enquirers the club list and not recommended specific people. Things seemed to improve a little then, that is until the following AGM. I had often been phoned up by the chairman before to do or present things in a slightly different way, to leave certain things in abeyance, to see that details or figures were 'adjusted slightly' so as to appear to be more or less than they were. It didn't seem to matter to me very much, I enjoyed the job and was pleased to help out if it enabled the club to run smoothly."

"What about that AGM?"

"Which one?"

"The one where there was all the rowing," Simon was sitting forward in his chair now.

"Ah, well, in the agenda a member had put forward a motion for a postal ballot instead of the show of hands because, they said, the chairman and members of committee loaded the meetings with their cronies so that the votes always went their way. There was a very heated debate."

"I know I was there and it was bloody well true, they did."

"Well, to cut a long story short, as you know, the motion was carried. We just carried on as normal for a few months until dear old Mrs Mallin died and Mrs Francis had to resign because Mrs Mallin used to bring her to the meetings......"

"Skip that, what happened then!"

"Well, they decided to co-opt onto the committee and the chairman just phoned me one evening and told me who had been co-opted. I was a bit surprised because there hadn't been a committee meeting. When I said this the chairman told me that it had been decided at short notice, he had phoned around the others but couldn't get hold of me. Call me naive if you like but that was the first time I'd ever encountered such ploys. I said that surely the club rules stated that we should have had a meeting but the Chairman assured me that it was in order, they had done the same thing before. A few more months went by and...."

Simon looked at his watch, "Damn, I must go, I'm due at my brother's house for dinner tonight. Look, how about I take you out for a drink sometime and you can tell me more."

"I'd like that. I'll wait to hear from you."

Viv drove home happily, it hadn't gone as she had anticipated but, this was even better. She had got his interest, it wasn't how she had intended to get it but, it had worked and that was all that mattered, she had a date. Hugging all the dogs when she got home, she changed into jeans and, throwing on a jacket, she took all but the one very old bitch for a long walk, she just wasn't up to it now and preferred the comforts of home. There was a definite spring to her step, if she could hold his interest, he would gradually get to know her and would ask her out again.

"More potatoes Simon?" Beryl passed him the plate. He certainly seemed in a good mood tonight, had he made it up with Fiona?

She hadn't phoned her recently, "I haven't heard from Fiona for a week or so, is she alright?"

"As far as I know. She seemed fine when I saw her judging. We did have a bit of a row though so I don't expect to hear from her for a while."

"I'm very sorry to hear that. What did you row about?"

Peter kicked her foot under the table and glared at her, she ignored him.

"Nothing much, just to do with dogs, surely Pete told you? Now, to change the subject, that was great Beryl. What's for pudding?"

That'll be all I'll get from him, she thought, men are so infuriating, "It's bread and butter pudding."

It was quite cold when he parked the car up the hill from the cottage, there were no cars in the drive and the lights were on. He imagined himself sitting by the Aga with a hot cup of coffee, Fee on the opposite side talking and laughing, he sighed, he had just got to do something to get back with Fee before it was too late, he'd even swallow his pride and beg if that was what it took. He'd had enough of this bloody awful existence. He took off the hand brake and coasted down the hill slowly before starting the engine.

CHAPTER NINETEEN

"Give Donald a hug for me won't you and thanks again Duncan for calling, please give my regards to Barbara." Fiona smiled as she put the phone down, she really looked forward to Duncan's monthly call now. She loved hearing about Donald's development, new things he said, what he liked playing with, wonderful pictures that he had drawn. He was obviously going to be a genius, well, according to his proud father.

She sighed as she put on her old anorak, her gloves and scarf, there had been a biting cold wind all day buffeting the trees back and forth; quite a few of the dogs had stayed in their kennel. Still thinking of Duncan's call and his praise of Donald, she realised that it would be Christmas in no time at all. Several boarders had already been booked in and she would obviously be full for Christmas. She must get her shopping done before she got too busy. She smiled in anticipation as she thought of the pleasure she would get in roaming around the toy shops. Laura's boys were really getting past the toy stage but Donald and Amanda still enabled her to indulge herself, at least for the next few years.

She adored the brightly lit shops with their vast array of colourful toys, picking up and renewing acquaintance with old favourites, remembering the happiness that she had got from certain toys, especially for her the dolls. She pulled her hat down further over her cold ears, yes, the dolls, so beautifully dressed, so life like, she would look at them for Amanda, then there was Donald, all the boys toys were so interesting, she could spend hours looking at them and seeing how they worked.. What fun she would have had if only.... she sighed deeply and moved on to the last kennel.

Saying goodnight to the dog and checking that the heating was on, she locked up and set off back to the cottage. Thank goodness she wasn't seeing Paul this evening, in fact she wasn't seeing him at all this weekend. He had gone to the Driffield show today where Simon was judging and he had a lot of work on tomorrow. Paul had tried to persuade her to go with him to the show but she had excused herself saying that, as she couldn't show, she didn't really have a lot of interest in what Simon would put up. He had been a little surprised at her explanation but had not pushed her. She was glad because she wasn't one hundred percent sure herself why she didn't want to watch Simon's judging. Natalie had also tried to persuade her to change her mind, she was taking Jamie and was so hopeful. Fiona didn't want to tell her that she had little chance of winning under Simon and, as she didn't want to see Natalie's disappointment, she declined. I'll get myself an early dinner she thought, it will warm me up and, if either of them calls later on, I'll be free to chatter, she shivered and warmed her cold hands by the Aga.

Natalie was the first to phone just before seven thirty, "Fiona guess what. Simon gave me a first in Post-Grad. That qualifies him for Crufts again! I've been dying to tell you the good news, so I've decided to get one of those mobile phones and then I can phone you from the show itself. She babbled on telling her who had been showing and who she had seen and spoken to but Fiona was only half listening, she was trying to fathom out why Simon would have given Jamie a first, "Natalie," she interrupted Natalie's flow of words, "Natalie, just out of interest, how many dogs were there in your class?"

"Seven. Why?"

"And they all turned up?"

"Yes, all seven."

Fiona frowned, that made it even more perplexing, either Simon had changed his style of judging or Natalie had bribed him and she didn't think either solution was feasible. She suddenly realised that Natalie was saying something else..... "and I was so pleased for her because she hardly ever gets anything."

"Wait a minute Natalie, whose this you're talking about?"

"I told you Viv Butcher, she got a first too. It was in the Limit Class."

"Viv Butcher!"

"Yes, wasn't that nice, she asked me to have a cup of tea with her at lunchtime. She was so pleased, over the moon in fact."

"I bet she was." Fiona's mind was working overtime on this snippet of information, "Look Natalie I must go but many, many congratulations on getting a first with Jamie. I'll see you soon."

Had Simon lost the plot totally or was the man ill? She just couldn't believe that he had put both Natalie and Viv up. Neither could do anything for him and it went against all his rules for judging, she obviously needed more input on this. She dialled Paul's number but only got the answerphone, "Hello Paul, it's only me, just wondered how today's show went. Could you give me a call please when you get in." She felt very unsettled and wondered who else she could phone, Caroline? No, she went into the sitting-room and turned the television on but wasn't really able to concentrate on the images. Something very funny was going on, this was definitely not Simon's style, but then, she had forgotten to ask who had got the CC's. I bet they weren't nobodies.

She sat on in front of the television wondering whether to phone Simon. Deciding that it was better than sitting there, she went into the hall and dialled his number but it just rang and rang. By eleven o'clock, nobody else had phoned and Simon was still not answering his phone so she made herself a cup of hot chocolate, called to Sally and together they went upstairs. She spent a rather restless night going over recent conversations with Simon and wondering what it was that she was missing.

Simon had heard the phone ringing but decided not to answer it. He knew that it would either be someone phoning to say how disappointed they were in his judging (they didn't win) or someone phoning to say how pleased they were and, if it was Viv, he didn't want to talk to her at the moment. He had surprised himself a bit in giving her a first, the dog was certainly worth it but obviously had never won a first in Limit before. While he had been looking at the final line up, he looked at Viv's dog and suddenly saw in his mind, the pile of neatly folded clothes in his bedroom. She hadn't told anyone yet, certainly not Fiona, that was obvious, perhaps if he kept her sweet she wouldn't say anything to her. If she did then that would finish any chance of getting back with Fiona and that didn't bear thinking about. That Natalie Bennett, well, she was a dark horse, her dog's name had been mentioned quite firmly by his old pal Ted Roberts in one of the pre-show telephone conversations. She couldn't be as sweet and innocent as she appeared because someone at the top was pushing her. He wondered if Fee knew. Fee, he had looked and looked for her face around the ringside onlookers, he wished she had been there, he had felt quite flat, it just wasn't the same when she wasn't there. They now wouldn't be able to compare notes afterwards, something he had always enjoyed.

As he laid in bed that night he couldn't get away from the nagging feeling he had had recently that something was not quite right, something had changed. He had definitely felt it too when Ted phoned the other night. Ted had always been a pal, perhaps he should have a quiet word with him. He certainly didn't have any future Champ shows in the offing except Germany and as for his dogs? Shaking his head, he switched off the light, bashed the pillow and went to sleep.

Natalie put the phone down and smiled, how kind of Paul Aston to ring to congratulate her, he had been very complementary about Jamie and had also been very complementary about her presentation and grooming of the dog. She knew that he sometimes took Fiona to the theatre or for a meal but was there any more to it than that? What a lucky girl she was, he seemed such an educated, well-dressed and interesting man, a bit like Richard in fact. Yes, she liked Paul Aston.

Viv sat curled up on the settee with all the dogs around her. It had been an absolutely marvellous day. The best she'd had in a long while, yes, even better than looking at Simon's naked body, well, almost. Her dog was qualified for Crufts and Simon was obviously beginning to see her in a different light or else he wouldn't have stuck his neck out like that. What a shock it must have been to some of the 'in' crowd. I bet tongues are wagging now, she thought, and, smiling she stroked the head of the nearest dog. She was a bit concerned that he would get a lot of stick from the 'inner circle' because someone must have had their nose put out of joint in order for her to win in Limit. He hadn't answered his phone when she rang earlier, she hoped that he wasn't already regretting his decision. Perhaps he was with Fiona, although she would be furious at her win too. Viv wondered what her next step should be now; she must be to talk to Simon again, that was obvious, he had seemed very keen to know the inside story of what had happened to her on that committee. Funny that because she had thought that he was too well in not to know what went on.

Yes, she'd wash her hair first thing in the morning and invite him round for lunch. She bet that he lived out of a tin if she was any judge of men, he'd be pleased to have a proper meal and, who knows, perhaps, she might be able to thank him properly. She fell asleep on the sofa and the dogs, noting this, lay still and shut their eyes too.

She woke up in the early hours of the morning, stiff, cramped and cold, the dogs it seemed had all wandered off to their beds. Stretching, she smiled, today she would ask Simon round.

"Hello. Good God Viv it's only eight o'clock, what's the matter?"

"I'm sorry Simon if I woke you but I so wanted to thank you and to ask if you would like to come round for a spot of lunch today if you're not doing anything else. Nothing grand but it would give me chance to finish telling you about my problems with that committee."

He took a minute to think, was he getting in too deep here? He'd have to make it clear that there was no future in it but, somehow not antagonise her. The poor devil was lonely and he certainly knew what that felt like.

"Well, I'd like to hear the end of the story but.... Yeah, OK. What time?"

"Shall we say one o'clock?"

He had hardly put the phone down when it rang again, "Hello Simon, it's Fiona."

"Hello Fee to what do I owe this honour?"

"Oh, don't be funny with me Simon. I want to know why you put Natalie up and Viv Butcher!"

"It's early, shouldn't you be letting the dogs out?"

"That's just like you answering a question with a question. Come on, why did you do it."

"Why do you think, because I got phone calls and listened to what they were saying"

"Who on earth phoned you about Natalie? Nobody could have phoned you about Viv because everybody mistrusts her."

"To your first question, that's for me to know and as for Viv - you'd be surprised."

"Oh Simon, don't be so exasperating."

"Look how about I come round and tell you all the gory details."

"Oh all right then, come for lunch."

"Ah, I can't do that, previous engagement. I'll pop round this evening."

"What previous engagement?"

"That's for me to know and ...."

"Don't start that again. I'll see you about seven then and don't be late."

CHAPTER TWENTY

This is better than a cheese sandwich thought Simon as he sat surveying the table in Viv's kitchen. When he had arrived, the atmosphere had been a bit awkward, Viv seemed nervous and he had felt slightly uncomfortable himself being in such an intimate situation and had wished that he had refused the offer of dinner. Viv was bustling round between the cooker and the table and Simon noted with pleasure as a dish of roast potatoes, two sorts of vegetables and a roast chicken appeared on the table. Viv smiled as she looked at his face, he could have no idea how she had dashed out to the local supermarket for a fresh chicken and some vegetables just after he had agreed to come. She had spent the rest of the morning, preparing the dinner and hastily cleaning round. He smiled as she said, "Do come and sit down Simon, don't let it get cold. Would you like a glass of wine? I've only a white, is that alright?"

"Yeah, fine."

To his surprise, he really enjoyed the meal and as he drank his coffee, he relaxed and looked at his surroundings, feeling much better with a good dinner under his belt. The furniture was nothing special, but it was adequate and looked comfortable. He wondered if she owned the house or rented it, again, it was nothing special, an end of a modern terrace of four houses, built perhaps in the sixties, reasonably sized rooms though. The dogs all appeared to live in the house and looked healthy enough. "What sort of a garden have you got Viv?"

"Big enough. I have flowers in tubs and things and the dogs have the rest as grass. There's a couple of fruit trees as well. It's nice in the summer because it's South facing and has lots of sunshine; the dogs love it. Funny, he'd never given a thought to how Viv lived. She seemed a different person in her own home. On the grapevine she was known as a bit of a 'goer' and always up for it if a CC was on offer, but apart from that!

"What are you smiling at Simon?"

"Oh nothing, just the dogs. They look well don't they."

"Would you like another cup of coffee?"

They chatted about various dogs past and present, shows and mutual acquaintances for a while and then Simon asked her to continue the story about the committee.

"Where did I stop? Had I got up to the AGM?"

"Yeah, the one with the ballots."

"Yes, well, as it happened, several people had put themselves forward for the committee that year and about five or six people had been nominated to judge our next Champ Show so the ballot was important. The chairman phoned me up one evening to ask me who had been proposed for the committee. On hearing the names he told me who we did and didn't want on the committee and who would be the best person to judge the show. When I told him that I didn't know how this was possible he just laughed, told me I was green and then proceeded to tell me exactly what to do."

"And what was that?"

"Do you know Simon, you are almost the first person I have told this to since it happened. I was so threatened at the time that if I revealed what went on I'd be....."

"Threatened?"

"Yes, anonymous letters, phone calls the lot."

"Saying what?"

"Oh, the usual, that if I said anything, it would all be denied, I would be made the scapegoat, my dogs would suffer in the ring and, worst of all, my dogs would not be safe."

"Good God."

"You do realise don't you that there is nothing in writing, it's all verbal communication so you can't prove anything. What could I do? As the chairman, president and treasurer are all dead now, I suppose it doesn't matter any more."

"So, what did you do to rig the ballot?"

“Oh, well he told me to phone round everybody I had sold a puppy to or who were good friends of mine and who were members, of course, and suggest that it would be in the club’s best interests if only certain people were voted for also that I strongly recommended these people as being good at their job. He told me to do the same when members phoned to ask who were the best people to vote for and, this was what really shook me, he told me to refer to the previous secretaries files and look for a file or a piece of paper marked ‘Ballot Papers’. When I found it, it contained a list of people who had apparently never bothered to come to meetings in the previous five to six years. I presumed that the chairman must have asked her to do this knowing that the question of ballot papers would be coming up in the future.”

Simon had let his coffee go cold as he listened intently, “What the hell did you have to do with them?”

“I had to check through them to make sure that no-one had died and then make out ballot papers, with their correct numbers, for them, but not send the papers, just fill them in myself. If the people concerned hadn’t phoned me by the last posting date....”

“But how did you get them to the auditors?”

“I posted a couple in different places and gave some to the chairman and treasurer to post as ordered.”

“Good God, such bloody organization. What happened then?”

“The right people got on, the committee were happy and nobody was any the wiser.”

“And then what.”

“Well, if you would like to stay for tea I could tell you but it’s a long story and I’m sorry Simon but, being a working girl, I’ve got some washing and housework still to do. Otherwise, it’ll have to be some other time.” She smiled to herself, she hadn’t planned it but it was working out very nicely; a bit like the ‘Arabian Nights’.

“That’s a damned nuisance, I’ve made other arrangements for this evening Viv.”

“Pity.”

“Yeah, it is. I was enjoying that. Thanks for the dinner Viv. See you again soon. Bye.”

Viv returned to the little kitchen and sat down, she looked across at the dirty plates on Simon's side of the table and then touched them lightly with her hand. It truly was the best day and the best meal that she had had in years.

After Fiona had spoken to Simon she too had rushed out to the nearest supermarket and bought a large pizza. She wasn't overfund of them but she knew that Simon liked them and, just before seven o'clock she took it out of the Aga, it looks delicious she thought, "Sally will you tell me why the hell I am bothering to do this?" The question remained unanswered as Sally was more interested in sniffing at the aroma. Hearing a car stop outside, she opened the kitchen door,

"Hello Simon come in."

"You all right? It's getting a bit nippy out there. How are the pups?"

"Fine thanks, ready to go except for the bitch I'm running on. You never told me how your litter went. Couldn't be bothered to let me know I suppose."

"If there had been any pups I would have done. I'm a bit dubious now that I was seen off with that bitch."

"You seen off!"

"Yeah, things are beginning to look that way. Anyway enough of that. Have I got news for you."

"What."

"Do you remember when Viv left the Cumbrian committee and there was all that talk about her. No, it was before your time, well she has been telling me what actually happened and you'll be amazed at......."

"She has been telling you. When?"

"The other day when she came for a stud and this lunchtime she told me....."

"This lunchtime! So she was your previous engagement was she. It's beginning to make sense now"

"What? As I was saying, she invited me for lunch and she told me..."

"Don't bother I don't want to know; but it's clear to me now how she got that first in Limit."

Simon looked at her for several seconds and then shrugged his shoulders, what was the point of trying to explain, she had already made her mind up, "Any chance of a cup of tea?"

In silence she poured two cups of tea and cut the pizza into portions, placed plates and knives on the table and brought the cups over. Her mind was bursting, how could he destroy their beautiful lovemaking by laying that ghastly woman! How could he come in here when he'd been with her today! It was disgusting! How could he... she paused for a moment, a plate of pizza in her hand, what about her and Paul? They had had sex on several occasions now... but that was different, that was sex it was not what she and Simon had had. Perhaps Simon had only had sex with Viv? Oh surely he couldn't have done all their wonderful things with her!

"Hi there, wake up, are you going to put that plate on the table?"

She looked into his eyes for a brief moment, she still loved him after everything and she still wanted to make love to him. What a bloody mess! The sooner she could get Paul to propose the better. She really ought to see her solicitor and start the divorce, there was nothing to stop her now.

"She sat down and handed him the plate of pizza, "Well, I'm waiting?"

"For what?"

"Why did you put up Natalie, for starters."

"I told you."

"I don't believe you. Natalie, I'm sure, doesn't know about such things."

"She may not but one of her friends does."

"Do you mean Audrey Chatsworth?"

Simon put a finger alongside his nose and tapped it.

"Oh Simon, you are exasperating. Why won't you tell me. I suppose you're going to say that they told you to put up Viv at the same time. Well, I don't believe you."

After that, the atmosphere was decidedly chilly and Simon didn't stay long. As he went out of the door he turned, "Fee are you sure that you're OK. Look, I only had lunch with Viv to hear her story. It would amaze you, honestly. I don't fancy her Fee. I love you. You know you've only got to say and I'd be back here like a shot."

Fiona busied herself with clearing the dishes and turned her back on him.

"OK Fee. Have it your own way. Oh, I nearly forgot, I think Sassy is coming in season, is it still OK for Saxon? I really could do with the money."

"Yes and goodnight Simon," she closed the door after him.

Waking to a cold, but bright sunny morning, Fiona bustled round and then saw to the pups, a task which always took much longer than it should have done because she loved to sit in the pen and play with them afterwards. Well, they're all clean for a short while at least, she felt it of prime importance to sit in the pen and talk, cuddle and play with them. It was socialising them for the human world they were going into. Natalie knocked on the door and opened it, "Fiona, it's only me, ah, there you are. I've just popped round to see if you would like to come out for a quick coffee?"

"I'm sorry Natalie but I have a lot to do today."

"Pity, I thought that we'd go to those dear little tea rooms that have all those yummy cakes and then we could start our Christmas shopping."

"Christmas shopping! In that case, let me make a coffee for you, you'll need it. Gosh, I haven't given it a thought."

As they sipped their coffee Fiona asked. "Natalie, have you seen much of Audrey lately?"

"No, but she did phone last night and, do you know I forgot to tell her about my win at Driffield."

After Natalie had left and while she was busy with the older dogs, Fiona thought about Christmas, it wasn't true what she had said to Natalie that she hadn't given it a thought, she wanted this Christmas to be special, she was hoping that Paul would ask her to marry him. She had already phoned her solicitor and made an appointment to see him later in the week about divorcing Simon, though even the thought of it made her stomach tighten, but she couldn't get the picture of Simon with Viv out of her mind.

Natalie was thoroughly enjoying her day in town. Now that Candida and Jason her husband, were coming for Christmas she wanted to brighten up the house with some new Christmas decorations, the old wooden beams and the inglenook fire places so lent themselves to the festive season. She had decided to buy a large tree, growing of course, and decorate it. She hadn't felt as happy and confident as she did now, since Richard died. She woke up in the mornings keen to get up and start the day, she was looking forward to the coming year and it was all because of one thing, the dogs and the friends that she had made like Fiona and Paul. She had even met up with old friends like Audrey and Ian. She would have a full diary of shows next year and she was hoping to have another litter. Life was looking good again.

Audrey had even phoned her last night about a stud dog for her forthcoming litter. It appeared that Audrey had been talking to Paul Aston at Driffield after he had got the CC and BOB with his dog under Simon. She had suggested to Natalie that it would be a good idea to use Paul's dog because Paul was going to export him to America shortly. Such a kind act, to think of her, she had been going to mention it to Fiona and ask for her opinion but she had seemed rather preoccupied this morning. Perhaps she had better phone Paul Aston first, he might not want her to use such a top-class dog and then she could tell Fiona. She would phone this evening.

"Hello, may I speak to Paul Aston please."

"Paul Aston speaking."

"Oh, hello, it's Natalie Bennett here."

"Hello Natalie, to what do I owe this honour?"

"I was talking to Audrey Chatsworth the other evening and she suggested that I use your stud dog, the one that is going to America. My young bitch Juno is due in season any day now, she is Fiona's breeding and I would so like a nice litter from her."

"Ah, that line should go in very well with Androcles. Are you aware that I charge a little more for this dog. He does throw excellent puppies. Strong with good conformation."

"That's no problem. Then I may use him?"

"Certainly, just let me know when she comes in."

She put the phone down and went back to the lounge, yes, next year was going to be wonderful. She paused on her way back to the lounge, she could have a party! All partying had had to stop when Richard became so ill but now..... the more she thought about it the better it seemed. Christmas? No she wanted to be selfish and to enjoy Candida's visit without interruption; they would be here for such a short time. New Year would be a good idea, yes, a party to let the New Year in. She would still have the Christmas tree in the hall. Even better, I could get Mr. Meredith in to redecorate this lounge, it hasn't been decorated for years. Yes, something lighter and brighter. She went to the writing bureau for some paper and a pen in order to make a guest list. Fiona first and foremost, Simon?, she had better ask Fiona about that. Audrey and Ian, Frank, her neighbours Diane and Will, Caroline Amery and her husband, Viv Butcher and guest, and of course, Paul Aston. She started another list for refreshments.

CHAPTER TWENTY-ONE

The alarm on the radio trilled out in the darkness, Fiona sleepily fumbled for the switch, "Oh no, it can't be morning yet. Sally are you awake," she yawned and a wet nose pressed into her hand. "Hello my lovely girl. It's time to get up, it's the LKA today, and it's the last show of the year thank goodness."

Her clothes for the day were all laid out and ready to put on, a habit she had acquired early on in her showing life. At this time in the morning she had to work on autopilot. Damn, she thought as she quickly dressed, just when I needed a good night's sleep I have to get up at five o'clock. She had slept badly and it was all Simon's fault bringing Sassy to be mated last night. It had all gone well but it had made her feel very close and intimate with Simon as they both stood there with the dogs tied; in fact, she had felt so aroused that she had been rather short with him afterwards and had even refused him a cup of coffee saying that she needed to get to bed for an early start. She had then spent most of the night tossing and turning, wondering what Simon would do when he got the letter from her solicitor, he hadn't mentioned it so he couldn't have got it yet, she would have to chivvy the solicitor up. She hurried downstairs and made a quick cup of tea and did a piece of toast for breakfast.

Checking that everything was alright, she went out into the dark, cold morning to get Saxon and put him in the estate. It was very cold and she shivered as she put him in his travelling cage. Just then the lights of Natalie's car came into view as she turned into the drive. Together they settled Jamie into the estate, stowed all their gear and set off.

"You're quiet Fiona. Are you feeling alright?"

"Yes, I'm fine Natalie, just a bit tired that's all. Had to do a mating last night."

"Oh, one of your dogs?"

"Yes and no, it was a Simfell but one of Simon's. He wanted to use Saxon but, as the timing was all wrong, we tried out Sammy. He was very good and we got an excellent mating."

"I mated Juno this week."

For a brief second Fiona took her eyes off the road, "You mated Juno this week. Who to?"

" Paul Aston's dog Androcles, the one that is going abroad."

"But... you were going to use Saxon."

"Well, I know that you had suggested it but.... Well, Audrey said..."

"Audrey! Do you mean your high and mighty friend Audrey Chatsworth?"

"I do wish you wouldn't keep saying that Fiona, she is an old friend of mine."

"Well she is, 'well in' then is that better?"

"Are you sure that you're feeling alright?"

"Of course I'm sure. So these marvellous puppies will be due next February then."

"Hopefully yes, Paul said that he would be interested in seeing them, he wants a dog puppy himself, if there is a nice one."

"Yes, well make sure that you don't charge him for it."

"Pardon?"

"Nothing, forget I said it. What did you think of Paul's dogs."

"Oh, I didn't go to his house, he offered to come to me."

"Did he."

"He is such an intelligent man, so knowledgeable about so many things. He was very interested in the architecture of my house and has promised to look up it's history for me. It was something that Richard and I were always going to do but we never seemed to find the time."

Fiona felt a stab of unease at Natalie's words, she hadn't seen so much of Paul lately, he had been so snowed under with work that he had only taken her out for a meal a couple of evenings and stayed the night once. Was he going off her? Please no, not now! This wasn't turning out to be a very good day so far.

"Now to change the subject completely, Fiona would you like to come to a party at my house on New Year's Eve."

"That sounds lovely Natalie. I love New Year's Eve parties. We used to....."

Although Natalie started talking again, Fiona didn't hear a word she said, her mind was on the wonderful parties that she and Simon had had at the cottage and now, there would never be any more. She didn't think that it was the sort of thing that Paul would like.

"and I'm even having the lounge decorated for the party. It was time that it was done anyway."

"Oh, that'll be nice. Are you going to invite Paul?"

"Yes, that's if he can come. He said that he was very busy at the moment."

The grey light of a cold winter's morning accompanied them as they drove into the NEC car park and stopped the car. They both sat still for a minute or two watching other exhibitors stiffly getting out of their cars and yawning then giving themselves a mental shake and getting on with the business of unloading the dogs and gear. A whole lot of dedication and effort goes into this game Fiona thought as she too yawned.

With the dogs settled on their benches, Fiona sat down to look at the catalogue, she knew that both Paul and Simon had entered for today's show but had Viv Butcher? Yes, the wretched woman was in Open with her and Saxon, damn the woman, Paul had reckoned that Saxon stood a good chance of getting his second CC but, when she had told Simon that last night he had burst out laughing, "Come on Fee, its Freddie Harwich judging. You know damned well that he always toes the line. Everyone has known for weeks that Frances Douglas is getting the bitch CC and BOB so that she makes up her bitch. They're both on the same show committee. The dog CC will very likely go to Stan Horrocks."

Fiona shivered, it seemed to take a while before these vast buildings warmed up, not enough bodies here yet she thought as she pulled out her flask and poured a cup of coffee; she put her hands around the steaming cup and shivered again.

"Hi Fiona, how are you?" She turned round to see the ferrety little face of Caroline Amery standing in front of her.

"I'm fine and how are you?"

"OK. How do you rate your chances today?"

"I've no idea but I'm keeping my fingers crossed, It isn't a very big class so I should get a card of some sort."

Caroline's bright eyes studied Fiona's face. Yes, she did look a bit drawn and black-eyed. Did she know about Viv and Simon? When Viv had told her the other day that Simon had been to her house twice she had immediately phoned up Sue Musday and Shirley Goss. Such news was too good to keep to herself, by now the whole Cumbrian world would know, surely someone would have let it slip to Fiona by now, "Right, well must be off, good luck if I don't see you before the class."

Fiona rubbed her hands together, she still felt cold.

"Hello Fiona, how are you managing?" Standing in front of her this time was Phyllis Watford, another well known gossip.

"Hello Phyllis I haven't seen you for ages. I'm fine thanks and how are you?"

"I'm very well considering, you look a bit under the weather though, not surprising under the circumstances."

"What circumstances?"

"You know, well I must be off, good luck anyway."

She watched as Phyllis moved along the benches, there must be some bit of gossip that she was unaware of, no doubt someone would tell her soon. I wonder why she didn't tell me what it was? The tannoy suddenly burst into life with the information that judging was starting in all rings in ten minutes. Good, she thought, let's hope he doesn't take too long on each class and then I can relax.

"Hello my dear, how are you?" Mrs Emsworth was looking at her in a sad way.

"I'm a little bit tired today but otherwise I'm fine thank you and how are you?" She thought that the dear soul was looking rather frail these days, it was only the dogs that kept her going.

"I'm very well my dear. Now you will look after yourself won't you?"

It was funny how everyone seemed so concerned for her, she must look a hell of a lot tireder than she was. Perhaps she was going down with a cold, she certainly felt cold. She made her way to Natalie's bench, "Want any help?"

"No thanks Fiona, I've just about got him ready, he looks alright doesn't he?"

"Um. He's looking good," she watched as Natalie walked him to the side of the ring in preparation for the next class. Although it was a reasonably big class with some fairly well-known faces in it, Jamie was pulled out first. Fiona was very surprised, she was beginning to smell a rat. Could it be 'Audrey' engineering all this she wondered because the dog was good but not that good and Natalie was still a relative newcomer. She would have to have a word with Simon again and ask him if it had been Audrey who had spoken to him before his show. She went back to her bench to prepare Saxon for the Open class.

She stood in the ring feeling worried, cold, and out of sorts, whether Saxon had sensed that she was tired or whether it was the atmosphere she didn't know but, he hadn't walked as well as he normally did. All the other dogs seemed to really drive around the ring with their owners all bright-eyed and bushy-tailed, she must try to keep him alert and keen as she waited. Freddie asked her to move the dog again and she could tell as soon as she moved off that he wasn't going to cooperate fully. When Freddie then waved her into the first spot she was amazed, she knew that Saxon was good but....

"That was very lucky wasn't it. Congratulations." Viv, who had been the only one not to be placed in the class smiled and patted Saxon's head, "but then some of us can't be lucky all the time can we." Fiona smiled, her heart was pounding, she just had to motivate Saxon before the challenge, if Saxon didn't walk any better, he wouldn't stand a chance, there were some good dogs here today. Natalie came up, "I'm so nervous Fiona. I can hardly breathe. I do hope he doesn't play up."

"Well you don't look nervous. You always look very smart and not a bit worried so, 'may the best man win'. Good luck Natalie."

The steward called out for all unbeaten dogs and as they walked into the ring the adrenaline began to build in Fiona, Saxon did walk better, due she thought, to the excitement he could now feel coming from her. She was willing him to look good, to stand well and he did, her heart was beating fast as the judge walked down the row of six dogs, please, please pick Saxon. That would be two CC s and all done on her and Saxon's merit this time and no Alan Burgess to please! She looked up from the dog just for a second to see the judge walking towards her with the green card, his hand outstretched. She had got the CC! Overjoyed, she shook the judges hand and, with tears in her eyes, she took Saxon round on his lap of honour unaware that the person behind her with the reserve CC, a 'name' was cursing her to all eternity. This would have been a third CC for his dog and would have made him into a champion. He already had several studs lined up for him on the strength of it.

CHAPTER TWENTY-TWO

"Hey, two down, one to go."
She felt familiar arms circle her waist and a warm kiss on her neck, turning she smiled at Simon.
"Yes, isn't it wonderful. Have you been in yet?"
"No, not till Limit. Just thought I'd come and congratulate you, although how you've done it this time..."
"Simon, stop it. This time it really is the dog. I haven't slept with anybody, I haven't slipped anybody anything and I haven't entertained....... anyone."
"And I believe you Fee."
"Do you?"
"Yes I do, you are so naive my girl that yes, I believe you. Now, how did you come up here today because I was going to suggest that I took you home and that we stopped for a celebratory meal."
Fiona looked at him for a second or two remembering the first time he had suggested that. It had been the first time that they had made love.
"Ah, I know what you're thinking Fee. Well, nothing would give me greater pleasure but, I did mean just a meal. Mind you if you want me to come back home with you, I'd not be adverse to the idea."
"I'm sorry Simon but I came up in the estate today and brought Natalie with me."
"Oh, pity, never mind, another time, I've got so much to tell you Fee."
As she watched him walking back to the other side of the aisle she felt tears prick her eyes. Wiping them away she told herself not to be so stupid, those days were gone, she turned and stroked the dog's

head, “Do you know Saxon, I really must be tired today,” the dog looked at her not quite certain of the words but hoping that it meant more food.

“Hello Fiona, forgive me but I saw you wiping your eyes. Are you all right? How are you coping with it all.”

“Hello Doreen, long time no see. How are you?”

“Oh, managing, managing. I was lost at first when Ken died but the dogs were a great help. I expect that you have found that. Haven’t quite got around to showing yet but I hope to this summer. I’ve been catching up on all the gossip today, nothing changes does it. I heard about you and Simon. I’m so sorry, Ken and I thought that you were the perfect couple.”

“Did you, I never knew that.”

“Well anyway, as long as you’re alright,” Doreen kissed her on the cheek and patted her shoulder, “Hope to see you in the summer.”

When Doreen was out of sight Fiona got her make-up bag and went to the lavatories. She looked at herself in the mirrors, yes she looked pretty awful, no wonder everyone seemed worried about her. She applied make-up and eye-liner, a warm coloured lipstick and then, standing back, combed her hair. That’s looks better for challenging for the BOB she thought.

Later, as she walked into the ring to challenge the bitch CC, which had been won by Fran Douglas as prophesied by Simon, she began to feel brighter. Saxon moved beautifully this time but, unfortunately, the bitch got the BOB. Simon came straight up to her as she came out of the ring, “Well done Fee. He looked a picture but, well, it was a foregone conclusion wasn’t it.”

“Thanks Simon and I’m sorry you only got a reserve in your class today.”

“Seems to be the story of my life lately. Take care going home. I’ll give you a ring later.”

She looked round for Paul, she hadn’t seen him all day apart from when he was showing in the ring and, before she could get to him, he had disappeared. Natalie came over, “Are you ready to go Fiona?”

“Yes, I was just looking for Paul, have you seen him?”

“Not since he was in the ring.”

As they drove home Natalie seemed exceptionally quiet and Fiona wondered if what she had said about Audrey Chatsworth had upset her, "Natalie, is something wrong?"
Natalie started as Fiona spoke to her, "No, nothing."

"Are you disappointed that you only got a VHC?"

"Good heavens no."

"Well, is it something I've said?"

"No, it's nothing you've said."

Fiona gave up, she was tired and just wanted to get home, if it was important, no doubt Natalie would tell her in her own good time.

It was about ten o'clock, and her eyes were almost closing as she stirred her hot milk, suddenly she was jolted awake by the sound of the phone. Blast the phone, who could be ringing now.

"Hi Fee, You got home OK."

"Yes of course, why the sudden concern about my driving?"

"Er, did anyone speak to you today?"

"Of course they did, look Simon I'm tired, could we get to the point of this call."

"Nobody said anything about Viv, well about Viv and me?"

She suddenly felt cold, "No, what about Viv and you?"

"Nothing absolutely nothing but... Look, can I pop round Monday after work?"

"Yes all right, I'll make some dinner."

All day Monday her mind was only half on the work she was doing, she couldn't wait for the day to end and for Simon to come. Viv and me, what did he mean, Viv and me, surely he hadn't, he wasn't, damn the man why didn't he come. That evening as Simon ate voraciously, she picked at her meal, Simon hardly spoke except to comment on the food.

"God Fee, this is the best meal I've had in ages."

Fiona, who couldn't wait for the meal to end, hurried him through the pudding and onto coffee.

"Now, tell me what all this is about you and Viv."

"Well, people as usual are making two and two into five and I didn't want you to get the wrong end of the stick."

"For goodness sake Simon, will you tell me what is going on!"

As Simon drank his coffee he explained to Fiona how he had been again to Viv's house in order to hear the end of her story, "and Fee, let me tell you, you don't know the half of it. Even I was surprised at one or two things she told me although I have heard things like it before."

"And you believed what she told you?"

"Yeah, it had the ring of truth to it. Just listen and stop interrupting, she was really put through the wringer because she was going to blow the gaffe on the committee, lies went round about her dogs throwing malformed puppies, her dogs were threatened, anonymously of course, she stopped getting judging appointments and she stopped winning much and this went on for years.... still is. In fact, all the things we've heard about her aren't..."

"For goodness sake Simon, you don't believe all that rubbish. She's just trying to soft soap you and get you on her side."

"No Fee. You know what a reputation she has for being a troublemaker. Well, that was put round to stop people talking to her."

"Rubbish, you know that Shaun fellow who lived with her for a while said that she was awful. Into every bed that would have her so that she could get on. You ought to watch out she might be telling you all this to get you into her bed. Unless of course..? Ask yourself, how was it that people knew you'd been to her house twice?"

"That Shaun robbed her blind, she told me and..."

"Have you slept with her?"

"I didn't go to her house to sleep with her and I didn't."

Fiona got up and started to clear the table, she knew that Simon had heard from her solicitor but, as yet, he had not replied. She ran some hot water and was putting some washing-up liquid into the bowl when Simon came up behind her, "Fee, please don't ask for a divorce, please Fee, I love you, nobody else, always have, always will. I just want to come home and put the past behind me. Please let me Fee."

She stood with her hands in the hot, soapy water, he was crying! She had only ever seen him cry once and that was when Barry, his son, was killed. Her heart seemed to be beating right through her ribs, she loved him, he made life fun, but she just couldn't trust him, anyway she had decided to settle for the comfortable easy, quiet life with Paul. If he proposed this Christmas, she would accept and then she would stop seeing Simon because it hurt too much. She turned to tell him of her decision, "Simon I'm going to m....." She got no further. Simon was quietly standing there looking utterly defeated, his eyes brimming with tears, "Oh Simon," she opened her arms and he stepped into them.

She turned and opened her eyes, she had been having a wondrous dream where she had been so happy. She curled her body around Simon's warm body and had started to fall asleep again when she became fully aware of the situation. It wasn't a dream, he was here. She suddenly recalled the events of the evening, how she had cuddled him and comforted him, how he had started to kiss her so passionately and how she had kissed him back. Without a word being said between them, they had gone upstairs and quietly removed their clothes, he had stood across the room from her and looked at her body, no-one had ever looked at her like that, without a word they climbed into bed and made love. There hadn't been the usual foreplay, the usual passion. There had just been a desperate hunger, a desperate need for each other. As they climaxed together they had both cried. Turning, she looked at his familiar features, they had forgotten to turn out the lights, and tears started in her eyes, what was she to do. Slipping out of bed, she put on her dressing gown and went downstairs followed by Sally who went straight to the kitchen door. Good heavens, they hadn't let her out last night, or locked the door! "Off you go girls," Sally ran out closely followed by Sapphire and Stella. She made a pot of tea and took the tray upstairs, "Simon, Simon, wake up I've made a cup of tea. I know it's early but I think you should go home."

"Home... I thought I was home," they looked at each other for a moment and then he took the proffered mug, "I see, well I'll drink this then and be on my way."

He refused breakfast and got into his car.

Although it was a bright, cold sunny day and she received her first Christmas cards in the post, Fiona felt flat and strangely worried about Simon. He had been different, she had never known him like he was last night. The phone rang, damn she thought, she hadn't yet put the answerphone on, "Hello Simfell Kennels."

"Hello my dear. I must apologise for not contacting you sooner but I had several people to see while I was up there. I hear that congratulations are in order."

"Yes Paul, Saxon got his second CC. I was so thrilled."

"Well done. Now my dear, I wondered if I might pop round this evening?"

"I'm sorry Paul but, I was going to have an early night. I have felt really tired ever since the show."

"In that case, you must certainly do that. I'll ring you tomorrow. Sleep well."
When the post came the next morning, as well as another Christmas card, there was a letter from her solicitor to say that Simon had been in touch and had given him the name of his solicitor.

CHAPTER TWENTY-THREE

Natalie had to put some of her parcels down in order to lock the car door, she had been up to London on the train to do some Christmas shopping but just for odds and ends this time. She had seen a dress in one of the big department stores which had taken her fancy and, on a whim, she had decided to buy it. The dress was not the sort that she usually wore, it was a deep, translucent green and rather clinging but she wanted to impress Paul at her New Year's Eve party. As she started to walk towards the front door it opened and Jessie's smiling face appeared, "Can I help you with those Mrs Bennett?"

"Oh no Jessie, thank you. It's only a few bits and pieces for Christmas. Nothing heavy."

"It won't be long now before Candida arrives with her husband will it, so Mrs Bennett, I've given the bedroom a really good dusting and vacuuming and I've made up the bed. It's all ready for them."

"Thank you Jessie. I'm sure that you are looking forward to seeing them as much as I am. We'll have so much to talk about. Now, shall we have a cup of tea?"

Later that afternoon, she walked around the house deciding where to put the flowers that she had ordered for tomorrow. The newly decorated drawing room looked so much better, the pale emulsion paint setting of the colour of the oak beams so well. She wanted everything to look welcoming when they arrived. Her life had changed so much since Candida went away, she was happy and hopeful now and she wanted the dear old house to reflect this. She was due at the hairdressers first thing tomorrow morning, she wanted her new hairstyle to look it's best when Candida and Jason arrived. She was also going to wear a new suit which she had recently bought at a rather nice boutique in the town. It was dark blue and well tailored and she had bought a blue silk blouse to wear with it. She smiled as she completed the tour of the house, yes, this was going to be a wonderful Christmas and New Year. In her last letter Candida had asked if they would be meeting this Paul Aston who seemed now to appear in every letter that she received from her mother! Natalie had immediately phoned Paul and asked him if he would like to come for lunch on the 23rd of December and he had readily agreed.

It was beginning to look hopeful that Juno was pregnant so she would obviously be mentioning Paul a lot more in her future letters when she told Candida about the puppies. She looked at her watch, yes, there was still time, she must go over to see Fiona. Worried that Fiona had been rather distant and preoccupied since LKA and concerned that perhaps the mating to Androcles instead of Saxon had upset her, she had phoned Caroline Amery to ask her advice. Caroline had been very interested and had told her that, although some of the big breeders did have cliques and that you had to use their dogs, she didn't think that Fiona was like that but, you could never be sure. She then laughed and said that she thought that perhaps Fiona had more on her mind at the moment than Androcles. Pressed to explain her remark, Caroline refused and told Natalie to ask Fiona.

As she drove into the kennels Natalie saw Fiona walking a couple of the dogs, she waved and Fiona waved and called out to Natalie that she wouldn't be long.

"Hello Fiona, I hope that I haven't come at an inconvenient time?"

"No, I'm pleased to see you, sit down and I'll pop the kettle on the Aga. Gosh, it's nearly dark already."

Natalie thought that Fiona looked very pale and tired, "I expect you're getting terribly busy with boarders are you?"

"Well yes, but I manage, most aren't coming in until Christmas Eve anyway," she made the tea and got out some biscuits, "Sorry they're only boring ones, haven't been out to the shops recently."

"I went early this morning but only for a few little extras. I suppose you've finished your Christmas shopping."

"Christmas shopping? Heavens no, I must get out tomorrow and do something," she had bought most of her presents and cards a short while ago but had done nothing in the last couple of weeks about food.

The business with Simon and Viv and the divorce had driven that out of her mind but now time was of the essence; she must impress Paul.

"Thank you for reminding me Natalie, I suppose I hadn't realised that it was quite so close."

They chatted on for about half-an-hour or so and Fiona brightened up a little but Natalie continued to be concerned. Fiona didn't seem to be very upset when she told her that all the signs were that Juno was pregnant so, what was it that was troubling her so much? "Fiona, I must go and let you get on but before I do, are you sure that there's nothing troubling you and, if there is, can I do anything to help?"

"No everything's fine Natalie, but thanks for the offer. I'm so pleased that you are going to see your daughter tomorrow, I know what that means to you and, if I don't see you before, I hope that you have a lovely Christmas."

"Thank you Fiona. In fact, thank you for everything. You are a really sweet person and a good friend."

Fiona smiled as she saw Natalie to the door, you wouldn't think that I was sweet if you knew what was happening she thought. After her solitary meal that evening, she sat down to compose a list of food and other items needed for Christmas. Paul was coming for Christmas Day and Boxing Day. He was bringing his dogs and putting them into one of her kennels. Everything had to be perfect, especially, if he did ask her to marry him. She had told him of Natalie's invitation for New Year's Eve and had found that he also had been invited. Perhaps they could announce their engagement then?

During the next few days, Fiona, with the assistance of Ruth, managed to get all her shopping completed. She was busy wrapping presents for Laura's four children and for Donald, when the phone rang, "Hello Fiona it's me Beryl. Peter says that I'm interfering but, would you like to come to dinner on Christmas Day. I have to tell you that I have already invited Simon. He hasn't let me know yet but I'm sure that he'll come. You know how he loves a good meal."

"No Beryl, thank you for asking but no for two reasons, I can't leave the boarders and I have already made other arrangements."

"Oh," there was a long pause but, Fiona was certainly not going to fill in the details, "Oh I see. Well, how about New Year's Eve?"

"Sorry Beryl, I've already been invited to Natalie's party."

"Oh well, when are we going to see you?"

"As a matter of fact, I was going to phone you later. Ruth is coming in tomorrow so that I can take my presents to Laura's children and Donald. I thought that I might be able to pop in to see you then.if it's convenient"

"Of course you can, at least we'll see you. I shall look forward to it. Peter will be at home, he's had an awful cold but we can get rid of him somehow and have a good natter," she laughed and said goodbye.

Having taken something to make her sleep, she seemed to be doing that a lot lately, Fiona had to force herself awake when the alarm went off but, realising that today she was going to take the Christmas presents to the children, she got up in order to see to everything before she left. This made Christmas for her, to take the children their presents, she loved choosing the different toys and gifts, she loved choosing the different paper for each of them and putting pretty matching ribbons on the various boxes and parcels. Stopping outside Laura's house, she picked up the appropriate bags full of presents and walked up the path, Laura flung open the door and put her arms around her, "It's lovely to see you Fiona, come in, come in and get warm. We don't see enough of you these days."

Laura's house was it's usual jumble of clothes half hanging on pegs, discarded shoes and trainers on the floor and piles of washing in the kitchen; even the dog greeting her rapturously; rushing up to her and putting it's paws on her waist.

"Ignore the mess Fiona, as you know, I just can't teach my lot to be tidy."

"It's lovely, yours is a real family home not a show house. There'll be plenty of time to be neat and tidy when they've left home. Anyway, I love the decorations and the tree."

"Do you, I'll tell the kids, it's all their own work."

As old friends do, they chatted about this and that for an hour or so until Fiona suddenly looked at her watch, "Is that the time! I must fly, I've still got to take Donald's present and see Beryl and Peter."

"Oh yes, how are Beryl and Peter?"

"They're fine I think except Peter's had a cold."

"And Simon? You haven't mentioned Simon."

"He's OK. He used one of my dogs for a mating recently."

"Oh, I see, so nothing's changed then. Are you sure I can't tempt you to another cup of coffee and some more biscuits?"

"No, I really must go it'll be dark in no time. Have a lovely Christmas Laura and wish Michael and the children a Happy Christmas from me and thank you for your presents. I shall open them on Christmas morning."

"I'm sure that the children will phone you as usual in the holiday and Michael sends his love."

"I'll look forward to hearing from them. Bye Laura. Happy Christmas."

Laura gave Fiona a big hug and watched pensively as she walked to her car.

Calling on Barbara was very different; when she knocked on the door Barbara opened it and said, "Do come in Fiona but you can't stay for very long I'm afraid, Donald doesn't like it if I'm not there to pick him up the moment he comes out, he's at the nursery party."

"That's fine Barbara, I'm running late anyway, look here are Donald's presents. I do hope that he enjoys them and I hope that you all have a Happy Christmas."

"Thank you, I'm sure we shall. I've no doubt that Duncan will phone you on the day, and now...."

"Of course, well, goodbye."

Fiona breathed a sigh of relief as she got into the car and headed for Beryl's house. She hated going to her former home. In her mind it was still as she had left it and she resented any changes that Barbara made. Illogical it may be but, she still resented it! What a shame that she hadn't been able to see Donald.

"Hi Beryl. Hi Peter, how's the cold?"

"It's nearly gone now thanks, just catarrh left. You know how it is."

"Poor you, well, I'm sure that Beryl's looked after you."

They talked about this and that as Beryl prepared a rather late lunch for them all and laid the table.

"Only some home-made soup, hot rolls and cheese Fiona. I hope that's OK?"

"Perfect, it'll warm me up. I always like your soup, what flavour is it this time?"

They sat down and, as they ate, the conversation was manoeuvred round by Beryl to the subject of Simon, "We haven't seen him for a while Fiona have you?"

"No, not since LKA."

"Peter has phoned him of course but he seems very down at the moment, hasn't got much to say at all. Did you know that the dog that he mated miscarried?"
"No, I didn't. He hasn't phoned to tell me."
"Worried about his phone bill possibly. He doesn't actually say but Peter has got the impression that he was relying on this litter for some cash. That's right Peter isn't it."
Without looking up from his plate Peter replied in the affirmative.
"Do you know if he is hard up Fiona?" Beryl returned to her pet subject.
"No, he's never said anything."
"Mm well, he phoned us last night to say that he couldn't come for Christmas he was going somewhere else. Do you know anything about that?"
"No, but I've got a good idea. He's very likely going to Viv Butcher's."
Beryl's eyes opened wide, "Viv Butcher's! Who is she?"
Fiona felt a bit mean as she explained who Viv was and why she thought that he would be going there and that he had been there several times before now. She hated seeing the stricken look on Beryl and Peter's face, it was patently obvious that they knew nothing about it. Knowing how much they had hoped that she and Simon would get back together, it must have come as a shock. She would dread having to tell them about her engagement to Paul soon.
"Well, I must be off, Ruth wants to leave at four o'clock. Thank you for a lovely meal Beryl. I do hope that you like your presents and thank you for mine. I promise I'll phone on Christmas morning. Bye," she kissed Beryl and hugged Peter, "See you soon,Bye."
As she drove home she recalled the recent conversation with Beryl and Peter, they were going to be so upset when they heard her news. It was obvious that Simon hadn't told them about the divorce; she hoped that they would still be her friends when she married Paul. What about this miscarriage and Simon being hard up, he'd never said anything to her about being short of money. She would have to find out about both those things.

CHAPTER TWENTY-FOUR

Viv came in from the grooming shed in the garden, she had a heater out there but, even so, she felt cold. Her dogs were all now running around the garden, they enjoyed their regular grooming sessions and almost vied with each other to be the first to be groomed. She always tried to keep them in top show condition just for her own satisfaction. Having washed her hands, she went into her main room and stopped for a moment to admire the Christmas tree. When Simon had agreed to come for dinner on Christmas Day her spirits had soared. Being an only child and now that both of her parents had died; she had spent several Christmas Days with just the dogs and the TV for company. It had been so exciting to rush out after his phone call to buy a tree and some decorations for it, crackers, wine, nuts and a small turkey. Just like other people.

She had chosen a small living tree with roots so that it would be a lasting memory of this Christmas when she planted it in the garden. She had chosen gold as the colour theme for the decorations, for so many years she had read the women's magazines about how to make your home look festive with new ideas for decorations for the table and the tree and now she was able to do it She smiled again at the glowing tree and sat down, immediately all the dogs jumped up on the settee beside her vying with each other to get onto her lap,she stroked them all in turn as she said their names. Chris her husband had been against having animals because they tied you down and interfered with one's social life. He had hated anything to do with Christmas as well other than the food, saying that it was all sentimental rubbish. The one Christmas that Shaun had spent with her had been utterly miserable as his idea of Christmas was to get blind drunk and be sick all over the carpet. She wrinkled her nose with disgust at the memory of it.

Simon was definitely not like that; she knew that he and Fiona had had parties for New Year's Eve. There had been some who had gloried in telling her about them knowing that, although she lived within reasonable distance of Fiona and Simon, she had never been invited. Not for the first time lately, she found herself wondering what exactly had gone wrong with that marriage. It had to be something to do with Fiona, after all look how she was carrying on now with Paul Aston. In time she got to hear all the gossip at the doctor's surgery. Could she have had someone before Paul? I wonder if she and Paul have been invited to Natalie's party? Settling back into the cushions she switched the TV on with the remote control, how nice it would be if she could watch her favourite programmes with Simon. Well, it wasn't long now to wait 'til Christmas.

At the same time that Viv was watching a programme on the television, Simon was answering a phone call from his brother Peter, "Yes, how many more times Pete, I'm OK, I've told you."

"Now Simon, if you are in any financial difficulties, you know that Beryl and I would be more than willing..."

"For heavens sake Pete, I don't want your money, I'm OK got it."

"Alright, alright, you always were an independant so and so. Anyway, I've made the offer and while we're on the subject, who is this Viv person that you are spending Christmas with instead of us?"

"That's changing the subject as far as I'm concerned."

"Don't play games with me, who the hell is she and what's wrong with her that you have to be so secretive? What about Fiona?"

"Well, if you must know, she is a woman that I've known for years, she shows Cumbrians and kindly invited me for Christmas dinner."

"So, why has she invited you for Christmas dinner?"

"Do you have to repeat everything I say? Because she fancies me I suppose."

"What! Then why the hell are you accepting."

"Perhaps because I fancy her. It does happen you know."

"I'll say it again. What about Fiona? I thought that you were getting back with her."

"Huh, well I wasn't going to say anything but since you've asked..."

"Divorced!"

Simon proceeded to explain that it was Fiona who had asked for the divorce and not him. He had wanted to get back with her but she hadn't wanted that. He told him that he had delayed replying to the solicitor until he realised that there was no hope but now, as far as he knew, it was going through.

"But she was here this afternoon and she never mentioned it to either of us."

"Guilty conscience? Didn't want to upset you ? Or didn't want you to try to change her mind Don't ask me, ask her."

"Beryl is going to be devastated, you know how fond she is of both of you. I must go and tell her the news. Well, take care Simon. You know I'll go along with whatever you decide. Cheerio."

Simon sat down heavily in the armchair, well at least they knew now. The fact didn't lift his mood but made him feel even worse than he already did. He'd always known that he and Fiona would eventually get back together again. He knew that his blasted pride had got the better of him and that he shouldn't have left but he'd thought that, after a while, when things cooled down..... That was almost the least of his worries. What with the Vet's bill for the miscarriage, the rent due again soon, no extra money coming in from matings, his bank balance was at rock bottom. He hadn't even paid Fiona for that last mating in fact, it was no good, he'd have to get a loan for next month's rent. He couldn't afford to enter for any more shows for a while, certainly couldn't afford to entertain anyone. There was hardly any booze in the place. Why the devil shouldn't he go to Viv's, he was, it seemed, turning into an outcast like her though why the hell he was he couldn't fathom out. Fiona hadn't invited him for Christmas, Viv had, so they might as well join forces against a common enemy. His gloomy thoughts were interrupted by the phone ringing again, "Simon, is it true that you are you going to Viv Butcher's for Christmas?" It was Fiona.

"Hello Fee. Nice to hear from you. Yes, she has kindly invited me over to her house. Why? Don't say that you want me to come to you instead."

"If you have to even ask why then I might as well put this phone down. You shouldn't be even seen with her let alone go to dinner with her. It'll do you no good in the ring you know."

"Oh, quite the diplomat now. I thought that that was my role."

“Do shut up and stop being clever. You know perfectly well what I mean.”

“OK are you going to invite me for Christmas dinner then?”

There was a long pause before she answered, “I can’t, I have already invited someone else.”

“Ah, so now it’s my turn. Why have you invited someone else. Who is he? I presume that it's a 'he'.”

“This is getting us nowhere. I saw Peter and Beryl today and they said that you were hard up. Is that right?”

“Don’t worry, I’ll pay you for the stud as soon as I can. I’m......”

“Don’t be so insulting Simon. I haven’t rung you for that, I only....”

“Why didn’t you tell them about the divorce?”

“What! Oh you're impossible.” He heard the phone disconnect.

Simon had hardly sat down before it rang again, he picked it up, “Got over your temper now?”

A man’s voice said, “Pardon, is that Simon Philips?” It was Paul Aston’s voice.

“Yes it is."

"Hello Simon it's Paul Aston."

"Yes, I know."

"Haven't seen you for a while. How are you getting on?"

"Fine."

"I was wondering if we could meet up for a drink one night. Say tomorrow about seven at the Horse and Groom?"

"Why?"

"No reason. Have you seen Fiona lately?”

“No. Why?”

"Well, how about that drink?"

"Sorry I've got a prior engagement."

"Ah yes, I've heard, the delectable Viv."

"None of your business. Bye."

Simon sat looking at the phone, the bloody creep, what the hell was that all about. It was funny that he'd called, most of his so-called doggy pals had better things to do now than phone him; it had been different when he could splash out money on those parties. He sighed as he remembered those parties that he and Fee had at New Year; they had done so well afterwards. Not that they hadn’t worked damned hard for the wins. He could see Fee, all dressed up dishing out drinks to everyone, including bloody Alan Burgess. Hadn't seen much of him lately, the word was that he wasn't at all well. Serve him bloody well right. No, they'd been good do's, I wonder what she's doing this New Year. He could phone her and invite her out -- no money damn it. Well, he'd invite her here. He picked up the phone, "Hi Fee. Have you cooled down now? How would you like to come here for New Year's Eve?"

"I'm sorry Simon but I am already going out for New Year's Eve."

"Where?"

"To Natalie's if you must know."

"Why Natalie's?"

"She's having a party."

"Is she, well, perhaps another time. Bye."

So Simon thought, I bet Paul has been invited. Why didn't Natalie invite me then? Surely Fee didn't hate him that much that she told her not to invite me! His deliberations were interrupted by the phone ringing.

"Hello Simon it's Viv."

"Hello."

"Simon, I've received an invitation from Natalie Bennett to a New Year's Eve party. It's says 'and guest' so would you like to come with me?"

The silence lasted so long that Viv wondered if he had heard her, "Hello Simon."

"Yes, Hello Viv. Thanks for the invite but I'm already going," he wasn't bloody going as her guest. No way!

"Hello, is that Natalie, Simon Philips here. Sorry to ring you so late but it's about your party..."

"Oh Simon, I'm so glad that you can come. Fiona told you then."

"Er, yes she did. Thank you for the invitation and I shall look forward to seeing you."

CHAPTER TWENTY-FIVE

Fiona opened her eyes and looked at the bedside clock, the display read five-thirty five. It was Christmas morning! She had always woken early on Christmas morning, even now, the small child within her was excited at the magic of it all. She lay there imagining all the children in bedrooms all over the world, pushing their toes down to the chilly regions at the end of the bed to find out if there was that thrilling sound of paper rustling. She pushed her feet down to the end of the bed and sighed, no there was no rustling. Paul, laying beside her, turned in his sleep, she smiled; he was a very kind man but he really wasn't into the realms of fantasy. He would have been very surprised if she had told him that she hoped, against all reason, that he would have left a rustly present at the bottom of the bed. One year Simon...... she suddenly felt very guilty, how could she lay here having had sex with Paul and think of Simon! She quickly slipped out of the bed and whispering to Sally, she grabbed her dressing gown and went downstairs, Sally at her heels.. Having had a cup of tea, she prepared the turkey for the oven, everything must go well today. She would take a cup of tea up to Paul, shower and then see to the dogs. Simon always did Christmas.....

When they sat down to dinner in the early afternoon, Paul produced a small packet and placed it beside her placemat, "Happy Christmas Fiona." As she opened it her fingers trembled slightly and the paper was hard to tear, finally a jewellers box was revealed. "Oh Paul," she said as she opened the box to reveal a pendant necklace, "Oh Paul it's........ beautiful. Thank you."

"I thought that you'd like it."

"Oh yes," she got up and kissed him, "It's lovely."

She had spent ages wondering what to buy him for Christmas and had finally settled on a new dressing-gown, a leather wallet and a bottle of whisky. He seemed very surprised and almost annoyed that she had got several presents for him. Simon had bought lots of things, some just silly little things to make her laugh but.... she hurriedly got up from the table and cleared the dirty plates.

The rest of the day passed pleasantly with Paul quietly appreciative of everything that she had planned and cooked. They listened to the Queen's speech and during the afternoon they chatted and played card games. In bed that night listening to Paul's regular breathing, the little girl sighed, where had all the magic gone? Had it gone forever because she had, at last, grown up?

Simon had been late in arriving at Viv's on Christmas morning. He was in a foul mood and barely apologised to Viv who had been frantically looking out of the window for the past hour wondering whether to take the turkey out or leave it in, whether to turn the potatoes, cook the Brussel sprouts and, all the time, worrying herself sick that he wouldn't come at all! The first and second course were almost eaten in silence with Viv having to force the food down her throat which was tight with unshed tears.

By the time she placed the pudding on the table Simon, who by now had drunk at least a bottle and a half of wine, was beginning to relax and talk, "Do you know Viv, well I know you do but, do you know that dog showing is a stinking bloody, crooked mess. I mean, do you know that, after all I've done, all I've achieved, all I've bloody achieved!" he stopped to fill his glass again, "Do you know that after all I've done.... I've said that haven't I, well, after everything, I'm being blacked! Do you know what that means?"

"Yes, I do."

"Do you? Yes, of course you do, not like Fee. Well, I mean, she should be the one by rights not me. I didn't mess up. I didn't slee....... I mean I did what I was told didn't I Viv?"

"Yes, I suppose you did You must have done."

He refilled his glass which seemed to miraculously have emptied itself, "D'know Viv I can talk to you. You know what goes on. You understand, so tell me, why me? Why have I been blacked?"

"Are you sure that you have, I mean you might have just had a run of bad luck." She quietly removed what little there was left of the wines from the table. She had plans for this evening and she didn't want a repetition of last time!

Simon tapped his nose with his finger, "Because I know, because Te.... because an old mate of mine had the dec... the decency to phone me yesterday and wish me a Happy Christmas. He knows I'm hard up and he told me not to wa... waste my money on the Champ shows. That's how I know."

"Who was this old mate?"

"Ah, promised I wouldn't say. Promised. Did me a favour for old times sake and I promised not to say. Don't want to get him in trouble so I promised see. D'you know, you're all right Viv, a mate, come here and I'll give you a big Christmas kiss." He got up from the table, walked round to her a little unsteadily and gave her a kiss on the lips, she responded warmly and he kissed her again and again, she could feel the passion rising in him and held him to her as hard as she could, he started to pull her jumper up as he was kissing her and she had to remove her arms from around him, he pulled it further and kissed the swell of her breasts where they emerged from her brassiere. She was pulling the jumper over her head as he was pulling her bra down to kiss her nipples when the front door bell rang. For a moment she remained still, the neck of the jumper tight across her face, her nipples had hardened under his warm lips and she was breathing hard as his hands slid up her thighs and into the leg of her panties, it rang again and a voice called, "Viv are you there? I know you're there Viv. Please it's an emergency". Cursing she pulled away from Simon's questing fingers, put her jumper on and went to the front door.

"Hello my dear, I'm so sorry to bother you but Frank has had a really bad turn and I thought you would know which doctor was on call today. Sorry to bother you dear."

It was one of her neighbours who was also a patient at the surgery who was standing there looking very troubled. Viv took her hand, "That's all right Jessie. It's Dr. Freeman. You know the number to ring don't you?" She watched as the old lady made her way down the path and closing the door, went back to Simon. He was sitting on the settee and, as she went to sit beside him she removed her jumper and bra, "Now, where were we."

Simon sat quite still and looked a bit embarrassed, so she took his hand and placed it on her thigh, "I was rather enjoying that Simon," she started to stroke him through his trousers, "These are a bit restricting aren't they," she stood up and leaned over him to undo his belt and let her breasts hang near his face. Suddenly he seized them in his hands and started to kiss her nipples running his hands up her legs he started to pull her panties down, "Wait a minute Simon," she stood up and quickly took the rest of her clothes off and stood in front of him holding out her hands to him.
Simon didn't move for a moment or to and red-faced put his hand to his forehead, "Viv, I'm bloody sorry but I can't. Drunk too much I think. Had quite a bit before I came. Sorry."
She knelt down beside him, "Please Simon, please try, I want you so much. Just play with me just cuddle me, anything."
He sighed and shook his head, "Sorry Viv. Perhaps another time," he looked at his watch, "Viv look at the time, I'll have to go and feed the dogs."
"Simon please, surely they could wait for a hour or two or even three?
Three hours! Bloody hell. "Perhaps another time Viv when I'm sober. If it's to be three hours I want prior notice!"
Viv started to say something and then stopped, better not come on too strong, she didn't want to destroy everything she had gained, "OK but that's a promise I shall hold you to."
Once out of the house he drove round the corner and then sat there for a while until his head cleared a bit, he then drove home as fast as he could.
He'd sat up so late last night mulling over Ted's call that he hadn't even taken Fiona her present. He saw to the dogs, got into the car again and went to the cottage. It was only a box of her favourite chocolates and one of those ornaments she collected but he knew that she would like them both, he had intended putting them by the kitchen door last night but tonight would have to do. They'd still be a surprise. He stopped as he was entering the drive, Paul Aston's car was still parked there. Imagining what was going on inside, he reversed rapidly out onto the road and went home to get as drunk as he could. He should have taken Viv, he hadn't been that drunk, what a bloody fool

he was, there it was offered to him on a plate and he'd refused! It would have served Fiona right if he'd gone all the way.

After lunch on Boxing Day, Candida was talking to her mother as they loaded the dishwasher together, "You seem to think a lot of this Paul Aston?"

"He is a very pleasant man, an accountant, used to know your father some years ago. He has been very helpful and kind. What do you think of him?"

"I like him, he's interesting to talk to."

"Yes, he is. Jason seems to get on well with him too doesn't he."

"And he's coming to your party as well?"

"Yes, along with a lot of others. Now Candida," Natalie smiled at her daughter, "don't go getting all romantic."

"No Mum, but I do hope that you have a lovely party. It's time that you had a bit of fun. Write to me and tell me how it goes won't you.. I'm sorry that we can't stay for it. It will bring the old house to life."

"Yes, I will, now, how about that game of Scrabble."

That night she lay in bed and listened to the familiar sighs and creaks as the old house settled for the night. It was so very comforting to have Candida back at home, to hear noises and movement around her. She got up and turning on the bedside light went and stood in front of the cheval mirror. She ruffled her hair, cupped her breasts and then smoothed her hands over her hips. Was she still attractive to the opposite sex? Perhaps she could lose a pound or two, not too much because it could make you look older and scrawny. She hadn't shown Candida the new dress and strappy sandals that she had bought for the party and the new make-up. Cupping her breasts again and pulling her tummy in she turned sideways and smiled at her image She then nodded and went back to bed. Yes, she would miss Candida and Jason when they went but she was looking forward to this party and next year very much.

CHAPTER TWENTY-SIX

Viv felt sick with excitement, she had had to work in the morning although it was New Year's Eve, since when she had walked the dogs, grabbed a spot of lunch, although she wasn't hungry and gone through her entire wardrobe twice and discarded every outfit as unsuitable for tonight's party. Then there was the question of sandals or shoes! The trouble was that most of her clothes nowadays were serviceable and suitable for walking or showing dogs. Her 'best' clothes were no longer fashionable, she hadn't been out to any sort of party or formal occasion for ages. She looked at her watch, Good Lord, if she didn't make up her mind soon she wouldn't have time to shower and do her hair and make-up, tonight was so important, she wanted to look her very best.

Fiona stared at her reflection in the long mirror, this dress enhanced her figure and the highlights that she had had put in her hair had brightened it up, she was sure that Paul was going to propose tonight.

Since he had gone home on the 27th., he had rung her twice saying how much he had enjoyed his visit and especially her company. He had also said that he hoped that, when things were sorted out with Simon, they would be together much more and that he had high hopes for the New Year. She was so pleased to hear him say this, the worry about him not proposing to her at Christmas had receded, of course, she should have realised that Paul would want to do things correctly. She held her hands up to the mirror, the nail varnish perfectly matched the colour of her dress, she had even painted her toe nails. Yes, I think that he will propose tonight, she looked round at the bedroom to see that it was neat and tidy for tonight. She was applied some perfume and was just spraying some around the bedroom when the phone rang, "Fiona, its Beryl, Fiona I've been so miserable since I phoned you last night. I'm sorry, you have every right to do what you want without interference from me. Peter kept stopping me from speaking to you, he said that I had no right to interfere but it was such a shock to hear that you were divorcing Simon, I couldn't help it. I love you both and know that you should be tog........ There I go again. Anyway Fiona, please forgive me and let's still be friends. I'd hate to lose my adopted sister."

"Oh Beryl, I'm so glad that you called. I know that you're upset but, it is for the best. You'd like Paul, he's rather quiet and a little bit staid but he's very kind and interesting. You and Peter must come over and meet him."

"Mm, well I don't know about Peter, he is still so angry with Simon he might not be very good company, but I should like to. Now what are you doing this evening?"

"Going to a party at Natalie's house. I'm just putting on the finishing touches."

"In that case I'll say Happy New Year to you from us both and I'll call you again in a few days."

"And a Happy New Year to you as well. Love to Peter. Bye Beryl." Fiona looked at her watch, almost time to leave, Paul said that he might be a little late so it had been decided that she would go in her own car.

Simon finished ironing the shirt and put it on, he looked at his watch, yes, there was just time if he hurried, he finished dressing, got into his car and drove to the top of the hill near the cottage. This way he would know if she was going with Paul, he'd decided that he wasn't going if she was, he just couldn't bear to watch her fawning up to someone else. He saw her car leave the drive and ducked down out of sight as it passed. She was on her own; he waited for about ten minutes and then started the car. Fiona thought that she saw Simon's car parked near the top of the hill but told herself not to be so fanciful. She would really have to stop thinking about Simon.

"Dennis, for heaven's sake will you hurry up, we'll be late."

"For crying out loud woman, you were in that bathroom for hours, how was I supposed to shave?"

"You know that I want to get there early. When all that lot get together it should be very interesting under the circumstances. I just can't wait."
Dennis came out of the bedroom having now shaved, shrugging on his jacket he came down the stairs to where Caroline was impatiently waiting, "Now, run it past me again, who is going out with whom and who must I not mention it to?"

"Oh Dennis you're impossible. Just don't say anything to anyone, alright."

Natalie walked slowly round the dining-room and the drawing room, Jessie had kindly come in to tidy up and Brian had laid the fires and filled the log baskets, the table looked very nice and the caterers had arrived, she was just re-arranging a chrysanthemum in one of the vases when the door bell rang.

"Hello Audrey, do come in, hello Ian, how are you, nice to see you again."
Natalie excused herself from her guests and walked into the kitchen to look at her watch, it was now almost twenty to eight and only Richard's old partner Frank, Audrey and Ian Chatsworth and Harriet and Larry her neighbours and friends for many years, had arrived. The caterers wanted to start serving dinner at eight fifteen. Audrey and Frank were reminiscing about days gone by as they sat by the fire in the drawing-room. She looked at her watch again, perhaps she should phone Fiona. It was so long since she had given a party that she was tense, don't be ridiculous she told herself they'll come. At that moment the door bell trilled, Natalie smoothed her dress over her hips and went to answer the door. "Hello Caroline and this is your husband. How do you do. I'm so glad that you could come. Let me take your coats." They stood waiting for her in the large oak- panelled hall and Caroline looked at her husband and raised her eyebrows.

Natalie re-appeared, "Do come into the sitting room and get warm, there's a log fire in there," When she had done the usual introductions and provided the newcomers with a drink, she again looked at her watch. I'd better phone she thought but before she could do so the door bell again sounded in the hall. She opened the door to reveal, Fiona and Viv Butcher standing outside.

"Are you on your own Viv?" Natalie enquired.

"No, Simon's coming later." There was a small silence in which Natalie looked at Fiona with astonishment and Fiona looked at Viv with hatred. Natalie quickly took them into the sitting-room and made the necessary introductions but even as she was doing this the bell sounded again. This time it was Simon carrying a poinsettia plant in a pot, "Hello Natalie, hope you like these things." As Simon entered the sitting room Natalie felt the tension rise as both Fiona and Viv looked in his direction. She felt a little apprehensive at this unexpected turn of events.

"Good evening everyone, I'm Simon Philips."

The situation was retrieved by two more friends of Natalie's arriving. The level of conversation rose as people started to chat and Natalie breathed a sigh of relief. it was another ten minutes before Paul Aston appeared making profuse apologies for the lateness of his arrival. The guest list was complete and Natalie was able to invite everyone into the dining-room.

The large, old refectory table was covered with a beautiful damask cloth, the silver cutlery gleamed (thanks to Jessie Mason) and the crystal glasses glittered and shone in the light. There were place names and everyone sat down. Simon, of course, was next to Fiona, and Paul was next to Natalie. Viv had to be content with Frank. The caterers immediately started to pour wine for those who wanted it and to serve the first course. Busy talking to Paul, Natalie didn't notice at first that Simon and Fiona were hardly speaking but Frank and Viv were having a great conversation! She wondered whatever they could have in common. Audrey was talking to Caroline but Caroline's husband had his head down and was just eating his food. He seemed completely overwhelmed by the occasion. Ian Chatsworth was chatting to Harriet. The dinner was a success, Natalie breathed a sigh of relief. When the coffee was being served she noticed that Viv was now talking across the table to Simon. Paul spoke to her, "May I say Natalie, that that was an excellent meal. Very much appreciated on my part."

"Thank you Paul. I do so like people who enjoy good food."

They had been chatting for most of the meal about the house. Paul had found out a bit of the history of it and she had invited him to come over again some time so that he could really look around. There were, she understood, some interesting architectural features in the cellar. Paul had accepted with alacrity.

Coffee and liqueurs were served in the drawing-room, Fiona elected to sit on a settee and found that Simon immediately sat next to her. Paul sat on the other side of her and engaged her in conversation. Simon then got up and started talking to Viv. Caroline and Dennis sat quietly watching everyone and sipping their coffee. During the next hour the party appeared to divide into groups. Natalie's friends were chatting happily about holidays past and in the future, Audrey, Paul, Fiona and Natalie were standing together in earnest conversation, Simon was talking to Audrey's husband, Viv was again talking to Frank and Caroline was straining her ears to hear the various conversations

They were still in the drawing-room when trays of filled glasses were brought in by Natalie and Paul just as the clocks started to chime the hour of midnight. Everyone raised their glasses and wished each other a Happy New Year. Without warning, Viv put her glass down and tried to encircle Simon with both arms in order to kiss him but, he pushed her arms away and moved swiftly across the room to where Fiona was standing with Paul. Brushing Paul aside he held Fiona tightly and kissed her long and hard. Paul looked furious but refrained from causing a scene. Viv, however, moved across the room too and tried to come between Fiona and Simon, "My turn now Simon." She said sliding her arms under his jacket and kissed him refusing to let him go.. Simon broke away from her mouth, and pushed her away, "Get off Viv."

"No, no I won't Simon, you're mine now." She had drunk a bit too much wine at dinner and, coupled with the liqueurs, her tongue was loosened, "Don't you realise I love you. I know that you love me. Look at that night we spent together." There was a gasp from Fiona, Paul looked slightly surprised but pleased until Viv turned to him and said, "What are you smirking at, you're no bloody angel."

Audrey and her husband made hurried excuses for leaving. Caroline and Dennis just sat down again on the settee and looked embarrassed, Natalie's friends quietly drifted away to the kitchen..

"I didn't spend a night with you, well I'm bloody certain I didn't make love to you. I was too damned drunk to know or do anything."

"You did. You did," Viv was shouting and holding on to his arm.

"I've had enough of this. There's no way drunk or sober that I'd make love to you. Now, let go of my arm."

“What about Christmas Day then, don’t tell me that you weren’t enjoying me then.”
Caroline wriggled on the settee and licked her lips, Dennis, now red with embarrassment, straightened his tie. Caroline leaned forward, nobody was going to believe this. What a party she was having.

Simon turned to Natalie who had been standing nearby throughout the scene, “I’m very sorry about this Natalie, I think it’s best that I go. Thank you for a lovely meal. Come on Fee get your coat."
At that moment Audrey, Ian and Frank came down the stairs having collected their coats, Natalie quickly showed them to the door.
Fiona had tears in her eyes as she shook her head and turned to Paul.

“Don’t worry Simon, I’ll see that Fiona gets home safely,” Paul said putting his arm gently round her shoulders.

“Oh yes, I’ve seen your car round at Fee’s some Saturday evenings. Trying to get in there are you. Well you're not bloody sleeping with my wife, we're not getting divorced! Come on Fee.”
Paul opened his mouth to say something and then thought better of it.

“Fee come on!” Simon tried to propel her towards the hall. Paul stepped in front of him, “Simon, Fiona does not want to come with you.” He put out an arm to ward him off and Simon, misinterpreting the action, hit him hard in the face and Paul went down like a stone. It was at that moment that Natalie walked back into the hall having seen Frank and Audrey and Ian into their cars, “Paul, oh Paul, she hurriedly knelt down. Can you hear me Paul?” Paul slowly opened his eyes.

“Will someone get me a small brandy please.” Natalie appealed to those around. However, as the neighbours were still in the kitchen and Caroline’s husband was helping her into her coat; it was Fiona who hurried back into the dining-room for the brandy.

Shamefaced, Simon mumbled an apology to Natalie and left. Viv, who had tried to stop him from going, burst into tears and sobbing loudly went in search of her coat. Caroline murmured a few platitudes, Dennis nodded his head and they both scuttled away into the darkness. Fiona knelt down with the brandy but Natalie took the glass from her and, holding his head up, got Paul to take a few sips. He quickly recovered, wiped his bloody nose with a handkerchief and stood up, “Natalie, how can I apologise enough. We have ruined your lovely party. I’m so sorry.”

"It was not your fault Paul."

In the meantime, Fiona had quietly disappeared and got her coat, "I think that I ought to go Natalie. I do so apologise for Simon's behaviour. He has a few problems at the moment. I know that doesn't excuse his conduct but.... well, thank you for a lovely evening."

The neighbours left shortly after and when they were on their own, Paul and Natalie sat on either side of the log fire drinking a cup of coffee.

"Thank you so much for staying on Paul. That was quite an upset."

"Wouldn't dream of doing anything else. You had obviously put a lot of time, thought and effort into organising this party. I can only apologise again for the behaviour of the others. It was inexcusable."

"What is the matter with Simon?"

"The grapevine has it that he is in serious financial difficulties. That, I think is why he is trying to get back with Fiona."

"Oh dear, poor man, and what about Viv Butcher?"

"Ah, that is another long story Natalie and none too savoury, I don't want to burden you with the sordid details. Please don't think that all exhibitors behave like this. Thank goodness Audrey had gone." He mentally made a note to phone the Amerys and Viv. He didn't want this little episode to do the rounds of the shows. With this in mind he made his excuses and left. He had to phone them before the morning. Too bad if he woke them up.

CHAPTER TWENTY-SEVEN

Viv sat in the armchair surrounded by her dogs. They were all very quiet, occasionally licking her face, they sensed that she was unhappy. She poured herself another glass of whisky from the bottle she had bought for them to celebrate when Simon came home with her from the party! She screwed her face up and she took a big mouthful of the amber liquid, "Do you all know that you are the only good things in my life?" The dogs all wagged their tails, Mum was feeling better. Viv poured another glass of whisky. She felt so alone, she knew that she'd never sleep tonight, she'd better take one of those sleeping tablets. She got up and went to the bedroom followed by Missy the oldest bitch. Missy jumped up on the bed where she usually spent her nights keeping Viv's feet warm. She looked up in surprise as Viv went downstairs again, tired, she closed her eyes and snuggled down on the duvet.

Why had everything gone so wrong in her life? Why did her husband, Chris, have to be like he was? Why couldn't she have been like everyone else and married, had a family and been happy? Then she would never have got into dog showing, she wouldn't have met Shaun, she wouldn't have been Secretary of that blasted club. She wouldn't consequently have had her name and reputation so blackened that nobody wanted to know her. How could they be so evil? She had asked herself this question so many times in the past, so many lies, so much hurt and heartache and all for a piece of coloured paper. What small insignificant people they were if they had to destroy other peoples happiness so that they could win a piece of paper. She took another sip of whisky. I must take this bloody sleeping tablet or I'll lay in bed thinking of Simon, she burst into floods of tears again. We could have been so happy together, I'm sure we could, she dabbed at her tear-swollen eyes and looked around the room. Had she taken that blasted tablet? No, she'd have remembered. She took one with some of the whisky and then topped the glass up, "I love you all," she said to the dogs, "you are my best friends. My only friends now, and you love me too don't you." She sniffled as she drank the whisky, "In fact, you're my only family too. There's no-one else in the world who cares. Simon doesn't," she started to cry loudly again, she so wanted Simon to like her, to love her. She wanted a friend to talk to in the evenings, when she felt happy or when she felt down. She wanted someone to have breakfast with someone - she poured another glass of whisky. Why don't I feel tired? That's because I haven't taken my pills. Perhaps I'd better take two tonight, or even three, I shan't sleep otherwise.

The phone started ringing in the hall, for several seconds Viv didn't stir but then she thought that it might be Simon phoning to apologise so she tried to get up to answer it. She was just making a very unsteady walk towards the hall by holding on to the walls, when it stopped. Wearily she retraced her steps, must go to bed she thought, I'll just have a little drink with my sleeping tablets and go to bed. Missy will be wondering where I am.

Caroline nudged Dennis, "The phone's ringing. Whoever can it be at this time? Must be urgent. Hurry up." Dennis staggered down the stairs to answer it, he had been in a deep sleep and resented being woken, "Who is it?"

"Hello, is that Dennis Amery?" It was a man's voice.

"Yes it is. Whose that?"

"It's Paul Aston here. Sorry to bother you Dennis. I hope you weren't asleep but I just had to phone you and your wife about that deplorable scene at Mrs Bennett's house last night."

"And?"

"Well, I'm sure that you will agree that it would not be in any of our best interests if this were to come out as gossip in the dog world."

"Why?"

"As I said, it would not do any of us, and that includes your wife, any good in the ring if this little incident were to become common

knowledge. I'm sure that your wife will understand when you give her the message. Well, I'll say goodnight, sorry to have disturbed you."
Dennis climbed back into bed and pulled the duvet over his cold body.
"What was that all about?"
"That bloke Paul Aston. He said keep your trap shut about tonight or else it'll do you harm in the ring."
"What's new. Couldn't it have waited till morning." Caroline turned off the light and tried to pull more of the duvet to her side.

Fiona went to bed although there were only a few hours left before she had to let the dogs out; sleep, however, proved to be impossible. She tossed and turned, the scenes from the last few hours replaying themselves in her head. Finally, with a grunt of annoyance, she got up, put on her dressing gown and went down to the kitchen and made some tea. She could not get out of her mind the image of Simon hitting Paul. What had she done to this usually quiet, kind man. Until all the business with Alan Burgess and afterwards with the baby, he had always been so level-headed, she had never known him lose his temper like that. Perhaps his financial situation was much more serious than he was saying. Perhaps he was ill or something, well there was only one way to find out, she would go round to his house this morning after she had seen to the dogs.

During the course of the morning, Duncan phoned to wish her a Happy New Year from them both and Donald and to tell her that one of his clients had invited them to his house at one of the well-known ski resorts.

"How wonderful Duncan, I'm sure that you'll all have a marvellous time, especially Donald with all that snow, When do you go?"

"At the beginning of February."

Duncan asked if she had any plans for the year ahead and how the dogs were getting on, she chatted for a few minutes and then excused herself. Now that she had made up her mind to speak to Simon she wanted to get it done with.

Stopping outside the house was a bit of a shock, it was a middle of terrace, turn of the century house which had definitely seen better days. The houses on either side had been renovated which made the one that Simon was living in look even worse with peeling paint on the door and rotting wood in the window frames. There was no reply when she rattled the letter box there being no bell or knocker. Damn! she thought, after all this effort he's out. She rattled the box again and realised that there was no barking. Perhaps he's out with the dogs. She went back to the warmth of the car and decided to wait for twenty minutes. After fifteen minutes had passed she saw him appear in her rear view mirror. So he had been out walking the dogs. She got out of the car as he drew level and. he looked up, a broad smile lit his thin face, "Hi Fee."

"Hello Simon, I thought that, after last night, we should have a talk."

As he opened the door, she thought that the house smelled damp. As he settled the dogs down and put the kettle on she looked round the cheaply furnished room with it's old wallpaper and it's dirty window, "Oh Simon, how can you live here."

"Fairly cheaply."

"But Simon, it's awful. Couldn't you find something better?"

"Yes, I reckon I could move toViv's house, but, contrary to what you heard last night, I prefer this."

He sounded so cynical, so bitter, so defeated. He had always seemed cheerful when he had come to the cottage. She had had no idea!

"I suppose you've come round to tell me off for my inexcusable behaviour last night?"

"No Simon no, I've come round to see why you did it."

"Why I bloody well did it? Don't play the bloody innocent with me Fee, you know why I did it. In spite of everything, I still love you. I love you so much that the sight of that bloody wheeler-dealer with his arm around you nearly drove me mad. Have you been sleeping with him?"

"What do you mean, wheeler-dealer?"

"Don't try to change the subject Fee. Have you been sleeping with him. Yes or no."

"I'm not answering you until I know what you mean."

"I've been finding out about our mutual friend and...."

"Oh no, you're not on again about all this fiddling and blacking and..... everything."

"My God Fee he's in it up to his bloody neck."

"Oh Simon, when are you going to realise that it's all in your mind. I know that it helped us, the presents, the parties, the free studs, the expensive puppies etc but that happens in all walks of life. You make it all seem like an organised Mafia or something. It's ridiculous. Look you got into the Masons but it hasn't done you any good has it, Something else you got wrong."

"When the wheeler-dealers want you out even the Masons doesn't help. Ask Viv Butcher, she'll confirm it, she's really been through the mill, blacked, character assassination, threats to her, threats to her dogs, the lot, and that was only small time, not the big dealers. Ask her!"

"I will, don't you worry. But I didn't come here to talk about all that. Are you in serious financial trouble because I want to help."
Simon looked at her for a moment and sighed deeply, "No Fee, thanks for the offer but I'll manage."

"Well, are you ill and not telling anyone?"

"No, fit as a fiddle."

"Couldn't I help you then to find something better than this. Look you'll get some money from the business when the divorce is settled. Let me lend you some now."

"Thanks, but no thanks. Incidentally, you never answered my question did you."

Caroline tried to phone Viv to ask her if Paul had told her to shut up but she was obviously out. She didn't really like Viv she had heard such stories about her but she had felt dreadfully sorry for her last night, it was painfully obvious that she was in love with Simon Philips and what was all that with Fiona, Paul and Simon. She was bursting to tell someone but, she didn't want her new little boy to miss out in the ring, what a nuisance.

Natalie tidied up the sitting room, she had so looked forward to this party and it had ended in that dreadful scene. Thank heavens Frank and Audrey had gone, having been outside at the time she wasn't quite sure what had started it. Diane and Will had kindly popped in this morning to help tidy up a bit. Over coffee they had intimated that they were very surprised that her doggy friends behaved like that. They had said, however, how charming Paul was, such an interesting man. She sighed, at least that had gone how she had hoped. He had been most attentive over dinner and had shown a genuine interest in the house saying how clever she had been in her choice of furniture, he had quite a knowledge of antique furniture. She would try to call Fiona again, perhaps she was in now.

No-one other than Paul and Caroline had tried to phone Viv and it wasn't until she didn't turn up at the surgery on the 2nd January that anyone thought to call round. Ellen Noakes, the other receptionist at the practice was walking back down the path having got no answer, when the door of the next house opened and a man said, "Is she there?"

"I couldn't get an answer."

"No, not surprised, those bloody dogs have been kicking up a hell of a commotion for ages. Howling and whining, it's nearly driven us mad."

Ellen stopped, that was funny, Viv adored those dogs, she wouldn't leave them in that state. She went back and knocked again and called, "Viv are you there?" The dogs all rushed up to the door barking furiously. It was only then that she noticed the curtains were still drawn.

CHAPTER TWENTY-EIGHT

The shock waves went around the Cumbrian Terrier bush-telegraph within twenty-four hours. Caroline revelling in being the one to start the drums beating. She had phoned Viv's number several times the day following the party to ask Viv if she too had been told to keep quiet and it wasn't until the next day that she finally got a reply, it was a man's voice asking her why she was phoning that number. She was then told that it was not possible to speak to Viv at the moment. Her suspicions were immediately aroused and she wondered just what was going on. That evening she persuaded a reluctant Dennis to come with her to visit Viv, he complained that they had never visited her before so she would think it a bit odd to do so now; nevertheless, he dutifully drove Caroline to Viv's address. Even as she put her hand on the gate and looked at the darkened house, a neighbour came out of their front door and asked if she was looking for Viv Butcher and it was he who told her the grisly details.

At first, shattered by the news she could only swallow hard and nod her head but, as the man went back indoors she and Dennis quickly got back into their car, "Dennis, what a shock. I didn't expect that!"

"No, we only saw her the other night. I wish that I'd spoken to her now. It's your fault, you told me to keep my mouth shut."

"Don't be silly, of course it wasn't my fault, but I wonder if it had anything to do with that argument?"

"Don't know do we. Might never know now."

As soon as she got home Caroline phoned Fiona, Natalie and Simon, and, although Dennis kept reminding her of the phone bill, she then settled down to phone several other Cumbrian exhibitors. The general comment was, "Who'd have thought it. I always thought that she was as tough as old boots. Didn't think that she was the sort to commit suicide. I suppose it was suicide."

When she put the phone down Fiona was very upset, although she had not liked Viv she would never have wanted this to happen to her. If it was suicide, she must have been in such despair for her to do something like that. Was it because of that row at the party. She suddenly had a picture in her mind of Viv's face when Simon had shouted at her. Oh no, she put her hand to her mouth, surely not, surely she hadn't really been in love with Simon. She must phone him, knowing Simon as she did she knew that he was going to feel terrible, but his number was engaged.

Natalie was sitting in her kitchen in tears, that wretched party she thought. I wish to goodness I'd never thought of it. Could it have been that scene that was behind it all or was there something else. She didn't know her well enough to say. She tried to phone Fiona to ask if Viv had been very ill or something but her line was engaged. She wiped the tears from her eyes and moved the dogs from her feet. Heavens she thought, I wonder what is happening about her dogs? I'll try to phone Paul.

Paul was very shocked at the news, "Look Natalie, it's obvious that you're very upset. Would you like me to come round? Does Fiona know about this?"

"Yes, Caroline said that she had told her but I haven't been able to get hold of her."

"Funny she didn't phone me. I'll try and give Fiona a call and then come round. She might like to come too." However, when he phoned Fiona, her line was engaged.

"Natalie, how are you?"

"I'm all right I suppose Paul. I feel so responsible for all this," she looked up at him with tears in her eyes.

"Nonsense, you are in no way responsible."

She sighed, it was so comforting to have him standing there in the hall. It was so nice to have a man to lean on again, "Would you like some tea Paul?"

"Yes, but you sit down and I will make it for you," he took her hand and led her into the sitting-room. She smiled and sat down;. it was so long since a man had made tea for her.

"What!" Simon shouted down the phone, "What did you say?"
Caroline told him what the neighbours had told her about the police having to break into the house and Viv's body being taken out on a stretcher all covered up so that she had to be dead.

"No, you've got this wrong Caroline. Not Viv."

"Well, the neighbours were pretty sure. One of them is looking after the dogs for a while. The police said that they would make arrangements to have them picked up and taken to a kennels."

"But she doesn't have to be dead."

"Well, as I told you the neighbours said that she was. Anyway, I must go now Simon. Sorry to be the bearer of bad news."
I bet you are he thought as he put the phone down. It rang again almost immediately but he didn't answer it. My God, the silly bitch killed herself. He suddenly heard himself shouting at her at Natalie's party. Oh my God, she didn't do it because of that; because of me. No, she only had the hots for me, only wanted a bit of fun, surely she hadn't been serious. He sat down heavily and reached for the glass of wine he'd been drinking prior to the call. He'd thought that everything that could go wrong had gone wrong. He brushed his fingers through his hair and groaned. Bloody hell! Was he responsible for her committing suicide? The phone rang again, the bush telegraph was getting going already, "Sod off whoever you are," he shouted to the vibrating phone.
Fiona let it ring for two or three minutes before she put the phone down, poor Simon he must be out and won't know yet. She would go round to his house and wait for him It might be better coming from her.

His house was in darkness when she arrived and, although she waited for a couple of hours, he did not return; she knew that he had to be out because the dogs didn't bark. Where on earth could he be? Very cold and tired, she again looked at the dark windows of the house, started up the car and went home. Back in the warmth of the cottage, she wondered whether she should have knocked on the door again. Perhaps he was at Beryl and Peter's, she'd phone them, "Hello Peter, I just wondered if Simon was with you?"

"No, haven't heard from him since New Year's Eve. Why?"

"Nothing really, just a doggy matter. Tell Beryl I'll phone her soon."

She tried his number several more times that evening but got no reply.

Paul phoned Fiona just as she was going to bed, “Fiona my dear, are you all right? It is dreadful news about Viv Butcher isn’t it.”

“Yes, I’m all right Paul. Terribly upset of course, what a waste of a life.”

"Would you like me to come and stay with you?"

"No thanks Paul, I'm alright, just going to bed in fact."

They chatted on for a while and Paul insisted on coming to see her the next evening. I don’t like to think of you sitting there on your own.”

“That's very kind and thoughtful of you Paul, but I assure you there's no need, I’m quite alright.”

Thank heavens I haven’t got a litter she thought as she hurried through the daily chores of feeding cleaning and exercising the dogs. After an early lunch and having not had a reply to her repeated calls that morning, she again made her way to Simon’s house. As she stopped the car she suddenly had a terrible thought, no, surely not, not Simon, she hurled herself from the car, ran up the path and hammered on the door. All the dogs started barking furiously and her heart nearly stopped, that’s what Caroline said that Viv’s dogs had done. “Simon, Simon open the door, Simon, Simon, Si...”

The door opened, “What the hell....”

“Oh Simon,” she threw herself into his arms and kissed his face oblivious to the stubble on it. “I thought for a minute that you were, that you had..... Oh Simon.” She kissed him again and again and he put his arms around her and kicked the door shut.

She pulled herself away, “Simon, where have you been. I rang and rang. I even came round last night but you weren’t here.”

He sighed and rubbed his chin, “Er, no.”

“Have you heard the news about Viv Butcher?”

“Yes.”

She looked at him, his eyes were almost sunken into his face, he hadn’t shaved and he looked haggard, “Oh Simon, I’m so sorry. Were you in love with her?”

His head jerked up, “No, of course not. Fancy saying a bloody silly thing like that.”

“Well, you don’t have to get cross with me, I’ve been terribly worried about you.”

"I don't have to get cross with you.! This is all your bloody fault!" he shouted.

"My fault!"

"Yes, your bloody fault, everything, all your bloody fault. All this, he swept his hand round the room, all the business at the party, all your bloody fault."

"What do you mean. You can't blame me for Viv's death." By now they were both standing up and shouting at each other, the dogs had retreated into the kitchen, laid down and closed their eyes.

"Yes, I bloody can. I've been awake all night thinking about this. If you hadn't been so bloody stupid as to sleep with Alan....."

"How many more times do I have to tell you. I did not sleep with Alan Burgess!"

"As good as! If you hadn't done that, none of this would have happened. I wouldn't have left. Viv wouldn't have been after me..."

"Oh, so you admit that she was after you. You slept with her didn't you! she said so at the party, so don't get all high and mighty with me. You're no bloody angel." She emphasised her point by poking him in the chest with a forefinger.

"That's not the point, it's still all your fault that I wasn't with you. You can't deny that. Your fault that I left, that I'm broke, your fault that I'm living here in this pigsty. So, therefore, it's your fault that Viv was after me."

"What about my baby, our baby. What about that!" Her voice became choked with emotion and tears came into her eyes, "That's why you really left. You couldn't bear the thought of having a baby round the place. It would interfere too much with your precious, bloody dog showing. You put the dogs before our baby, before me. You cheated me into marrying you so that you could grease palms for your precious dog showing, you used my friends to get into the Masons and now you've cheated again over the German dog show by forging my signature, and why, all for your own, bloody glory."

"That's not how it was at all I......"

"That is exactly how it was and it was all your fault! I can never trust you ever again Simon and that's why I'm going to marry Paul."

There was a sudden and complete silence in the room while they just stood and looked at each other then Simon straightened up, "Well, in that case, there is nothing more to be said." He opened the door to the narrow hall and with an outstretched hand, inviting her to leave. Without saying a word she brushed past him and walked swiftly out of the house.

CHAPTER TWENTY-NINE.

The weather turned very wintry during the next few days, there were severe frosts at night and as Fiona got into bed one particularly cold night, she thought of Simon in that awfully cold, damp house. The poor dogs must be feeling the cold too, he wouldn't be able to keep them in show condition in that place. Perhaps she ought to offer to have his dogs until he found something better? Don't be stupid Fiona, she admonished herself snuggling further down into the duvet, he can't afford anything better and that would mean that you'd have them for ages with him coming round to see them all the time. Best to leave things as they were, she reached out and turned off the light.

Had everything that had happened been her fault? The question had been bugging her ever since Simon had insisted that she was at fault. No, of course it hadn't. That was just his side of events, he was just lumping all the blame onto her to salve his conscience. Simon, Duncan, all men did this to a greater or lesser degree because they couldn't be in the wrong! Yes. She had behaved in a thoughtless way, yes, she had consequently hurt Simon badly, but then he'd hurt her with his refusing to be seen with her at shows and his disinterest in his baby. The baby......... no, that was all in the past, she flung the bedclothes back, put her feet into her slippers and grabbed her dressing-gown. It's history, I'm going to marry Paul and be safe and happy and show my dogs. Whatever situation Simon is in now, he brought on himself, "Sally I'm going down for a cuppa, are you coming?"

The next morning was even colder and there was a threat of snow. Just before midday, Natalie came to see her, she asked Fiona if she would be available to help her if she had problems with the litter, Fiona agreed that she would, although a little annoyed at the request. She knew that there were many breeders who would tell her to ask the owner of the stud dog to help under the circumstances. They spoke briefly about Viv's death.

"Have you seen Paul since, Fiona?"

"No, he did phone to see if I was OK but that's all. Why?"

"No reason, I just wondered if there was any more information."

Natalie was pleased to hear this, she was beginning to realise just how much she liked this quiet, educated man and she was a bit concerned that there was a relationship with Fiona as Simon had suggested at the party, "Do you know why Simon was so angry with Paul?"

Fiona didn't answer for a second or two but concentrated on making another cup of coffee for them both. She was beginning to suspect that there was more to this questioning than met the eye.

"Not really, there was nothing to be angry about was there. I believe that Simon is in financial difficulties and I suppose he was just feeling a bit down and Paul happened to be there."

"Oh, I'm so sorry to hear that. Could it be anything to do with losing that litter?"

"Well, I don't think that helped and, of course, his other bitch missed earlier in the year."

"Oh, did he lose a previous litter? I didn't know. He'll be very cut up about Viv won't he? Caroline said that Simon and Viv were getting very friendly. It was the talk at all the shows apparently."

"Oh yes, he was definitely seeing her," Fiona's voice sounded angry, "stupid man."

Natalie finished her cup of coffee, "Well, I mustn't stay any longer. I'm terrified that the puppies will arrive early so, if you are all right Fiona, I'll be off. Thanks for the coffee," she got into her car feeling quite satisfied with the way the conversation had gone, Fiona didn't seem to be too concerned about Paul but she did seem very angry about Simon's relationship with poor Viv.

Paul came round to the cottage that evening and, once again, the conversation centred around Viv's death, "Now my dear, I have done my best to limit the damage to us by asking Caroline and the others to say nothing. We don't want our names dragged into some sordid affair between Simon and Viv do we. By the way, I presume from Simon's behaviour that he is not at all happy about the divorce. You are still going for a two year separation aren't you? It is the most civilised way of proceeding after all?"

"Yes, but why do you ask?"

"Because my dear, after the other night, it is obvious that he doesn't want the divorce and I don't wish to be cited as co-respondent. Does he know that we......"

"No, of course not. I haven't told anyone."

"Not even Natalie?"

"No, no-one."

"Well, in that case, I don't know about you but, on such a cold night, it would be very pleasant to cuddle up in bed wouldn't it, although I shan't be able to stay unfortunately."

Fiona agreed but, laying beside him with his hand cuddling her breast, she did wonder whether Simon did know about these evenings with Paul and, if he did, would he possibly want to cite Paul in the divorce? Could she cite Viv now that she was dead?

For the next two days heavy clouds dumped inches of snow on the ground and it became very arduous seeing to the dogs each day. It meant towelling each one down after a romp in the snow, to prevent them getting cold and making sure that their bedding was adequate and dry, her days seemed endless. Thank heavens that she only had one boarder. It was so cold that the heating in the kennels was only just adequate and the water bowls froze almost immediately. By the evening she was just too tired to bother about anything. Nobody came to see her because it was impossible to get up the incline of the drive. Natalie phoned to say that she had some trouble with frozen pipes and was very worried that Juno would have her puppies and she wouldn't be able to keep them warm enough. She had asked her handyman, Brian, to buy and install an electric heater in the whelping room. Paul phoned but only to say that he was very busy, as usual, causing Fiona to wonder if she would ever see him once they were living together. She had heard nothing from Simon but that was only to be expected. Duncan had also phoned to see if she was all right and so had Beryl but she was still feeling rather gloomy and depressed. She didn't even have the afternoon work at the bookshop to cheer her up as they were stocktaking and, always in the back of her mind was whether she really had caused Viv's death, albeit indirectly

Relief from misery came in an excited call from Natalie, Juno had had three puppies and all was well. Juno was now settled in her new quarters and seemed well and contented with her family.

"That's the best news I've had so far this year Natalie. Have you told Paul?"

"Yes, as a matter of fact he is coming round this evening to see them. He insisted."

"Oh, did he. He must have finished some of his work. Anyway, congratulations Natalie and I'll pop over as soon as I am able. The drive up to the cottage is still covered in ice and snow."

Paul stood looking at the bitch with her litter, "What an excellent litter Natalie, this room is perfect as a whelping room isn't it; being just off the kitchen." Paul turned and smiled at Natalie, "May I pick one up?" He bent down and picked up one of the pups, "This one in particular, he's a fine specimen. I shall stake my claim for him if you don't object Natalie."

"Not at all Paul. I feel honoured that someone with your expertise is even interested in my little family."

"Ah Natalie, never sell your stock short, never. First rule of dog showing. Be generous with praise for your own stock and a little mean when praising others."

"I shall remember that Paul, now would you like a cup of tea or coffee? Or perhaps you would prefer something stronger to keep the cold out."

"Whatever you are having Natalie."

She hurried out to the cold kitchen, without the central heating the old house was very cold indeed. She put the kettle on and then went to the dining-room for the whisky.

Seated on either side of the roaring log fire, Paul chatted away regaling Natalie with stories from the past. Shows that he had won, dogs that he had exported and who had done so well. Natalie sat there listening, she felt so happy in his company. She shifted in her chair, "I could sit here all night listening to your tales, they are all so fascinating. I am so glad that I started this hobby and so glad that I met you Paul," she smiled at him and reaching out gently touched his hand with the tips of her fingers. Paul did nothing for a second and then turned his hand so that he could hold her hand in his, "It was fortuitous for us both that we met again after all these years Natalie," he lifted her hand and placed a kiss in her palm.

A shiver of excitement went down her spine, he was interested in her! She hadn't been wrong, it was her that he was interested in not Fiona.

"I'm afraid that I must go now, it is getting late. You haven't forgotten your promise to show me over the cellars sometime have you?"

"No Paul, come whenever you like. You will very likely be able to tell me more about them than I can you. You seem so knowledgeable about old buildings."

"History and architecture have always been an interest of mine, and now my dear," he bent his head and kissed her gently on the lips.

After Natalie had closed the heavy, front door she put the bolts on and then smiling touched her lips, he likes me, he really likes me.

Paul was thoughtful as he drove home. What had prompted him to kiss her? He certainly hadn't intended to. He had intended to marry Fiona, she was good for him, didn't create ripples or anything in his ordered life well, that is until now. He hoped that the Viv affair would quickly die down and that Simon wouldn't cause trouble over the divorce. Now, however, there seemed to be another possibility on the horizon. He had wanted to have a friendship with Natalie because she knew the right people and because she was well provided for, both great assets in dog showing. She could easily help him to get into the charmed circle. He had not considered anything other than that but now? She was lonely, well off, pretty in a more mature way than Fiona, had a beautiful house, more money than Fiona and could put a lot of business his way.

He enjoyed his little nights with Fiona, especially now when she had calmed down a bit, he had been rather disturbed at first when she had wanted to run around naked through the house and had even wanted to kiss his... him; he pulled a face at the memory. He enjoyed sex as much as the next man but it wasn't right that a woman should behave with so little decorum. He allowed himself to speculate on making love to Natalie and was surprised to find that the idea rather excited him.

Peter came into the room frowning, "Do you know Beryl, I swear Simon's drunk again. He was talking rubbish. He makes me so mad."

"Why what was he saying? He is so unhappy you know and now that I've seen that place he lives in!"

"His choice, the bloody fool. Didn't know when he was well off."

"But Peter, that house is terrible, he must be frozen this weather."

"Oh yes, that's what he says, he's worried about the dogs."

There had been another heavy fall of snow and the TV news was filled with scenes of trapped cars, farmers trying to tractor food out to their animals in the fields and pregnant mothers being airlifted to hospital. Fiona phoned Natalie to ask if her puppies were all right and if she had managed to get the central heating going again. Natalie seemed to be on top of the world and chatted away happily for quite a while. She then tried to phone Paul to see how he was faring. He apologised for not having been to see her but he had a bad cold and did not wish to give it to her. Still feeling rather lonely, she then phoned Beryl and Peter to ask how they were managing in the extreme weather.

"Thank you so much for calling Fiona, you are a dear, We're both fine but we are a bit worried about Simon. Have you heard from him recently?"

"No, why?"

"Well, he wasn't managing too well a couple of days ago but, now we've had all this extra snow, we are a bit concerned. He must be so cold in that house, Peter tried to get him last night to ask him to come and stay with us for a while and I phoned this morning but there was still no reply."

"He'll have gone to work I expect, try again this evening. Let me know how you get on."

When Beryl phoned in the evening it was to say that there again had been no reply and Peter had decided to phone early the next morning.

CHAPTER THIRTY

Peter and Beryl slept badly and were up and phoning Simon by seven o'clock the next morning but Simon still did not answer the phone.

"He can't have gone to work yet Beryl. Something's wrong, I know it is. I'm going round there."

"I'll come as well."

"No, you phone the office for me and say that I won't be in today will you."

Beryl made a very quick breakfast for him and he set off on the slushy roads for Simon's house.

Getting no reply to his knocking and calling but hearing the dogs barking furiously, he made his way around the back of the houses. There was a door in the fence at the back of each house and, reaching over to undo the bolt, Peter made his way down the tiny garden to the back door which turned out not to be locked. The dogs started barking furiously and, as he opened the door, they all bounded out to greet him and sniff at his legs, "Hello you lot. Well you seem OK. Where's Simon?" The kitchen seemed clean and there was water in the bowl on the floor so Simon had to be around somewhere. Just as he was going to call Simon's name, Peter suddenly heard a spasm of coughing coming from upstairs. He ran up the stairs calling out, "Hello Simon, it's me, Peter."

Simon was laying in bed coughing and it was a few minutes before he was able to talk to Peter,

"Am I glad to see you. Make me a cup of tea would you I'm gasping and could you let the dogs out."

Peter noticed that he could hardly speak and was gasping for breath,
"I've already let the dogs out. This room is like a fridge. Have you got a water bottle or an electric blanket?"
"No but..." He started to cough again.
"I suppose you've been up and down looking after those dogs haven't you."
"Yes, of course."
"You're mad. Do you know that."
Peter disappeared and came back with a hot cup of tea and some toast, "Brought some toast as well. When did you last eat?"
"Not hungry." He sat up and drank the tea, "God, I needed that, thanks Peter."
"You're coming home with me so that Beryl can look after you."
"Can't, the dogs need...."
"Damn the dogs. Look I'm not taking no for an answer. I'm phoning Beryl now so that she can make up a bed for you and then I'm phoning Fiona to see if she will have the dogs."
"No, don't phone Fee. I don't want to bother her."
"Don't talk rot, you must be light-headed and feverish. Anyway, you've no say in the matter." Peter went out of the room and Simon heard him speaking on the phone downstairs.
"That's all settled. Come on, I'll pack a case for you and we'll leave straight away. Fiona says she'll pick up the dogs shortly. I'm going to leave your key for her."
Simon smiled weakly, "OK big brother, you win."
Fiona, well wrapped up, saw to her dogs and also prepared some kennels for Simon's dogs. Peter had sounded worried, Simon must be pretty bad for Peter to want to take him straight home but she knew that he would be well looked after there. Why hadn't Simon phoned her and said that he didn't feel well. Later that morning she crawled slowly out of her icy drive, thank heavens she thought that, like all dog exhibitors, she was used to driving in all conditions. The cold dampness in Simon's house rushed out to meet her as she opened the front door; no wonder he had such a bad cough. She collected all the dogs and put them in the back of the estate, "Well, you all look fit as fiddles. Heaven knows how Simon managed to look after you." She reflected on the dedication of dog exhibitors, other people just didn't realise how much they sacrificed for their dogs. How much time,

energy, thought, care, love and money went into their hobby of showing dogs, twenty-four hours a day and three hundred and sixty-five days a year, even when you were ill!

With the dogs settled in, she phoned Beryl, “Hello Beryl it’s Fiona. How is Simon?”

“Not at all well. He has a temperature and is coughing really badly. If he doesn’t start improving I shall have to get a doctor to see him.”

“I’ll come over and see him.”

“Er, I’m sorry Fiona but Simon says that he doesn’t want to see anybody.”

“Oh, I see. Well, I’ll phone again soon Beryl.”

“Are you alright?”

“Yes, kept busy of course. This weather makes hard work of everything doesn’t it.”

Fiona phoned every day and gradually the reports on Simon’s health got better, “He’s been very poorly you know Fiona. Just hasn’t been looking after himself. Just like a man.”

“Is he well enough for visitors now?”

“I don’t know Fiona. He still says that he doesn’t want to see anyone. He did ask if the dogs were alright and I told him that you had been phoning every day but.....”

“I see, well thank’s Beryl. I’ll call again in a few days time,” Fiona put down the phone and shrugged her shoulders. It hurt that he didn’t want to see her but then perhaps it was for the best.

On the spur of the moment, she grabbed her coat and locked the door. She had promised to go over to see Natalie’s litter, she’d go now, it would cheer her up. She always loved to see their dear little faces, it made her smile.

“They are absolutely lovely Natalie. So strong, she’s obviously got some good milk there and she seems to be looking after them well. Do you want me to send any prospective buyers onto you?”

“No thank you. I’m keeping one, Paul is having one and he has arranged for the other one to go to Finland. Isn’t that kind of him.”

Fiona was very troubled by this statement. Paul had not said a word of this when she had gone out for a drink with him yesterday evening. Why? She would somehow have to bring it into the next conversation, after all he had in effect pinched the mating from her and was now selling the puppies and not saying a word to her. She knew that he had a lot of work, tax returns or something so perhaps it had slipped his mind, "Has Paul seen them recently?"

"Oh yes, he has been so kind and helpful and popped over on several occasions. He's coming this evening as a matter of fact."

Fiona bit her lip, she had been about to say, "Oh, is he." She didn't like the sound of this at all, Paul had said nothing last night and it was obvious from Natalie's shining eyes that she fancied Paul! I should have seen this coming she thought, it would be ages before her divorce came through and Paul hadn't actually proposed to her yet although he still came round on a Saturday evening and stayed the night. Was he beginning to have second thoughts? Over the next few weeks, the weather improved and Simon got better so Fiona had more time to think about the problem of Paul, she came to the conclusion that she must suggest to him that he move in with her on a permanent basis. He could have one of the downstairs rooms as his office, his dogs would be kennelled here and they could make plans for the future. He was always talking about the merits and rewards of judging abroad, they could do it together.

The next morning, when she had come in to make a cup of coffee the phone rang, "Hello, is that Fiona, this is Caroline."

"Caroline?"

"Yes, Caroline Amery. Fiona, I've just been told that the result of the inquest on Viv Butcher was Accidental Death! Apparently, she hadn't taken enough sleeping tablets to finish her off and had left some in the bottle so she didn't mean to commit suicide! Fancy that! It seems that, if she had been caught in time that they might have been able to save her. Isn't that awful.!"

"Yes it is Caroline. I didn't really like her but that is such a sad way to die."

"Yes, well I must go. Oh, and by the way, I've tried to contact Simon to let him know but can't get a reply. Is he away?"

"Yes, he is. I'll tell him when he comes back."

"Oh, I nearly forgot, the funeral is at St Mary's church on the 11th at 2 o'clock. Do you think that you'll be going?"

"I expect so. Have you told Natalie?"

"Yes, I think I've covered just about everyone who might want to come. You won't forget to tell Simon will you because I'm sure that he would want to come."

That evening she phoned Beryl and told her the news and asked her to pass it on to Simon

CHAPTER THIRTY-ONE

Simon quietly slipped into the church, took a prayer book from the verger and sat in a pew at the very back of the church. Partially hidden by a pillar, hardly any of the mourners arriving afterwards noticed him. He sat there looking at the coffin draped with flowers, he could see Viv so clearly telling him about how badly the dog world in general had treated her. He looked around at the other pews recognising several faces, he smiled wryly as he recognised that two of them were from the very committee that she had mentioned. Caroline Amery was there seated quite near the front and he could see Natalie Bennett but not Fiona; he wondered if she was coming.

Fiona looked at her watch, one-forty, heavens, she thought as she raced out to the car, I shall be late. She had done a mating that morning and the dogs had been tied for fifty minutes, it had put everything back and she had so wanted to be early at the church. She guessed that it would be nearly empty, usually dog show people were very loyal to other exhibitors and most funeral services were well attended but, Viv Butcher, she had been seen as being such a troublemaker that Fiona felt that very few would turn up. There were quite a lot of cars parked on the road and she had to park her car quite a long way from the church, she ran along the pavement, up the church path and into the doorway of the church. She could hear organ music playing quietly in the background and breathed a sigh of relief, the service hadn't started. A churchwarden handed her a book of prayer and she walked into the nave to find all the pews absolutely full! A hand waved to her half-way down the church and she saw Natalie's face.

“Hello Fiona,” Natalie whispered, “I saved you a place but I was beginning to wonder if you were coming.”

“Thank you Natalie,” Fiona whispered back, “Got held up. I didn’t think there would be so many people....” she suddenly saw the coffin near the alter. It was smothered in the most beautiful flowers, “What beautiful......” but before she could finish her sentence the Vicar came to the centre of the choir stalls. He thanked everybody for coming and the service began.

Fiona sat slightly stunned, the person that the Vicar was describing, the person who helped so many elderly people at the practice, going shopping for them, gardening for them, the person who had taken in and found homes for so many rescued dogs, the person who was always willing to help at church fetes, surely this wasn’t the detested Viv Butcher. Surely this wasn’t the Viv Butcher who was always trying to win by any means, always speaking badly of people, causing trouble between people. Her thoughts were interrupted by Natalie standing up at her side, she hurriedly stood up and the church was filled with the sound of a large congregation singing. Fiona stood with tears in her eyes, Simon had tried to talk to her about Viv and she hadn’t wanted to listen. She had thought that he was just getting on his hobby horse of being ‘blacked’ but perhaps he had been trying to tell her something else. She felt very small and mean, Natalie tugged at her sleeve and she realised that everyone was sitting down again, she did also. Sneaking a look at Natalie, she could see that her face was calm and peaceful so she was not surprised at the goodness and kindness of Viv as expressed by the Vicar.

The service came to an end and everyone started to file out of the pews and followed the coffin outside where it was placed again in the hearse. There was to be a short service later at the Crematorium. Many people were wiping their eyes and Fiona caught little snatches of conversation, all praising Viv for her kindness, she looked around for Simon but couldn’t see him anywhere. Perhaps he hadn’t felt up to coming today, or was it that he was too upset by her death. She realised that Natalie was speaking to her, “Would you like to come back to my house for a cup of tea Fiona; these services are always upsetting aren’t they. Just look at the amount of flowers here, sprays and wreaths. She was a kind person and, it would seem, very much appreciated. I do wish I had taken the time to get to know her better.”

"Yes, so do I... now."

As soon as she got back from Natalie's she phoned Beryl, "Hello Beryl, how is Simon."

"Oh hello Fiona, I was going to phone you later. Simon isn't here, he has gone back to his house. I know what you're going to say but he was determined and you of all people know what that means. He wanted me to phone you to say that he would pick up the dogs at the weekend if that was all right with you."

"Of course it's all right with me but why couldn't he ask me himself?"

"Don't get cross with me Fiona, I'm only the messenger but I do know that he shouldn't have gone to that funeral today either. He isn't one hundred per cent fit yet but he muttered something to Peter about still feeling guilty and wanting to support her. He is very low and dejected you know Fiona, Peter says that he has never seen him like this, I'm quite worried about him."

Having said goodbye to Beryl, Fiona immediately dialled Simon's number but got no reply. Curse the man she thought, I still worry about him, I always will. Why can't I stop loving him? She wanted to tell him that, if he insisted on picking up the dogs, he would have to pick them up tomorrow morning if possible. Paul would be coming over in the evening and she didn't want another scene.

She had hardly put the phone down when she heard a car stopping outside the door, Paul came into the kitchen, "Hello my dear, I'm most terribly sorry but something has come up and I shan't be able to come tomorrow evening."

"Oh Paul, I had planned a special meal for Valentine's Day," she had wanted to create a pleasant atmosphere so that over dinner, she could tell Paul about her idea of his moving in with her.

"I'm so sorry to disappoint you my dear but...."

"Never mind, there was something that I wanted to discuss with you so could we make it early next week instead?"

"Of course, I shall look forward to it."

Simon came over to collect the dogs on Saturday morning, "Thanks Fee they all look marvellous. Thanks for looking after them."

"Don't be silly, It was a pleasure, it reminded me of..." She stopped just as she had been going to say 'when we lived together'.

"Anyway, I'm grateful. Thanks again. Goodbye."

"Oh don't go yet have a cup of coffee, I've made some scones too. You look as if you could do with fattening up. While you're here, I'd also value your opinion on that young lad I kept from the last litter. I really don't know whether to keep him or not or which judges will like him." She was babbling but she so wanted him to stay and talk to her.
Simon smiled, "OK Fee, but only for a short while. I want to get back."

It was just like old times, having looked at the dog, they sat in the warm kitchen talking about Saxon, Sammy and the young hopeful Sanders and their future chances. They discussed the merits of some new food that Fiona had been asked to try by one of the dog food manufacturers and how she thought it compared with their present feeding programme. The suitability of various stud dogs was considered for certain Simfell bitches which led them on to the breed in general and the way in which it was going, whether it was getting too big or not, too heavy or not, losing certain characteristics. It was only when Fiona got up to put the light on that they found that they had talked the afternoon away.

"Heavens, it's going dark and I haven't seen to the dogs."

"I'll help you."

"No you won't, you're still convalescent. Beryl would shoot me if I let you out there in this wind."
They both laughed as Simon walked to the door, "Right then, I'll say cheerio and thanks for the tea and the chat. Bye Fee."
For the first time since he had left her, he went without kissing her. Fiona felt upset and lonely, "Bye Simon, take care," she called as he drove away.

When she went back into the kitchen to put on her anorak and boots, she saw a box of chocolates on the table with a note, 'For you Fee. Thanks for everything and Happy Valentine's Day.'

Natalie's nose was shining, her cheeks were bright red and her hair untidy, she grabbed the powder puff on her dressing table and dabbed at her nose and cheeks. She then quickly ran a comb through her hair. Heavens she thought, I'm putting on too much weight, this skirt is getting awfully tight around the waist. She frowned and smoothed her hands over her hips. It must be walking the dogs and showing them she thought, because both occupations seemed to give her such an appetite. Frowning again she decided to change her jumper for a looser one to hide the bulges. Paul Aston was coming to see the puppies tonight and she had invited him to stay for dinner.

Dabbing her nose again with the puff, she hurried downstairs to check on the dinner. She then went into the dining-room, serviettes, she'd forgotten those pretty serviettes that she'd bought especially for today. Placing them on the table, she smiled. Yes, they did make the table look very attractive, prettier perhaps than the more formal damask ones. Just then the dogs started to bark as a car stopped in the drive. She patted her hair and ran her tongue over her lips, "Natalie," she said, "Natalie you're being utterly ridiculous. This man is just coming to see the puppies not a fifty-something widow who is putting on weight!" She smoothed her skirt over her hips and opened the door, "Hello Paul., I'm so glad that you could come. I know how busy you are."

"It's my pleasure. These are for you," he handed her a bunch of red carnations.

"Would you like to see the puppies before we have dinner?"

Over dinner he again regaled her with stories of his previous dogs and how well they had done in the ring. The topic then changed to his passions for Architecture and old buildings. Natalie was an interested listener and the meal went very well. Over coffee he asked her about Richard and his illness, and about her daughter Candida. They then talked about forthcoming shows and he advised her which to enter. He thought that Jamie had a bright future. They talked about Audrey Chatsworth and other mutual friends high up in the dog world and found that they had several other friends in common.

Over their coffee which they had sitting by the sitting-room fire, the conversation changed to more general topics during the course of which, Paul told her that he had had a passion for trains both large and small ever since he was a boy. Natalie exclaimed, "I don't believe it. Richard was the same, in fact, in the attic at this moment is a complete Hornby set with masses of lines and stations and everything that you can imagine. I'm saving it in the hopes that Candida might one day present me with a grandson. If you like, I'll ask Brian who helps me with the garden to get them down for you to see."

"I should like that very much indeed but now, I must thank you for an excellent meal and depart."

Natalie rose and went to open the sitting-room door just as Paul went to do the same, she brushed against him and he put his hand on her arm to steady her. She blushed and looked up at his handsomely rugged face, neither of them moved until he bent his head and lightly kissed her on the lips, "I hope you didn't mind Natalie only you looked so pretty."
Blushing furiously she looked up at his face again, "No Paul, I didn't mind at all," and she stood on tiptoe to kiss him again, "After all it is St. Valentine's Day."

CHAPTER THIRTY-TWO

Paul rummaged through the sideboard, he grunted as he stood up with a bottle of Cognac in his hand, he had a lot of thinking and organising to do and needed something to stimulate his mind. He had always found in the past that a good drop of Cognac worked wonders. A grateful client had given this particular bottle to him just before Christmas and he had only just remembered it. Pouring a generous amount into the goblet, he sat down in his leather armchair, taking pleasure from the look of the amber liquid as it circled round the glass. His professional life had never been better, in the world of dogs his years in the show scene were being rewarded and he was hoping for even higher things this year and definitely next year. He knew that certain things were in place and he was now in a position to help them along and profit by them. This was not the problem, well indirectly maybe but, as his personal life overlapped with the show scene, it could become quite a problem if he didn't get it right.

He was more than contented with the arrangement that he now had with Fiona, it suited his needs and, in time, when her divorce came through and, when she had progressed more in the dog world, he would move in with her and marry her. That had been his intention ever since his skiing accident but now, there was another piece of puzzle to add to the jigsaw, now there was Natalie. He would have to consider the relative merits of both as far as he and his future were concerned. Fiona was slim and attractive, Natalie was rather plump and homely looking but that could be altered. Both were able to socialise well and would be an asset in his business dealings and in the show scene. Both owned their own property, he had ascertained that neither had a mortgage to be considered. Fiona did have established kennels and that was a plus on her side. Even so, Natalie's property must be worth more than Fiona's, even with the kennels. Both were good cooks, another important aspect to be considered as he did enjoy good food well cooked. Fiona was a pleasant and willing partner in bed. Ah, what about Natalie. He had been a little surprised at her response the other evening. Her kiss had been warm and promising more but, and here was another problem, he was pretty certain that Natalie would not be as accommodating as Fiona so it would be a leap of faith if he married her. She certainly wouldn't be as attractive naked as Fiona. Um, he needed a little more Cognac.

He had always been attracted to Fiona ever since Simon had introduced her to him but, it had been obvious from the start that she was besotted with the damned man. The idea of actually marrying again had only really surfaced after his accident when it became very apparent that, as he got older, he was now fifty-three, he would need someone to care for him. He had only then seen the merits of this action as far as the show scene was concerned, Fiona already gave CC's in one breed, under his guidance she had started to ask for and get judging in other breeds and to fulfil their requirements to go on their judging lists. He himself already gave tickets in five breeds, if she could be helped to achieve the same......

He again swilled the brandy around the sides of the goblet; of course he could get Natalie started on the judging scene, by pulling a few strings he could have her up to CC level in no time, he had never thought to sound her out about judging, he must correct that oversight and quickly. She was already very friendly with quite a few people in top places, in no time, if they played their cards right, they might both be in the charmed circle. She had no other ties, her daughter being married, but then neither did Fiona, now that he had managed to distance her from Philips with regard to the show scene. Simon had gone backwards while she had gone forwards and, in fact, would continue to do so this year, he'd always known that Simon was eager and ambitious and would, therefore, not be able to stomach the fact that Fiona was going to the top and he wasn't. Trouble was that he had not put anything in place this year for Natalie, he must set about that immediately if she agreed to judge, he liked to keep all his options open for whatever he decided to do in the future. Having helped several people with their small financial problems in the past, he knew that he could always call in a small favour like that. He sipped the warm liquid in the glass, yes, for the time being it might be best to carry on as normal with Fiona, why not, and see how quickly he could progress things for Natalie.

In the meantime, however, he must ascertain whether Natalie had a favourable attitude towards judging and, more importantly, he must reinforce his statement to Fiona that, until they were married, it was best to keep their little Saturday night arrangement to themselves. He picked up the phone, "Fiona my dear, I have been missing you. Can I look forward perhaps to seeing you next weekend? Yes, good, until then."

Natalie looked at the pastries tastefully set on the plate and sighed. No, she mustn't, she really must stop coming to this delightful tea-room, she must lose some weight. Since the evening with Paul she had felt so happy, so excited and confident, full of ideas, she had bought herself a new swimming costume and had asked her neighbours, Harriet and Larry, if she might use their heated pool. Already she felt better for it and her skirts were definitely a little less tight around the waist. That kiss from Paul had been the kickstart she needed to do something about her figure. She decided that she had been starved of male love for too long and she liked Paul. If she were to marry him it would improve her social like tremendously, with mutual friends and mutual interests, she could do a lot worse. He was financially sound, that was obvious although she had also made a few dicreet enquiries through Frank, just to be on the safe side. Sighing again she asked for the bill, "It was just a pot of tea," smiling and infinitely pleased with herself, she left the temptation behind.

She stopped and looked in a shop window at some beautiful lingerie and nightwear, yes, there was that to consider too, if the romance with Paul developed she supposed that he would want to make love to her and...... yes, she must definitely not eat any more cakes or biscuits. Fiona was coming to see her this afternoon, she was so slim and never had to diet, she would give her all the cake that she had made yesterday and get it out of sight.

"Do have another slice Fiona, you're so slender, I don't know how you can eat cake and stay as you are. I only have to eat a little and I get fat."

"Thank you Natalie, it's delicious. You're not fat, in fact, I think you've lost a little weight recently. Have you been on a diet?"

"No, I've just been trying to exercise a bit more. Keep fit really."

It pleased Fiona to sit in Natalie's beautiful drawing-room and relax, the old house had a quiet, peaceful atmosphere, it's own personality, the soft light coming through the mullioned windows made her feel almost soporific...

"How do you think you'll do at Crufts Fiona?"

Crufts was on the horizon and she had been working on Saxon even more than usual, in company she was quite sure with every other hopeful exhibitor. To win at Crufts was everybody's dream and the people who visited Crufts in their droves couldn't have any conception of the time and thought and self-sacrifice that went into every exhibit they saw on the benches. She had been to a few Open shows recently to get him used to the ring again after Christmas.

"Gosh, I was nearly asleep, I didn't realise how tired I was until I stopped."

"It will be all this extra work you're doing for Crufts. I'm so sorry that I shall miss it but I wouldn't want to leave the pups for so long."

"No I agree, if I get a couple of good night's sleep before the big day, I'll be all right, it's such a long and tiring day. I'm so glad that it's on a Thursday this year, it's always the quietest day."

They chatted on for a while about the dogs until Fiona suddenly jumped up, "Good heavens look at the time. Sorry to dash Natalie and thanks for the tea and cake." She wanted to get back and be all finished with a hot meal in the Aga before seven o'clock. Simon had taken to popping in on a Wednesday on his way home from work, he never stayed for long and he didn't try to kiss her or even to touch her. He still seemed tired and depressed, no longer full of ideas and plans, she felt concerned and, for the past two weeks she had had a hot meal ready for him and it pleased her to see him eat it with relish, he was still very thin.

That evening, as she was dishing up the main course Simon asked if Saxon was ready for the big day.

"Pretty well ready. I'd like you to give him the once-over just before then."

"Pleasure, I understand that the word is out that you'll do well."

"Simon. Don't start that, let's have a pleasant evening."

"No, honestly, that is what is being said. I hope you do, he is a worthy champion."

"Who are you taking?"

"Me, oh I'm not even going, let alone taking anyone."

"But Simon, you've always gone to Crufts You have never missed it since I've known you. You must go. It wouldn't be Crufts without you."

"No, not this year, I don't think that I would feature at all and anyway, I can't afford it."

Fiona went to say more and then bit her lip, it was obvious that Simon didn't want to talk about it and it worried her. She remembered how, when she had first met him, he had been so enthusiastic, so dedicated, nothing and no-one would have kept him from Crufts, not even Mary his first wife!

He finished his meal and stood up, "Must be off, got to walk the dogs. Thanks for the meal and the company. See you next Wednesday and I'll check Saxon over for you. Bye Fee."

"Bye Simon, I'll see you then."

She watched as he got into his car and drove off, something was very wrong, all the fun and life seemed to have gone out of him.

"Hi Beryl it's Fiona. Do you and Peter see much of Simon now?"

"No, not since he went to that funeral and then straight home. Why?"

"No reason, just wondered how his health is now," she didn't want to tell Beryl about Simon's weekly visit because she would read much more into it and she didn't want to be questioned about her motives. She wasn't sure what they were herself.

"He sent me a beautiful bouquet when he left. He has phoned once or twice but that's all. Has he phoned you?"

"Me, um, no, he hasn't phoned me," this was the truth so Fiona didn't feel bad about deceiving Beryl. What she did feel bad about was the fact that neither Simon, Beryl or Peter had any idea that Paul was sleeping with her on a regular basis.

That Saturday evening, the watcher in the car at the top of the hill started the engine and drove away. He must stop doing this now that it was becoming a fairly regular occurrence. After all, if she was going to marry him! He mentally kicked himself as he done so often before. He had been making discrete enquiries about his friend Paul Aston and now realised that during those couple of years that he and Fiona had been so busy getting the kennel up and running and trying to get accepted in the circles of power, Paul had been equally busy in the circles of power and more successfully than he had realised. Fiona was destined for the top and he was destined for nothing so, good luck to her. He just hoped that she would stay friends.

CHAPTER THIRTY-THREE

Shivering, Fiona glanced at her watch, four-thirty, time to get on the road if she wanted to avoid the early morning rush to work. Checking once again that she had her passes, her grooming gear, lunch, flask, money, make-up bag and an extra pair of comfortable shoes (Crufts was always hell on the feet), she said goodbye to Sally and her daughters and told them that Ruth would be there about seven o'clock Firmly closing the door she made her way to the estate car where Saxon was already installed and waiting.

As she drove along the quiet roads she reflected on all the exhibitors travelling from places like Scotland, Ireland or Cornwall who had, no doubt, set out last night or even earlier to travel by coach or car, boat or plane to get to this prestigious show. She was tense with excitement, Crufts always had this effect on her, there was no other show like it and she knew that everyone else felt the same.

"Saxon, are you alright back there? It seems a long journey without Simon to talk to doesn't it." She had just realised that this was the first time she had driven to Crufts without Simon. He wasn't even going to be there to lend support, criticise the judge when she didn't win or praise the judge when she did! She had watched at the love and care, the skill with which he checked over Saxon yesterday evening and she had tried hard to persuade him to come, she had even offered him a lift but he had been adamant saying that, apart from anything else, he didn't want to leave the dogs so long, they got left enough as it was. He also didn't want the neighbours complaining too much.

It just didn't seem like Simon not to have arranged something in order for him to go to Crufts. She wondered if he was still not completely well, was there something he wasn't telling her or Peter? This occupied her mind for some time until suddenly she saw the signs for the NEC. The journey had gone quite quickly and with no hold ups. There would be a bit of a queue to get into the car park no doubt, but she was in good time and she would be able to walk Saxon a little before going in and then settle him down well before judging started. Laden with her various bits and pieces she joined the chattering, excited queue of hopefuls walking towards the massive halls.

As she made her way in she saw one or two other Cumbrian exhibitors and waved, she also saw some from other terrier breeds that she had got to know. The noise of dogs barking and people talking made her excitement and anticipation build even more and the adrenaline to flow. You couldn't help but feel the buzz that was Crufts. She collected her catalogue, found her bench and pouring a much needed cup of tea, she opened the catalogue to see who her rivals were going to be on the day, "Good heavens," she said out loud as she saw Viv's name as an exhibitor in her class. She must have sent her entry off before she died, perhaps it was just as well that Simon wasn't here, it might have upset him. She had speculated on the journey up whether it was Viv's death that was having this awful effect on Simon, perhaps he still felt responsible, her name had not come up in any of their recent conversations.

Her thoughts were interrupted by a voice she knew well, "Hello Fiona, how are you my dear?" Mrs Emsworth was standing there, a dog on a lead and her bag and travelling box in her hand, "I'm really getting too old for this you know dear. I think that this will be my last Crufts."

"Oh no don't say that Mrs Emsworth, it just wouldn't be the same without you. Let me help you with those things. What number are you? By the way, I've got a small present for you in my bag, I should have sent it to you for Christmas."

As she walked back to her bench having got Mrs Emsworth installed Fiona bumped into Caroline Amery, "Hello Fiona, have you seen that Viv had entered....." Fiona cut her short, "Yes, I have."

" Isn't that awful! Is Simon here today? He'll be upset when..."

"No, he isn't."

"Perhaps it's for the best. Well, have you brought something smart to change into today?"

"No, why?"

"Come on Fiona, don't play the innocent, it's been the talk for months that you're going to do well today."

"Well, nobody has said it to me. Who's told you?"

Caroline tapped her finger on her nose, "You'll see. You'll see. Wait until all the photographers appear. I always bring a clean blouse or jumper just in case. You are welcome to borrow mine if you like."

Fiona thanked her and looked around to see if she could catch a glimspe of Paul, she saw a TV celebrity being helped through the crowds but not Paul.

By now all the halls were filling up with exhibitors and visitors and the stalls were already doing a roaring trade. The tannoy suddenly announced that judging would commence in all rings and Fiona struggled through the crowd to get to the ringside, she wanted to watch the puppy classes, there was one entered, that she had sold to a man from Scotland, from the last litter. It had looked promising as a pup and had had some nice write-ups in the dog papers, she wanted to see how it had developed.

"Hi there Fiona, don't suppose Simon's here?" It was Bob Adams.

"Hello Bob, no he isn't."

"Thought not."

Immediately Fiona was on the alert, "Why."

Bob shrugged his shoulders and changed the subject, "Shouldn't leave that lad of yours unattended today if I was you."

Fiona looked at him for a moment and then excused herself and went back to the bench, everything seemed all right, Saxon didn't seem disturbed at all; of course, if people had been speculating on her doing well then perhaps she should err on the side of caution; she sat down, if only Simon had come she could have watched some of the classes. By asking other passing exhibitors which class was on, she was able to get Saxon ready for the Open dog class in good time.

As she made her way to the ring several exhibitors patted her on the back and wished her luck, others just stared stony-faced. She hadn't seen Paul at all. He was judging another terrier breed today and she doubted if she would see him now 'til much later. Her stomach was churning as she walked Saxon after the judge's inspection, she didn't know him at all, no-one did. Some said he was from Sweden, some said that they thought he was German while several others thought that he was from Finland. He looked very competent as he walked along the exhibits for the final decision. He pulled Saxon out into second place. There goes the CC anyway, so much for all the talk! The challenge was called and Fiona was told to stand by. The unbeaten dogs were called into the ring and the CC awarded. The steward then asked Fiona to go back to challenge for the reserve CC. She was overjoyed when the now smiling judge handed her the reserve ticket. She let out the breath that she had been holding for ages and shook his hand vigorously, smiling and laughing she hugged Saxon and then ran around the ring behind the CC winner. She had the reserve CC at Crufts! As she and the CC winner did their lap of honour, flash bulbs were going off all round the ring as the many overseas visitors took videos and snaps of the winners. The atmosphere was electric with people cheering and clapping, she came out of the ring with tears of happiness in her eyes and was immediately surrounded by well-wishers. Strangers came up and asked if they could take photos of Saxon and a German couple came up and asked to buy him. When she smilingly refused, they asked if they could purchase one of his future puppies, Fiona was on cloud nine.

By early afternoon, however, she was exhausted, the lights, the noise and the crowds coupled with early start and all the excitement since were taking their toll.

"Congratulations Fiona. I told you didn't I."

It was Caroline again, Fiona very much wanted to ask just how she knew but was too tired to bother. She did ask her if she would sit with Saxon for a few minutes while she got some much needed items from the many stands around the show. Caroline was pleased to do so, it would be nice to sit on a bench with that lovely ticket pinned up at the back of the bench. She very much doubted that she would do it otherwise so she gloried in the attention as one or two people came up and asked if they could take a photo of her and Saxon.

When Fiona returned it was nearing the time that exhibitors were allowed to leave the show, tired and weary she packed up her things and made her way to the exit not looking forward to the journey back.

As she got out of the car, the cottage door opened and Simon appeared, "Hi Fee how did it go?"

"Simon! What are you doing here?"
"That's no way to greet a friend."
"But why are you here? Is there something wrong."
"Long story, Ruth phoned me about six o'clock this morning, she cut her hand badly as she was getting breakfast and had to go to the hospital. I brought my dogs over here and saw to everything. I hope that's OK."
"Yes, but, how is she?"
"She phoned me when she got back, she had to have a couple of stitches but she's fine. Well, how did you get on?"
Over tea and beans on toast, prepared by Simon, she told him of the events of the day. He didn't say anything until she had finished and then said, "Yeah, thought you'd do well today. Good, he richly deserves it."
"Now why did you say that. Caroline said much the same. How did you know that I'd do well? I have never seen this man before, neither have I given him a good puppy, nor entertained him. In fact I haven't done any of the things that you used to say would help us win so, how did you know?"
Simon looked at her for a moment and shook his head, "You really don't know do you. Oh Fee I'm not going to be the one to tell you. Just enjoy it. I really must round up my dogs now and head off home."
"Tell me what?"
"My sweet love, you're not catching me like that. I'm off now."
"Must you? Well I can't thank you enough Simon. It was good of you to step in like that."
"Good of me! I've had a great day. Once again, congratulations. Bye."
She frowned as she watched his car go down the drive with all his dogs looking out of the back window, there was something that she was missing here. How had he known as well and why was he not prepared to tell her? She would have to speak to Paul.
The next morning she had an excited call from Natalie, "Fiona, wonderful news. Many congratulations, Paul has just told me the good news. Fiona! A reserve CC at Crufts!"
"Thank you Natalie, yes, it's marvellous isn't it. Something you just dream about. Tell me Natalie, did you know that I was going to do well?"

"What a funny thing to say, no, of course I didn't. Who was the judge I've forgotten."

"Some chap from Sweden I think, well, it could have been Germany or Finland or anywhere, no-one really knew. I certainly didn't know him."

"Finland, what a coincidence that would have been. One of my puppies is going to Finland. Do you remember I told you."

Fiona didn't reply and after a rather long pause Natalie spoke again, "Fiona are you still there?"

"Yes, yes, I was just thinking; didn't Paul arrange that sale for you?"

"What the one to Finland? Yes he did. It was someone who wanted one of his puppies I think and as he didn't have any, he recommended mine."

"I see, yes, well thank you for phoning Natalie, we must meet up soon and have a celebratory lunch or something."

"I'd love that Fiona, just as soon as the pups have gone. Wonderful news."

Fiona put the phone down and stood in the hall, her mind racing. No, no Paul couldn't have had anything to do with it. He wasn't like that at all, he had integrity and was kind, gentle and caring, he wouldn't be manipulative. No, in this case two and two did not make four. He didn't need to behave like that, he was well respected and very knowledgeable, he was comfortably off, he had an excellent job, he wouldn't, he couldn't be one of the people that Simon had always talked about, the power-merchants, the wheeler-dealers. He wasn't an Alan Burgess; at that her mind went into a complete spin. Oh my God, no, not that, surely she hadn't won because of the Saturday nights! No, No, please no. He loved her, he was going to marry her it was quite different. Shaking she wandered back to the kitchen and sat down heavily. Sally sensing that something was wrong came up and put her head on Fiona's hand. When had she started winning again? Had she been sleeping with Paul then? She refused to believe what her mind was telling her, no there had to be another simple explanation, good heavens, as far as Crufts was concerned she didn't even know if the judge was from Finland. Well she could soon find that out, she dialled Paul's number but the answerphone was on. Blast, she would have to wait until this evening.

"Hello Paul, it's Fiona."

"I was going to call you this evening. Congratulations are in order. I'm so sorry that I didn't see you but, by the time I'd finished judging, you'd gone. I did manage to have a quick word with the judge though. He was very pleased with his entry, said that all his principal winners had been of excellent quality."

"Do you know him? Is he Finnish?"

"No, I think that he was born in Sweden, or it might have been Denmark, I'm not sure. Why do you ask?"

"So you do know him."

"Never met him before. Why, does it matter?"

"No I suppose not, it's just that everybody was wondering where he came from that's all."

She breathed a sigh of relief, he wasn't from Finland he was Swedish. No wonder all this malicious gossip goes round at shows, people just get their facts completely wrong.

Spring was round the corner and she was going to really campaign Saxon. She was determined now to make him into a Champion. She was friends again with Simon, the daffodils were coming out in the wood and life was great.

CHAPTER THIRTY-FOUR

Winter was finally giving way to Spring, Fiona was delighted to be walking the dogs in the woods, the smell of the earth rose up as the dogs ran around and she took a deep breath, closed her eyes and smiled. The daffodils were out, the trees were budding and the stems of the bluebells were showing through the damp soil, clumps of violets were everywhere, this was the best season of all with winter gone and the warm summer days to look forward to.

She had started showing a promising young bitch related to Sapphire at one or two of the local Open shows and had had some success so she was hopeful of doing well this summer with her as well. She hadn't seen much of Paul for the last week or two because he had gone abroad for a judging appointment, he would then, no doubt have a backlog of work to catch up on. Simon had continued to come around on a Wednesday evening for a meal, she looked forward to planning the meal and enjoyed his company but still seemed different, quiet and a little reserved; it bothered her. He was actually coming over again tomorrow because two of his dogs had found something quite delectable to roll in on one of their walks and he had asked if she minded if he brought them over to bath and dry them off with the equipment in the kennel. Apparently they were 'stinking the place out'.

Natalie was singing one of her favourite Gershwin tunes as she started preparations for dinner that evening. She had retrieved the Hornby train set from the attic, with the help of Brian, and had invited Paul for dinner that evening so that he could see it. She had invited him last weekend but he had had to go out of the country for a judging appointment. It was such a pleasure to be organising a dinner for two again, when Richard had been well they had often given small, intimate dinner parties for friends and clients as well. Richard had always maintained that it helped to oil the wheels of industry. She smiled and the dogs, who had been watching these proceedings avidly, just in case something edible fell to the ground, wagged their tails. It was remembering the letter which she had received from Candida that morning that had made her smile, it was again full of questions about the new puppy and about Paul. Was she sure that Paul was trustworthy? Was he unattached? Divorced? Did he have any children? Apart from the fact that he was unattached, she couldn't answer the other two questions with certainty, but she fully intended to find out the answers this evening if possible.

She wasn't sure but she had a sneaking feeling that Fiona might be looking in Paul's direction now that she was divorcing Simon! She could very likely answer all these questions but Natalie didn't want to show her hand just yet. Years of playing bridge were paying off at last, time for action, there were no friends in love and war. Going up to her bedroom she glanced in the mirror, yes, the weight on her waist and hips was definitely going. The swimming, the walking and the lack of cakes and biscuits were certainly starting to have an effect. Would Paul notice? Looking in the wardrobe she selected a black dress than she hadn't worn for a few years, a designer label that was simple and timeless but sophisticated. Trying it on was a surprise, it fitted her better than it had before. Looking at herself sideways in the mirror she smiled again, at her reflection, yes, she was definitely looking forward to this evening.

Paul replaced the receiver without making the call, he should go round to see Fiona tomorrow night, he hadn't been for several weeks now but..... he was going to see Natalie this evening for dinner and he didn't know how it might pan out. She was obviously extremely keen to see him but he didn't think she was the sort to go to bed with him without some sort of commitment, he could be wrong. Fiona on the other hand always seemed keen to go to bed with him, sometimes a little too keen. She had this way about her that sometimes, after they had made love, she appeared a little restless and talkative, a little disappointed, it annoyed him slightly. Just at that moment his phone rang, "Hello Fiona, I was just thinking about you. Oh, no, I'm so sorry but I shan't be able to come over to see you this evening, dinner with a client I'm afraid. Yes, I'm disappointed too. Tomorrow? Again, I'm sorry, so much to catch up on you know. I'll try to pop over during the week. I'll let you know. Yes, I love you too. Goodbye."

Natalie took the bunch of cream roses, "Paul, these are beautiful. Thank you so much."

"I'm pleased that you like them. I wasn't sure which colour you preferred."

As they sat eating their meal, which Paul had noted, was extremely well organised, presented and cooked, he stole glances around the room noting the old timber beams, the period furniture, the quality of the china figures, the books and nodded with satisfaction.

"My dear, this is an excellent meal if I might say so. Excellent."

"Thank you, I do enjoy entertaining."

Over coffee they discussed forthcoming shows, the development of her new puppy and her prospects in the summer ahead. He advised her not to go to the Open shows with Jamie any more but restrict herself to the Champ shows. It was alright though to introduce the puppy to the show scene through the Open shows. She asked him about rumours she had heard about hereditary diseases in the breed and he was able to assure her that she had no problems with his line, others perhaps, but not his.

"Enough of dogs Natalie, where is this trainset that you promised to show me."

"Oh, it's upstairs if you would like to see it."

He followed her up the heavy oak staircase noting the movement of her hips, he didn't remember her being as slim but it was certainly an improvement. She turned the light on in one of the bedrooms, "Here it is Paul, all in a bit of a mess." He quickly noted the oak four-poster bed draped in pale blue, the whole room seemed to be tones of blue, very restful he thought. He turned his attention to the trainset, "This is a magnificent collection Natalie, this must be worth a fortune." He picked up various engines and carriages, rolling stock, stations, in fact everything for a tremendous lay-out and all in mint condition.

"If you liked, I could get Brian to assemble it in another room. I'm sure it would benefit from being used."

" That is remarkably kind of you Natalie but, if you wouldn't mind, I should love to have the chance to assemble it myself."

They looked into each other's eyes and Natalie smiled and then looked down at her feet, standing here with Paul in the bedroom was making her feel a little excited and she didn't want Paul to see it in case he didn't feel the same. Paul reached out and took her hand, "Natalie, I always thought that Richard was a lucky man to have you as his wife. I now know that he was." He leaned forward and kissed her lightly on the cheek. She looked up at him, she was blushing but the invitation was plain in her eyes.

What a dilemma Paul thought. Should I or shouldn't I. I'll take it slowly just in case I've misread this, there's too much at stake here. He gently pulled her towards him and kissed her lightly on the lips, her parted lips were warm and soft, "Forgive me if that offended you but I couldn't resist."

She put her hands on his chest and kissed him on the lips hungrily, "You didn't offend me Paul."

He stood there for a moment unsure how to proceed but then he gently took her hands and held her away from him, "Natalie, I feel very strongly for you but, perhaps we shouldn't rush things. Shall we go downstairs again."

The light went out of her eyes and she pushed past him and hurried down the stairs. Damn, damn, he'd made the wrong decision. Running down the stairs he found her in the drawing-room putting a Gershwin selection on the Hi-Fi. As the music filled the room he went up to her and asked her to dance. She turned into his arms but did not look up at him. He felt her ample breasts pressed against his chest and tightened his arms around her. They danced without speaking and, as the song changed, he lifted her head with his forefinger and gently kissed her on the lips. She responded immediately pulling him even closer and kissing him urgently, "Paul, Paul," she said breathlessly, "you are the first man to even kiss me in years.. I want......."

She stopped speaking and looked down at the floor, "Perhaps I've got it wrong, perhaps you don't feel... I'm not young and pretty, perhaps you don't... I'm sorry," she started to move out of the circle of his arms, but he pulled her back and kissed her firmly on the mouth, "You are a beautiful; woman Natalie, any man would want to...." He looked into her eyes, "Are you sure Natalie?"

"Oh yes Paul. Yes," just for a second she remembered that she hadn't asked him if he was divorced but as his lips touched hers again, she forgot about it, it seemed irrelevant at this moment.

Keeping his arm around her waist, they retraced their steps to the bedrooms, she led him into a very pretty bedroom which was obviously hers, "Paul, I've never done this sort of thing....I don't know what to do... I'm terribly nervous... I'm afraid that... It's been so long since I... I'm frightened that you won't like me."

He kissed her again and then gently turned her round and started to undo the zip on her dress, she slipped out of the dress but then stood still as he took off his jacket and shirt, "Have you changed your mind Natalie?" she was shivering as if she was cold but she shook her head, bit her lip and started to take off her shoes and tights, for a second she hesitated but seeing Paul remove his trousers and vest, she quickly removed her bra and knickers and stood there biting her lips and looking worried and unhappy. This seemed to arouse a lot of passion in Paul, he quickly removed his pants and took her in his arms, the warmth of her body excited him, "My dear you are more beautiful than I imagined. Your breasts are magnificent."

She looked up and gave him a tentative smile, it made him feel so protective of her, he gently led her to the large bed, pulled the covers back and laid her on it. He bent down to kiss her and she opened her arms to him.

Paul laid there in the darkened room puzzling over his feelings, this had been an enormous surprise. He had been more aroused and felt more passion for this woman than he had ever done before. Good heavens he'd made love to her twice! He hadn't done that for many years. He had certainly never felt this way with Fiona. This really was a turn up for the books. If he wanted, he could have all this on a regular basis and the house and all that went with it. He moved his body slightly, the light was just beginning to show through the curtains and he could see her face on the pillow and the top of her smooth shoulders, he let out a long breath and touched her arm, Natalie stirred slightly and moved her arm across until it connected with his body, she opened her eyes with a start and then smiled, "Shall we try again Paul. You are a wonderful lover."

It was mid morning when Paul let himself into his house. The poor dogs had been left all night. He hadn't arranged cover because he hadn't expected to be so long. Phew, he felt shattered but strangely elated. He'd see to the dogs and then sit down with a cup of coffee to try to make sense of it all. Good heavens, three times! She was so sweet and gentle yet so feminine that he couldn't resist her. The feelings that she awoke in him were unique in his experience, he had never loved anyone like that. Three times in one night and he'd arranged to go back shortly! Good God!

He woke up suddenly and looked at his watch, it was three-thirty, thank heaven he hadn't arranged to see Fiona. Fiona! Now there was a problem. He felt that he knew exactly where his future now lay and it wasn't with her that was if Natalie was willing to marry him! He'd see that Fiona was OK in the ring though. She deserved that.

At the same time that Paul was kindly considering her future show career, Fiona was helping Simon to shampoo the two offending dogs, "What a smell. Whatever did the dirty little devils roll in?"

"Lord knows but it's bloody awful."

They both burst out laughing and Fiona and the dogs blinked their eyes with embarrassment. She was so pleased to hear Simon laugh like that, it was just like old times. After the dogs had been under the dryer Simon put them back in his car.

"You'll have a cup of tea before you go won't you Simon."

"I'd best be off, don't want to hold you up."

"You won't, I've got nothing special to do."

Simon seemed to think for a moment before he replied, "Well, if you're sure."

They went into the warm kitchen and Sally ran up and greeted them, "Hello old Sal. How are you?" Sally, pleased to be the centre of attention, wagged her tail and put her front feet on his legs. Fiona made tea and got out some cake, "That was very kind of you to have that young bitch of Viv's."

"Least I could do. She looks very promising actually. Might even show her one day. The rescue found homes for the others you know."

"Yes, I heard. Are you going to National Terrier?"

" No, don't think so."

"Oh Simon. Why not."

"You know why not. Two things. No money and it's a waste of time for me."

Fiona didn't respond, they had been getting on so much better lately and she didn't want him to get onto this silly 'blacking' business again. Simon stood up, "Best be getting back, thanks for everything. See you."

Fiona turned off the television, it was boring and time was hanging heavy, Spring always made her feel restless, she must do some more decorating, the bathroom perhaps or her bedroom. The phone rang but, before she could speak, an excited voice said, "Oh Fiona, I'm so glad you're there. I've just got to tell you, Paul came over yesterday evening and, well... Oh Fiona, he stayed the night and.... Oh Fiona, we are so deeply in love. He's coming again soon and I can't wait to see him......"

Fiona didn't hear the rest of the sentence, or the next, her mind was in limbo, lost, what was this woman saying! She felt totally betrayed by them both.

CHAPTER THIRTY-FIVE

It all seemed very quiet, Sally nosed open the door and went into the hall, she saw Fiona standing there her head in her hands. Sally made a noise in her throat and looked up at Fiona, she made the noise again but still, for a moment, Fiona did not respond.

Fiona gradually became aware that Sally was making a peculiar noise and she bent down and stroked her head, "It's all right Sally don't worry, I'm alright, I've just had a bit of a shock" She went back into the warm kitchen and Sally followed her. Whatever was going on? Had she been misled by Paul all this time, no, she thought of all their outings, the theatre, dinners, railway journeys, Saturday nights! They had had such a good relationship, not the heights of fun or passion that was true but he had always said that he loved her and that they would be together soon. So what the hell did Natalie mean! Heavens he'd only been round, when was it, only a few Saturdays ago and now he was supposed to be deeply in love with her! There was only one thing to do to sort this mess out. She got up quickly and went out to the hall and dialled Paul's number. She only got the answerphone message. Damnation, he must be out, her dismay was rapidly turning to anger.

She walked around the house restless and unhappy, she put her jacket on and walked around the moonlit exercise paddock with thoughts tumbling into her mind and out to be replaced with more. Paul wasn't like that he was dependable, honest, kind he couldn't, he just couldn't behave like that. Natalie had read the signs wrongly or she was exaggerating, yes, that's what it was. Yes, that's what it must be, he had perhaps stayed the night, drank too much or something, she would tell Paul about the misunderstanding and he would have to let

Natalie down gently. Wait a minute though, he had put off coming to see her in order to go to Natalie's, he would have to explain that as well. With her mind made up, she ran back to the cottage and dialled Paul's number again but, again, she got the answerphone. Damn the man, where is he? Surely not.... She quickly dialled Natalie's number, "Hello, Natalie Bennett, oh, hello Fiona, no, Paul isn't here. Why is there something....."

Fiona slammed the phone down. Damn damn, where was the man? She called on and off until midnight but it was always the answerphone message. Thoroughly frustrated and with a splitting headache, Fiona called to Sally, locked up and went to bed.

Paul sat in the leather chair a goblet of Cognac in his hand. He still could not get to grips with what had happened last night. Good God he was really in love with this woman, he couldn't have done what he did otherwise! This bizarre situation had not come into his calculations. Not that it altered much, just Natalie not Fiona. It was obviously the very best course to take now. There was the little problem, however, of explaining matters to Fiona. He assumed that it was either her or Natalie who had been calling all evening and he didn't wish to speak to either of them until he had formulated his plan. He sipped the last of the brandy, one thing was certain, it was a matter of urgency to speak to Fiona. Although Natalie had been so very warm and willing, he knew that it was only because she felt that she loved him and he loved her. She would drop him like a brick if she found out about his Saturday evenings with Fiona! Good lord, tomorrow, he would have to go and see Fiona and as early tomorrow morning as possible; he frowned, the damage might already have been done!

By morning, after an almost sleepless night, Fiona's headache was even worse, she had tossed and turned all night thinking up solutions and reasons, if only she could talk to someone about this but, who? She couldn't talk to Simon, Beryl would say, I told you so, Laura wouldn't even begin to understand, neither would Duncan! How she wished that her father was still alive. Dragging herself out of bed and getting dressed, she went out and attended to the dogs needs.

By nine-thirty and already exhausted, she was sitting in the kitchen when Paul's car stopped outside. She jumped up and ran out to him, "Paul, I'm so glad to see you. I tried and tried to contact you last night. Where were you?"

"Hello Fiona, shall we go inside. We need to have a talk."

"Yes we do Paul, something dreadful has happened, Natalie phoned me yesterday and she seems to think that you are in love with her and......."

"That's why I have come to see you Fiona, I am in love with Natalie, deeply in love."

All colour went from Fiona's face as she stared at him, "But you can't be, what about us? What about all the things we said and did. You said that you loved me!"

"I truly thought that I did Fiona. Believe me, this has come as a great shock to me."

"A shock to you!"

"Yes my dear, a great shock. That is why I have come to see you straight away, to explain what happened."

"Oh, I know what happened."

"What we had together was so beautiful Fiona. You are a very charming and sweet person and I have felt very privileged to have known you and been loved by you and I don't want the memory of that sullied at all. For that reason and that reason alone, I am asking you to say nothing of our past relationship to anyone. I presume you haven't?"

Fiona shook her head,

"Then let's keep it as a lovely, secret episode in our lives."

Colour suffused Fiona's face as the full implication of what he was saying went in. "Are you telling me in plain language that you are dropping me for Natalie and that I'm not to tell her or anyone else, especially nobody in the show scene, what a dirty trick you've played on me."

"It will harm us both less in our personal lives and in the ring if you don't."

"Harm us less in the ring! You sound just like Simon! What the hell about me, my feelings, my love."

"Oh, come on now Fiona, let's be honest, you know and I know that you still love Simon."

"You've never said that before. It didn't seem to bother you on Saturday nights!"

Paul just shrugged his shoulders, "You know it's true Fiona."

"Will you please leave now Paul."

"Not until I have your promise to say nothing to anyone. You are doing very well now, don't jeopardise it all with a few hasty words. You are well on the way to making Saxon up and, no doubt, others in the future. You are well regarded in the judging scene again and, no doubt, several appointments are on the cards for the next few years, even appointments abroad. As I say, don't ruin it all now. You'll regret it."

"Are you threatening me?"

"Good heavens no, you do have a vivid imagination Fiona, I just know how these things escalate. I've seen it before, I've been in dogs for quite a while Fiona. You learn things and I don't want you to get hurt."

"Like Viv you mean."

Paul raised his eyebrows a little but did not reply, getting up he made his way to the door, "I have some flowers for you in the car. I forgot to bring them in."

"Oh, don't insult me any further."

He went out of the kitchen and returned with a magnificent bouquet of mixed flowers and laid them on the table, "I must be off now Fiona, do think over what I've said. You're a sensible girl, I'm sure you will see the wisdom in what I have suggested."

As the car drove away Fiona rammed the bouquet into the waste bin, "Damn the bloody hypocrite," she shouted and then burst into tears. She felt betrayed, betrayed and stupid, why hadn't she seen him for what he was! You just couldn't trust anyone, well, not any man, only the dogs were trustworthy, only the dogs really gave you their love. "Sally, where are you Sal." She looked around the kitchen, that's funny, where was Sally, she hadn't seen her for ages. Did she come out with her this morning? She couldn't remember, "Sally, Sally, where are you?" She looked in the downstairs rooms but couldn't see her. She must have gone out when Paul left. Opening the door she called her name several times but Sally didn't appear. She went upstairs with a sudden sense of foreboding to find Sally laying, as if asleep, in her cosy little bed.

An enormous solid lump seemed to fill Fiona's chest and she could hardly breathe, she slowly bent down and stroked the soft hair, "Sally wake up poppet. Sally!" There was no response from the dog as Fiona knelt on the floor and gently lifted the lifeless form from the bed. She

looked so peacefully asleep. She couldn't be.... She just couldn't be... Tears streamed unheeded down Fiona's cheeks as she knelt on the floor rocking the little form clutched tightly to her chest. She could hardly breath for the pain and strangled cries came from her mouth as she rocked to and fro, "Oh Sally, Sally don't go. I love you. Please don't go Sally. Please." The little dog lay in her arms, cold and unmoving. How long she sat there she did not know. It was the excruciating pain in her now stiff legs that made her finally move. She laid Sally down gently in her bed and then stiffly stood up and rubbed her lower limbs. Looking down at the still form laying exactly as she had every night for years, Fiona burst into renewed tears. "I can't bear this pain. It's too great. I just can't bear it," she shouted to the four walls of the room. She finally took some tissues from the box beside her bed and scrubbed at her eyes and blew her nose. Going downstairs the pain in her chest was terrible, she dialled a number, "Hello Simon, it's Sally she's.....," she could say no more, she just burst into renewed crying. When she could speak, she picked up the phone again but the line was disconnected. Could she have possibly made a mistake? Sally hadn't been ill, apart for a little heart murmur the Vet said she was in great shape, Fiona hurried upstairs again calling to Sally but Sally hadn't stirred, she knew in her heart that she wouldn't have done. She sat on the bed incapable of any further movement or thought. Some time later she heard movement downstairs and Simon's voice calling to her, footsteps thundered up the stairs and then Simon was there. He quickly looked at the dog and then, without saying a word, sat down beside Fiona and gently took her into his arms and laid her head on his chest. How long they sat there without speaking she did not know, gradually her tears dried up and the shuddering sobs and sighs slowly eased and then there was complete silence. After a while Simon moved slightly, "Come on Fee. Come on love, you're frozen. Come downstairs and let me make a cuppa for you."
He took her by the hand and she followed him downstairs.

CHAPTER THIRTY-SIX

During the afternoon Simon and Fiona wrapped Sally in a clean, white towel and carried her small body up to the woods where so often she had played. Simon dug a deep hole in the soft, moist, sweet-smelling earth and then laid her gently in it. Fiona was incapable of doing anything to help, sobs were wracking her slim body as she watched Simon fill in the small grave, “Oh Sally, my Sally,” she cried and moved as if to stop him.

“Fee you must let her go. Believe me, I know how you’re hurting.” Fiona was about to tell him that he couldn’t possibly know how she felt but then remembered how Simon had been when his son Barry had died. The memory helped to strengthen her and she put out a hand to him, “Thank you Simon.” He looked at her and she could see the unshed tears in his eyes. He hurt too and was trying not to break down and he had had to do everything. She took his hand, “Let’s say goodbye to her together.”

After a few quiet moments they walked hand in hand back to the cottage. Simon made some tea and they sat at the kitchen table. After a few moments silence Fiona looked up and said,

“I was just remembering when Duncan and I picked Sally up from Mrs Emsworth’s. She was such a lovely puppy. I suppose I ought to tell Mrs Emsworth sometime.”

“Yes, but not at the moment. I would never have met you if it hadn't been for Sally.”

“No, you wouldn’t would you. So much has happened since then and she was always with me, I don’t think I can manage without her,” Fiona started to cry again.

"Come on Fee, there are the other dogs to think of, which reminds me I must go, my dogs need feeding and letting out. I just came straight over here."

"Simon, I'm so sorry, I quite forgot. Of course you go, I'll be all right, I'll have to see to mine as well. Will you be coming back?"

"If you want me to I will."

"Yes please."

"I tell you what, I'll collect some fish and chips on my way back."

She had thought that she couldn't eat anything but, when Simon brought in the aromatic package and put the salt, vinegar and sauce on the table, she suddenly felt hungry.

"Don't let's bother with plates Fee. Just eat."

Fiona cleared away the paper and put the kettle on, she was still very quiet and Simon started talking to her, he related a conversation he had had with Peter concerning where he and Beryl were going for their summer holiday, he talked about his work, he told her about a particularly interesting programme on genetics that he had seen on the TV but, he got little response. He then spoke about the dogs and in particular Saxon, "Have you decided what you 'll do with him when he gets his champion status this year?"

Fiona's head jerked up, "Have you been talking to Paul?"

"Paul, what, Paul Aston, no I bloody well haven't. He's the cause..... Why ask me that?"

"He's the cause of what?"

Simon could see that, for some reason she was getting very upset and anxious and was worried that the conversation was getting deeper than he wanted, "Oh nothing, just me and my imagination. Forget it. How's Laura and the boys? Are they coming to see you for Easter?"

Fiona told him how much the boys had grown and that they were coming for a week in the Easter holidays to do some more metal detecting. She smiled, "You must come and help them again," but then her face crumpled and fresh tears filled her eyes, "They'll miss Sally, she so loved them coming to play with her. Oh Simon!" she burst into tears again and Simon got up and pulled her into his arms and held her close, "It'll be alright Fee. You'll see." He continued to murmur endearments and stroke her hair until the tears stopped and she sighed deeply and looked up into his face, "Simon, you've been wonderful to me and I don't deserve it. I..." He stopped her words by kissing her and, as his lips touched hers, warmth spread right through her mind and body. How stupid she had been! This man really loved her, had always loved her and what had she done with his love, she had almost slept with Alan Burgess and had slept with Paul. Paul! He didn't know about Paul, how could she tell him. She stopped kissing him and moved away, "Simon, I'll be OK now. Perhaps you'd better go. Your poor dogs will need letting out. I'll be all right now. I'll call you tomorrow."

For some moments Simon looked at her and then nodded agreement, "OK Fee, if that's what you want."

Birdsong awoke her in the morning, she had surprisingly slept all night. Remembering the events of yesterday she looked towards Sally's bed in the corner, but it was not there. A sob escaped her, Simon had been so thoughtful, he had even known how the sight of the bed would have upset her and had removed it. Again she thought what a fool she had been over the past year or so, she just had not been thinking straight. Paul had totally used her. She felt ashamed that she had not seen through him, all this business about keeping quiet because it might harm me in the ring. It would harm his chances with Natalie more like. It would harm him with Audrey Chatsworth and the other big-wigs more like. He'd been playing one off against the other. Did poor old Natalie have any idea what she was letting herself in for? He was one of the big wheeler-dealers, the organisers! Yes, of course, it all fitted in now. Her wins with Saxon, all the judging appointments she was getting, it all fitted the pattern. Had he ever intended to marry her? That was something she would never know now. Even she could see that marriage to Natalie would be much more advantageous, she was already friendly with people at the top, she had a lot more money and a lovely house, all very impressive for entertaining. How could she have been so stupid that she didn't see it before. Hadn't Simon briefed her about all this years ago. Simon! Did Simon know what Paul was really like? Was this why Simon said that she would have a good year? Was this why Simon had had such a bad year? She jumped out of bed and hurriedly showered and dressed. Would Simon be at home? She must tell him that Paul was not to be trusted, he might not know. She knew that it would be the end of their friendship when he knew that she had slept with Paul but, she had to tell him, she owed him that. His dogs meant so much to him.

She stopped dead, her hand on the kitchen door, she didn't have to tell Simon! If she was right then surely she held the trump cards now; she could persuade Paul to drop the 'black' on Simon and still retain her advantage as well. Simon need never know. Her silence with regard to Paul could pay dividends. She dialled Paul's number and then replaced the receiver as the phone rang. No, I must think this through first. I, for once, have the upper hand and I must use it to benefit both Simon and me. Simon and I have suffered enough from wheeler-dealers like Paul. She sat quietly drinking a cup of tea while she made her plans. She then dialled Paul's number again and asked him to call round that morning at eleven o'clock. She was calling the shots now and Paul, slightly worried by the tone of her voice, decided to do as she asked. He was more than a little annoyed that he had let himself get into this mess. Love had got him into a very difficult situation and one that must be handled with great caution. Thank heavens he thought as he got into his car that Fiona is so unworldly.

"Hello Fiona, it's a lovely day isn't it. How can I help you?"

The conversation that followed was not to Paul's liking. He was amazed that Fiona could be so direct. She spelt out exactly what she wanted from him in return for her silence. The 'black' was to be removed from Simon, Paul expressed his ignorance on this subject but she just reiterated her demand and carried on. If possible, she was going to try a reconciliation with Simon and, if she was successful, she expected that the Simfell kennels and the Simfell dogs would always be looked upon with favour in and out of the ring. Equally, she and Simon would be looked upon favourably when championship show judging appointments were considered both here and abroad. Even if she did not get back with Simon, the same demands applied. She also insisted that her friendship with Natalie be allowed to continue and that they should be included in any entertaining that they might do and she and Simon would reciprocate. Here Paul, who had remained almost silent up until now tried to protest about the continued friendship saying that this would be rather unseemly in the circumstances; but Fiona was adamant on the point. People, she stated, would become suspicious if they were not as friendly and the gossip would start and anyway, she wanted to continue her friendship with

Natalie. She, after all was the innocent party in all this! After a bit of blustering, Paul had to unwillingly acquiesce.

"Well, I think that's all for now Paul. I hope you'll both be very happy, don't forget our wedding invitation will you," she smiled at Paul and went towards the Aga, "Would you like a cup of tea to seal our agreement?"

Paul, by now red-faced and very angry, refused and hurriedly left. He drove home far too fast his mind working furiously, how dare she hold him to ransom like this. Who the hell did she think she was, a nobody, she would have been hopeless without his help. Was marriage to Natalie going to be worth it? He thought of their night together and of the other social benefits. Yes, he would have to agree to Fiona's demands whether he married Natalie or not anyway so for now...... He screeched to a halt in his drive and slamming the door went into his house and poured himself a stiff brandy.

Fiona called Simon at work and invited him to supper the following evening.

"Great I'd like that. How are you OK?"

"Yes, I'm OK. Thank you again Simon, I couldn't have coped without you. Sally keeps coming into my mind, little things she did when she was a puppy, her first show, her first litter, all sorts of things, I keep crying, it's awful but I'm determined to get myself sorted out."

That evening the watcher on the hill did not see any cars go to the cottage. He smiled, she hadn't sought consolation anywhere else then, that had to be a good omen.

CHAPTER THIRTY-SEVEN

As the next two weeks of Spring went by Fiona gradually accepted the loss of Sally and felt more confident about her future. She hadn't heard a word from Paul but felt pretty sure that he would adhere to their agreement because she had heard from Natalie several times and had seen her twice and each time her conversations had been full of Paul. His kindness, his generosity. how much they had in common; Fiona swung from wanting to tell her what a heel he was to being pleased that she seemed so happy.

Fiona had ordered a small headstone for the little grave in the woods and brought another relative of Sally's into the cottage. Now Sapphire, Sally's daughter, had pride of place in Fiona's bedroom. She had started decorating again, this time it was the bathroom. She had chosen a delicate sea-green colour and had bought towels and other accessories to match, feeling confident now about her future and about her showing had proved to be a great stimulus and morale booster. Simon still came to dinner every Wednesday and they were now able to talk in a far more relaxed manner. Today, she had phoned Simon to ask him if he would like to come to the cottage and stay this weekend just to see if they could get back together again. The mere thought of it made her stomach turn over. He could bring the dogs on the Friday evening as well, they so enjoyed being out of that small house and in the kennels with the other dogs. The dogs noticed that Simon had quite a bounce in his step as he walked them that evening.

Since that awful day when Sally died she had never mentioned Paul in any of their conversations. Simon welcomed this change in her attitude and was wise enough to remain silent on the subject; obviously

Natalie was involved but he was not going to rock the boat by asking. Just being with her was enough for the time being. It was extremely difficult to leave her on a Wednesday evening but, he was determined to take things easy and let Fiona dictate the pace. He often didn't even kiss her goodnight because he knew that he wanted more, much more but, for now he wouldn't push his luck.

Fiona had had nothing to do with Paul since their little discussion but, when Simon came in that Friday evening saying that he had been offered a Championship judging appointment in the Autumn of next year, she knew that it was Paul's way of telling her that he would keep his side of the bargain. Natalie was a different person, still keen on showing the dogs but full of plans for the wedding, dinner parties and holidays abroad. It was obvious that she was very much in love with Paul and Fiona was not going to disillusion her. She had found it very hard to say nothing when she had seen Paul fawning over Natalie at the Birmingham show. Several Cumbrian exhibitors had remarked on it to her and it had gone round the grapevine like crazy. Caroline had sidled up to her on the bench and had hinted that she personally had expected Paul to be with her, Fiona. Fiona had quickly squashed that knowing how Caroline could tittle-tattle, "Really Caroline talk about two and two making five, I knew that he was keen on Natalie all along. I was in a position to help him out when he had that skiing accident and he was just grateful. That's all there was to it." Caroline looked disappointed so Fiona knew that she had accepted her explanation.

It had seemed very odd making up a bed in the other room for Simon the previous night but Fiona still felt so guilty about her liaison with Paul; Simon had looked very unhappy but had thankfully not commented on the change. On the Saturday morning Fiona and Simon set up the little headstone in the wood together and, as they looked down at Sally's grave Simon remarked, "You know Fee Sally did me the biggest favour when she had that first litter, she brought me to you. I can still see you as you were when you opened that door, dressed in blue. Never forget it. I'll always be in her debt." Fiona looked up to see tears in Simon's eyes, "She loved you, you know, she missed you terribly when you went."

"Did she. Did you? Do you?" Simon turned her to face him, "Please tell me Fee do you still love me?"

Fiona looked back at the grave and the only sound for a while was the wind soughing in the trees.
She did love him very much, he had changed a bit, seemed calmer and less arrogant, seemed to consider her feelings more but, yes, she loved him still and she wanted him. She wanted to laugh with him, have fun with him, show with him, sleep with him, make love with him but, and it was a big but, should she clear it with him first about Paul. She felt that she couldn't have him back permanently, couldn't sleep with him unless she told him about her relationship with Paul. It was a dilemma and she just didn't know what to do. She couldn't risk losing him.

"Well? Fee I really do need to know where I stand." Simon's voice sounded strained and it brought her back to the present.

"Yes, I do love you and miss you when you go away but..... Simon, I must tell you something. Something which is on my conscience, something to do with...."
She got no further because Simon put a finger on her lips, "No Fee, don't tell me anything."

"But Simon, I must tell..."
She got no further because Simon started to kiss her, she pulled away from his mouth and tried again to say something but again he stopped her and, as his kisses got more passionate the old feelings started to rise in her and she abandoned herself to his kisses.

"My God Fee, am I getting the right message?"

"Yes Simon but, well, it's a bit cold here. Shall we go back to the cottage." Simon hugged her to him and laughed and then grabbing her hand, they walked back to the cottage. As she entered she could here the phone ringing.

"Oh no you don't Fee. Leave it for God's sake. I've waited long enough."

"No, you'll have to wait a bit longer, I'll answer it and then I can put the answerphone on."

As they walked hand-in hand up the stairs she told him that the caller had been Duncan and that he had asked her to be Donald's legal guardian if anything happened to Barbara and himself.

"Good lord, he's not ill is he?"

"No, you know Duncan, he likes to cross all the 't's and dot the 'i's. What have you got that pot of jam for?"

"Well my girl, you once promised me that, if I covered myself with jam, you would lick it off so, during the course of this afternoon...."
The dogs in the kitchen wagged their tails at the sounds of laughter coming down from the bedroom.

As they sat by the Aga in their dressing gowns drinking a nightcap Fiona said, "You're not going back tomorrow night are you Simon."

"Not if you don't want me to Fee."

"Then stay please Simon,." she held out her hand to him and then suddenly laughed.

"What's so funny."

"I've just thought, Beryl will be so pleased. She has always said that we were meant to be together," with his arm around her waist they went back to bed and the dogs settled down for the night.